TAPESTRY
OF LOVE

TAPESTRY OF LOVE

NEW DIRECTIONS
BOOK TWO

LINDA BYLER

Good Books

New York, New York

TAPESTRY OF LOVE

Good Books books may be purchased in bulk at special discounts for sales promotion, corporate gifts, fund-raising, or educational purposes. Special editions can also be created to specifications. For details, contact the Special Sales Department, Good Books, 307 West 36th Street, 11th Floor, New York, NY 10018 or info@skyhorsepublishing.com.

Good Books is an imprint of Skyhorse Publishing, Inc.®, a Delaware corporation.

Visit our website at www.goodbooks.com.

10 9 8 7 6 5 4 3 2

Library of Congress Cataloging-in-Publication Data
Names: Byler, Linda, author.
Title: Tapestry of love / Linda Byler.
Description: New York, New York : Good Books, 2023. | Series: New directions ; book two | Summary: "The second book in the New Directions series, this Amish romance will keep you guessing until the end!"-- Provided by publisher.
Identifiers: LCCN 2023017369 (print) | LCCN 2023017370 (ebook) | ISBN 9781680998627 (paperback) | ISBN 9781680998818 (ebook)
Subjects: LCSH: Amish--Fiction | LCGFT: Romance fiction. | Christian fiction. | Novels.
Classification: LCC PS3602.Y53 T36 2023 (print) | LCC PS3602.Y53 (ebook) | DDC 813/.6--dc23/eng/20230417
LC record available at https://lccn.loc.gov/2023017369
LC ebook record available at https://lccn.loc.gov/2023017370

ISBN: 978-1-68099-862-7
eBook ISBN: 978-1-68099-881-8

Cover design by Create Design Publish LLC

Printed in the United States of America

TAPESTRY
OF LOVE

CHAPTER 1

He met her at the train station in Harrisburg, a roiling mass of humanity, monstrous, clanging trains, acres of cement, steel poles, and carts trundled from who knows where. She spotted him through the crowd, his face wearing a look of anticipation, his eyes darting anxiously.

She lifted a hand, called out, but her voice was swallowed up in the hum and bustle of the crowd. She pushed back a stray lock of hair, straightened her bib apron, and shoved her way through, excusing herself, apologies to her left, then her right.

"Here, here I am, Levi," she called out.

The glad cry, the smile of recognition, and she was by his side, her hand clasped firmly in his, the only proper way of greeting in public among their people. His eyes spoke of his love, his pleasure in seeing her face.

"Susan!"

"Levi. Oh, it's so good to be home. Thank you for meeting me here today."

"I offered. I wanted to be the first one to welcome you back. How are you? Was the ride tedious?"

She laughed, told him of time creeping slowly, impatience a constant companion, the need to see her family overwhelming. They could barely gather their senses long enough to claim her luggage, to find their way from the station to the parked SUV, talk to the driver, and finally drive through the city and onto Route 283.

She sat in the second seat, her eyes taking in the beloved green fields of alfalfa, white dairy barns, black and white Holsteins on a lush pasture. Chicken and turkey houses hundreds of feet long. Blue Harvestore silos. As they neared Lancaster and passed places of business, heavy traffic, exits leading to ramps that led to the city, she knew her exit was close.

She had forgotten how green everything was. How brilliantly, electrifyingly green. The leaves on the trees, the lawns like carpeting, azaleas and rhododendrons in shocking hues of pink and red. She stifled a yelp of exhilaration at the sight of a horse-drawn gray carriage, clopping along the wide shoulder of the road to allow vehicles to pass unhindered. She stared happily as they passed the first produce stand, the shelves filled with spring onions, radishes, fresh brown eggs, shoofly pie, and chocolate whoopie pies.

Her heart sang of home, home, home. She was truly here, this lovely place with its abundant growth, its fertile soil, the hustle and bustle of commerce, businesses thriving on the tourist trade. Everything was structured, planned, in order, and running like clockwork. She felt the adrenaline pumping through her veins, wanting to open her own market stand, start a cleaning business, make quilts and sell them. She had never realized how much she belonged here in this humming center of trade, of talent and skill and hard, honest labor. How satisfying to earn a good wage, to live in a beautiful home, to care for a property with precise attention to detail, an art handed down by German ancestors.

And then she was home, the screen door flung open, and her mother running clumsily, the heaviness of her embrace, followed by her father, Mark, and Elmer.

Yes, her trip home had been long, seemingly weeks instead of days. No, she had not slept well, or eaten well, but here she was, safe and sound, back in the fold. She could smell her mother's chicken lasagna in the oven, and there'd be fresh asparagus from the garden and, best of all, a French rhubarb pie, the crumbs heavy with butter and brown sugar.

Levi would not stay for dinner, but he took her aside and asked to come on Saturday night. "Yes, oh yes," she said, smiling into his eyes, which shone so intensely into hers.

That first wonderful homecoming meal, complete with Liz and Rose, husbands and children in tow, charging through the door with arms flung wide, enveloping her in a showy emotional display of love and tears.

"You look dried out," Rose observed, holding her at arm's length, looking deeply into her green eyes. "As if desert winds have been attacking your skin."

Liz hooked an arm across her shoulders, said, "Pooh, there's no desert in Wyoming, that's Arizona. Duh." Which brought a withering look from Rose, and Susan laughed with abandon. She hugged them both and said she was truly and absolutely at home. Nieces and nephews clamored for attention and there was hearty handshaking from Amos and Dave.

It was too chilly for coffee on the back patio, so after dishes they all settled in the living room to hear Susan's account of life in Wyoming as a schoolteacher. She found herself choking up as she spoke of Titus, her eyes wet with unshed tears.

"He didn't take my leaving very well, I'm afraid," she said, in a low voice, rough with emotion.

"Don't feel guilty now," Liz cut in.

"I don't. Isaac is writing to a young widow, so he'll have a mother soon enough. Sharon is much more stable, lives in a world of dolls and make believe. And horses. Isaac is good with the children. It's just that Titus is . . . well, everyone says he hasn't been quite right since his mother died, and Isaac just lets him roam around with that dog."

"I thought you said he was good with the children," Rose objected.

"All except that. I just don't agree with Titus being allowed to follow his nose wherever he wants."

"Absolutely not."

"No."

Righteous nods, all around.

"So, describe this place where you lived," her father said.

In glowing terms, she gave a verbal picture of the breathtaking view of the expertly built home, the dark brown melding with the landscape so beautifully, the large barn, riding arena, the flagstone patio and furniture. But, she added, the place sorely felt the neglect and sadness of the deceased mother.

Always quick to pick up on possibilities, Rose asked about Isaac. Why couldn't she marry him and be the mother Titus and Sharon need? The forthright question took Susan off guard, but she righted herself quickly, and said in a level voice that she could never marry Isaac.

He was a giant, with titanium plates in his face, always filthy, smelling of diesel fuel and sawdust. He had zero patience for anything, talked way too loudly, laughed too loudly, or else pouted around the house like a spoiled child. He didn't brush his teeth enough, he never shaved properly, and he was missing half the time, leaving those children to fend for themselves.

No.

"Well, then, what about Levi? You can't leave him dangling the way you do."

"I won't."

"Mother, I hear wedding bells," her father broke in.

"Davey, now don't say that. It makes my knees weak."

They all laughed, then moved to the kitchen for more coffee and rhubarb pie and dishes of vanilla ice cream with chocolate syrup for the children. The subject turned to Mark and Beth's engagement and wedding in the fall, with Rose and Liz shrieking about how glad they were Mark was their brother. It would be lovely to go to a wedding as the sisters of the groom, treated like royalty and not having to do one single little thing all day except eat and talk. Oh, and sing. Yes, that, too.

Susan eyed her sister's new choice of dress fabric, the gray pebbly material stretched tightly around her arms, the skirt much too tight around her advancing hips, and thought, *Well, eat, yes.* But she wisely kept this observation to herself.

She was really and truly home, in the best way possible, surrounded by family, the ties that bind, the love surrounding them like strong ropes. Nothing could ever take her away from this as long as she lived. The realization of this truth was written in stone. As sure as an arrow from an expert marksman, her heart had found its home, with family and Levi.

SHE AWOKE TO the sound of traffic, the low hum of vehicles, trucks shifting gears, an occasional clopping of hooves, the rattle of steel wheels on macadam. The luxury of lying in her own bed between clean sheets, the beauty of her furniture and tasteful decor was almost too much joy. It was simply so good to be home.

The uncomfortable thought of Titus and Sharon waking up to their new *maud* (maid) pushed its way into her consciousness.

She'd met Tina, the twenty-eight-year-old housekeeper from Geauga County, Ohio. Where or how Isaac had found her that spring still wasn't clear, but there she was one bright morning, the week before Susan's departure. Dark-haired, dark-eyed, a tall, willowy figure and an arresting face, and enough confidence to fill the state of Wyoming, she was a delight as Susan showed her around. Her dry sense of humor was an unexpected asset, and Susan felt sure she would easily win Isaac's heart. The widow he was thinking about marrying probably would not work out after Tina's presence filled the house.

If Titus and Susan were okay, and Isaac became enamored of this Tina, she could comfortably move on with her life, store the Wyoming memories in her chest of bygone days, dust her hands of the year. It had only been ten months, actually, and yet it seemed much longer.

She'd seize this day, make the most of a Saturday at home, look forward to her evening with Levi. The whole future seemed bedazzled with stardust. No more treacherous horse riding or wobbly bike rides, either. No more unruly students and endless dust and sticky mud.

She was in Lancaster County again, the home of perfect lawns and macadam driveways, spotless barns and groomed pastures.

Her mother's breakfast casserole was so good, with ham and freshly steamed asparagus in eggs, milk, and cheese, a thick fragrant sausage gravy to ladle over it. She drank a cold glass of home-canned grape juice, patted her stomach, and grimaced.

"Mom, I'll get fat, being here again."

"Oh, you won't," her mother chuckled. "And if you do, you'll resemble Rose."

They shared a meaningful look, and they laughed good naturedly.

"I love Rose just the way she is," Susan said.

"Of course."

"Have you heard from Kate?" Susan asked.

"Not since January."

Her mother's face lost the glow of good humor and fell into a deep sadness. Her eyes darkened as her mouth softened, trembling slightly by the emotion overtaking her. Kate was her little girl, the bright one, the sunshine of the house taken out of the family circle by the unstable Dan, who was now convicted of many odd and numerous things, living in North Dakota in the oil fields. This bit of information had been shared by Dan's sister Barb, a sharp-tongued woman who kept no secret honestly.

"It's why she hasn't written. I'm sure she doesn't want us to know."

"Mam. Don't. She's just trying to protect you from heartache as much as possible. She's so selfless. You know that."

Her mother nodded, dabbed at her tears.

"I just wish I could understand what we've done wrong, Dat and I. Why can't Kate be here, Amish, in her place with the rest of us?"

Susan shook her head, told her not to take blame. God knew what He was doing, and there was a reason for this, even if they would never understand.

They washed dishes, cleaned the kitchen, then Susan sewed a new dress for her date with Levi, a pale pink, the color of summer roses.

Her heart sang in time with the whir of the sewing machine, the joy of allowing herself to love freely, to actually be able to say she was ready and willing to become Mrs. Levi Yoder. She reveled in the abandoning of old fears, brought about by the words of Isaac in Wyoming.

Finally, finally, her time had come.

She greeted her horse, stroking the silky neck beneath the mane, fed him an apple, and frowned at the amount of manure buildup in his stall.

Dat had never been meticulous about these things, and now where was he on a Saturday morning? Likely down at the Bird-in-Hand restaurant drinking coffee and chatting with the locals.

She looked out to see her mother emerge from the garden shed with a hoe, headed for the bean rows.

"Mam?"

She stopped, turned.

"You want to ride along to Leacock Shoes?"

"Why? I don't need anything. Besides, your horse hasn't been driven enough, he'll be too frisky."

"I can handle him."

But her mother shook her head and continued on her way to the bean patch, leaving Susan to harness Chaos and hitch him up herself, which she accomplished with no small amount of effort. He sidestepped, refused to back between the shafts, then pranced and shook his head up and down once the neck rein was attached. She found herself unable to get into the buggy, walking along beside it as she hung back on the reins, repeating a steady "Whoa, whoa there. Stop it now." Finally, she made a running leap. The horse sensed the loosening of the reins and made a flying lunge as she struggled to apply the brakes and haul back on the reins as hard as she could before they came to the well-traveled Route 340.

"Crazy horse," she muttered.

He balked when he had to stand still at the end of the driveway, waiting till traffic thinned, so she waited till he was done throwing a fit, then moved off smoothly, joining the flow of traffic. She fought a moment of unexpected anxiety, all these purring, gleaming vehicles surging past like colorful monsters, impatient locals and gawking tourists putting her under the proverbial microscope. She barely missed side-scraping a black SUV that took a quick exit and parked, the driver standing behind his vehicle with a cell phone held high, taking pictures or videos of the fast-moving horse.

Susan felt her throat tightening, her breath coming in bunches. She took a deep breath to calm herself, reaching for the turn signal switch as she approached Leacock Road. She watched the mirror, allowing a stream of vehicles to pass from the front before turning left.

She had forgotten the amount of vehicles moving steadily on the road past their house. She'd have to get used to it again. She certainly didn't miss the dirt, the dust and the mud, the potholes and unregulated rules of travel in Wyoming.

She was so happy to enter the store with the familiar scent of new leather and hand-sewn clothes manufactured on humming sewing machines by enterprising young seamstresses who made a significant difference in family finances with their talents. Children's clothes, broadfall trousers, coats and black bonnets, white head coverings, and especially those pinafore-style aprons for little girls, so complicated to achieve a good fit.

Mam said time changed things so much. There was a time when everyone made their own clothes, every mother responsible for the sewing, producing her own trousers, capes, and aprons, no matter how complicated.

You learned, acquired the skill, and passed it on to your girls, which was still the case for the most part. But what young housewife wouldn't pass up the frustration of repeatedly trying to make a *schwottz shottzly* (black apron) for her two-year-old, only to have that elusive neckline fit weirdly time after time? To go to any Amish dry goods store, select the fabric of your choice, and get a perfect pinafore-style apron for ten or fifteen dollars was, indeed, a blessed opportunity.

And so a trade was born, all in the name of progress.

Around the time the new covering material was introduced, no one missed the Monday morning ritual of soaking organdy coverings in laundry detergent, rinsing them thoroughly, heating water on the stove with shavings of Gulf wax, that old-fashioned paraffin, to stiffen the limp white fabric, ironing them with a sizzling hot sadiron, using a paring knife to put in the row of pleats rising above the front part of the covering. The new fabric meant a quick spray of Clorox Cleanup, a five-minute wait, a rinse under running water, and then they could be hung up to dry—no ironing, no stiffening. The best thing to happen to Amish housewives in a long time.

Sometime, in years past, the wringer washer had been introduced, with the same appreciation. The bathtub and flush commode, hot water heater and milking machines—all of it was contemplated, discussed, and accessible, finally.

And so the church evolved from kerosene or gas lights to batteries, those handy little rechargeable gadgets that powered everything from lamps to modified electric washers. Solar panels appeared on roofs, bringing even more appliances into use, and still electricity was *verboten* (forbidden), the proverbial carrot in front of the donkey's nose for some.

To keep the rules enforced, to know when to hold back and when to let go, required the wisdom of Solomon, for there would always be the liberals stretching the *ordnung* (rules) and the conservatives hanging on to the old ways.

Godly men in the ministry strove for an even keel, knowing that to keep the great ship afloat meant a healthy balance, the ship manned by God's love and wisdom, and so stayed close to the Source. Some loved the Amish way of life, reverenced the *ordnung* and took it very seriously, while others abandoned the teachings of the old ways, denounced their membership, and found another church more aligned to their view of God.

Susan found herself flipping through the adorable pink and blue baby dresses with aprons to match, daydreaming, wondering. To be a mother was every Amish girl's wish, to have a home and a husband, to take her place in the community as one of many. Her heart was fully taking in the abundance of God's blessing, being here among her people, the prospect of her life being so richly endowed with a newfound love.

Levi was older, yes, and so much more mature, so levelheaded, already a leader at the storage barn company, so she could rejoice in the future, thinking of a wise, kind-hearted, financially responsible husband.

Plus, very handsome.

She smiled to herself, said hello to a young woman holding a chubby baby on her hip, then moved away from the baby clothes, went downstairs and purchased a pair of Sketchers, then moved on to the dress shoes.

She found a middle-aged woman seated on a stool with three pairs of women's shoes strewn among the tissue paper and opened boxes.

She recognized Malinda Lantz, from church.

"Well, Susan! You're back?"

"Hi. Yes. I am, indeed."

"Welcome home. My, it's good to see you. Are you here to stay?"

"Yes." A resounding yes.

"Good. I was afraid you'd go out there and find one of those wild bachelors to marry you."

Susan laughed. "No such luck."

"Well, good. How's your mother?"

"Good, as far as I know."

"Her back was bothering her so bad in church."

"Really? She didn't say anything."

"Tell me, Susan. Which shoes should I wear?"

Susan looked at all of them, one as ugly as the next, but she smiled and pointed to one that appeared to be the same as all the rest.

"Yep. I thought so, too. See you in church tomorrow?"

"Certainly. I'm so glad to be back in my home church."

Malinda nodded, smiled, gathered up her shoes and was gone, leaving Susan to decide on a pair of shoes herself.

AT HOME, HER mother was taking a nap on the recliner, opening one eye when Susan walked in.

"Oh, there you are already. Can hardly get used to the fact you're actually at home. Did you get shoes?"

"Yup. I'm starved. It's three o'clock, and I had no lunch."

"You better get done what you're going to do. Levi will soon be here. Ach, Susan, I'm so glad you're actually dating now. So comforting knowing you'll be *fasarked* (taken care of)."

"Really, Mam. Becoming someone's wife means you're fasarked? Think about Kate."

"Don't, Susan."

"Sorry, Mam."

"It's just so hard."

"I know. I shouldn't have said that."

"It's okay."

"You know, though, she feels she is where God wants her to be. She feels she's there by God's will, to be a helpmeet to Dan until he gets his footing, whatever that phrase is supposed to mean."

"Kate has always been very dutiful, very attached to the ones she loves. Remember her black kitten? She carried that poor cat around for months, and when it was hit by a car here in front of the house, she never really got over it. So perhaps she knows what she's talking about, being devoted to Dan in spite of his shortcomings."

Susan looked at her mother, shrugged her shoulders, and let it go. There was no point worrying her mother even more by telling her the truth about Dan's alcoholism, so she fixed a sandwich, ate it, and pressed the new dress before going to her room to put away her laundry.

She hoped Levi would mention another road trip, perhaps enable her to travel to South Dakota to find her sister. Was Dan providing for the family's needs? Was she living a life of hardship the way so many wives of alcoholic men did? Or had he mastered his weakness and allowed her to have a better life?

She put her clean laundry in drawers, hung freshly laundered dresses and aprons on hangers, then sat on the small sofa and reached for her book. She found herself unable to concentrate, anticipating her evening with Levi, her mind wandering to Titus, hoping he would be okay in the summer months, hoping Tina would prove a good caregiver.

She'd surprised her entirely, appearing on the porch in the bright sunshine, saying she was there to take over after she left.

Susan had definitely taken a liking to her soon enough, but felt a bit miffed at Isaac, thoughtlessly bringing this girl into her house without warning, and she told him so.

He didn't answer, just sat on the couch like a big lump, his hair uncombed, a three-day fuzz over his face, and glared at her.

"I don't know why you think I had to answer to you. You'll be gone soon enough, so what do you care?"

Her eyes flashed green.

"It's not just me. It's the children. What about Titus?"

His own eyes were smoldering black coals.

"What about him?"

"You know how he is!" she shouted, the words tumbling from her mouth. "Why can't you ever consider someone else's feelings? You don't think farther than your nose reaches. You know how he'll react to a stranger."

"I told him."

"Really? He tells me everything, and he never mentioned Tina."

"I told him about an hour ago."

She found Titus curled into a ball underneath the covers, his hair wet with perspiration, his face sodden with tears, his nose running into his pillow.

She touched his shoulder.

"Titus."

"No. Go away."

"Titus, it's okay. Tina is wonderful. She'll be so much fun."

He hid his face, pulled the covers over his head. When she pulled them away, he sat up, threw back the covers, pounded her arms and her back with his fists, screamed and shrieked and yelled, bringing Tina and Isaac in leaps up the stairs, Isaac restraining him easily, Tina's face gone white.

The three of them had a mature conversation, with Tina listening intently, absorbing the story of the small boy's existence since his mother's passing, shaking her head at Isaac's lenient outlook. But Titus never said a word to her after that, never said goodbye, was not present when the driver came to take her to the Amtrak station. She searched the pines, the surrounding pastures for a glimpse of him as the vehicle moved down the drive, but had to give up and admit he was not around.

Sharon had already made up to Tina, so she kissed Susan, hugged her and said goodbye, a well-adjusted, well-behaved young lady. And Isaac stood beside Tina, held Susan's hand in a farewell handshake, his dark eyes blank as he wished her well, thanked her for all she had done.

She felt no regret, only an eagerness she could not contain as the vehicle moved faster on a good macadam road. She knew she would never return. Her life lay ahead of her, complete with a winding golden road, an arching rainbow of promise, a loving husband, and a new-found confidence in romance, in dating Levi without a fear of failure.

And she thought about how Isaac and Tina made a striking couple, giving them less than a year before love bloomed.

CHAPTER 2

They sat on the patio in full view of the neighbors until the air turned chilly and Levi suggested they move inside. Susan complied with a smile. They made coffee before Levi went to greet her parents, politely shaking hands, talking about the unseasonably frosty nights.

Susan watched the way he bent over her mother's hand, watched his smile, his absolute charm, and felt a new pride, a possession of this fine man. As usual, his clothes were impeccable, his trousers pressed, and he wore a fine, woven gray shirt. She felt thankful, joyous, and moved gladly to the living room after her parents retired to bed.

Levi leaned back against the couch, his face etched in the soft glow of the lamplight, his eyes bright with interest as she described Wyoming. She missed school, missed all her pupils, yes, but there was, simply, no place like home. She had missed life here in the East, had missed him.

"You can say that honestly now? You really do know what you want?" he asked.

"I do."

"Then I'll ask you again to be my girlfriend, and we will be an official couple. Dare I even hope this is true?"

She smiled, nodded, her eyes on his, and he gathered her into a soft and tender embrace, where she remained, gladly.

"Being in Wyoming taught me so many things. Isaac helped me to see how my fear of marriage was very selfish, thinking only of myself. Which is true. I also learned to love children more fully, to enjoy the exuberance they so freely display. I used to think of them as brats. Sorry."

She heard the deep rumble of his chest and knew he was quietly laughing.

"The children were so hard to leave. We had this surprise farewell partly, complete with a hot dog roast. Campfires are a big thing in Wyoming. Everybody loves them. So we had this really fun party and a big group hug. I got so many handmade cards, gifts from parents. It was like Christmas. I mean, nothing like the horse Isaac gave me at Christmas, but such sweet little gifts."

She felt him stiffen. His arm dropped away.

"What?"

She sat up, moved away, reached up to smooth her hair. She felt as if she had overstepped a boundary, disobeyed somehow.

"He . . . he gave me a horse at Christmas. I guess I didn't mention that in my letters."

"Did you bring it home on the train?"

"Levi! Really?"

She gave a nervous laugh, unsure of how she should absorb this mockery. This was not the gentle Levi she remembered.

"See, Susan, I never liked the idea of you living with that widower. You can't tell me he didn't fall for you. A horse? If that isn't a sign of wanting to impress, I don't know what is."

"No, Levi. You would have to meet Isaac to understand. He is not a romantic figure, not even an idea of one. He's a logger, for Pete's sake, going around smelling of diesel fuel, oil, and whatever ghastly smelling thing he pours into chainsaws. He's loud, obnoxious, has like, steel plates under his skin to hold his face together, constantly runs his giant hand through his hair, and because he doesn't wash them enough, his hair stands on end half the time. He belches at the table, lets his son roam the woods with his dog. No, Levi, Isaac isn't even in the running as a possible competitor."

"I'm sorry to appear jealous. That was mean. But, Susan, I'm crazy about you, and it's a normal emotion for a man to feel jealous of another man. And you lived with this guy."

"I did, Levi, but there were no feelings involved."

"Good."

She didn't understand the sudden stab of irritation after he said that. She pushed the feeling down, made a special effort to have an enjoyable evening, which she could honestly say they did after she poured root beer over vanilla ice cream and sat opposite him as they enjoyed the creamy, fizzy treat.

"What are Mark and Beth doing?" she asked him, puzzled that he hadn't mentioned spending time with them. She though he'd want to go out to eat, as a celebratory dinner, or go someplace he had always enjoyed.

"I don't know. Mark is so into getting married and settling down, seems like he never wants to do anything anymore. Saving his money."

Susan nodded. "Sounds like it."

"Well, Susan, it's getting late. I better let you get some sleep if you have church tomorrow. Thank you for the great snack."

"You're welcome."

He pushed back his chair, yawned, stretched. She got up to her feet, gathered the dishes, carried them to the sink. She smiled when she felt his hands on her shoulders, went gladly into his arms, and was grateful for the light peck on her cheek, the sincere "Goodnight, my darling Susan. I love you."

"I love you, too, Levi."

"I can only say my future has never looked brighter. I look forward to spending every weekend with you."

She followed him outside to help him hitch up his horse, watched the lights of the buggy meld with the string of cars on 340, then turned to go inside. She looked up into the night sky to find the star pattern she had been used to finding every night, but could only find a few, the night sky seeming far away, the lights and sounds of many people living and moving in a concentrated area reducing the beauty of the night sky.

No big deal, she thought, as she wiped the counter and looked at the clock.

Eleven. Not quite eleven o'clock.

Well, that was very thoughtful of him, to think of her needing her sleep if she had church in the morning. He was certainly very kind and sweet, and that bit about the horse proved how much he really cared about her. She took a deep breath, realized how wise she had been to set her course, to fully appreciate what a good man Levi really was.

She lay in bed with a smile on her face, a deep sense of peace of having chosen wisely, and now he had become even more caring, showing his Christian character by restraining himself with a light kiss on the cheek.

No use starting their courtship with too much touching, for sure.

He was just the perfect boyfriend, as sweet as she remembered. And now her own heart had been adjusted, a whole new world of love opening before her.

Thank you, Jesus. Thank you for all the blessings bestowed on me, as undeserving as I am.

CHURCH SERVICES WERE held at a neighboring farm, so she walked with Mark, who had not come home till after two in the morning, creating quite a bit of teasing. His excuse was that he'd fallen asleep, or maybe his horse had, he wasn't sure. Both parents tried to look strict, but gave up and laughed, allowing Mark to become quite jaunty as he walked beside Susan.

"Didn't Elmer come home last night?"

"No. He's hanging out with quite a bunch. You know Sam's Check's Abner?"

She nodded.

"His brother Amie is quite a leader with Elmer's group. Got himself a black Mustang, the loudest car in Lancaster. Dat isn't happy. Mam doesn't know it."

"Better that way."

"So what time did Levi leave?"

"Not till eleven."

"Eleven? That's early."

"Well, he's like he always was. Thinking of me. He said he doesn't want me to be tired in church today."

Mark nodded.

They walked together in silence, each one to their own thoughts, comfortable in the way brother and sister can be. After a while, Susan remembered to ask why he and Beth didn't join them.

"We thought it would be best for you to be alone on your first date. Levi was pretty nervous."

"Was he?" Susan laughed, happy to know how much she meant to him.

At church she was greeted with plenty of fanfare, the wanderer's return, the lone sheep back in the fold. Susan appreciated the attention, thanked everyone for their kindness, sat with the old friends and acquaintances, and again rejoiced in being home.

She knew the minister who preached the first sermon, the deacon who read Scripture, and the old bishop who expounded God's word in the second sermon. Even the eastern Dutch dialect was familiar and dear.

She helped serve lunch with happiness, knowing Levi would arrive that afternoon and they'd go to the youth's gathering together, as a couple, creating quite a stir. They would receive congratulations at the hymn singing, a time-honored tradition for a new dating couple.

On her walk home, the neat appearances of homes, the orderly layout of fields and fence rows, the brilliance of green and myriad colors of flowers only heightened her happiness, and when Levi arrived, she invited him upstairs to her room to sit on the small couch and see the things she cherished, her own personal space.

He admired the pictures on the walls, her furniture, her choice of rugs and pillows.

"Levi, that is so thoughtful of you, leaving at eleven last evening," Susan told him.

He blinked a few times before meeting her eyes, then smiled his easy smile, the one that melted her heart, and he took her hand in his, saying he would always remember to put her needs before his own.

They chose to wear the same color, now that they were a couple. He had on a navy blue shirt, so she picked a dress the same color, her cape and apron pinned perfectly into place. He complimented her on the beautiful color the navy blue brought out in her eyes, and she blushed, hardly understanding the flustered beating of her heart as he stood beside her at the mirror.

They were, indeed, a perfect couple.

She thought of Isaac and Tina, hoped with all her heart God would bless them as He had blessed her and Levi. This dating was not to be taken lightly, she realized, and told Levi that evening when they were alone. He agreed solemnly, nodded his head when she mentioned the responsibility of caring for one another the way God intended.

"I do believe so many young people enter a courtship thinking they're capable of giving their lives for each other, but really have no clue how to give up their own will," Susan said.

"Oh, absolutely," Levi agreed.

"So let's try to focus on the Christian aspect of dating, the caring and appreciation instead of the . . . the . . ."

She stopped, embarrassed.

Levi became very still and quiet. When he said nothing for quite some time, she realized she had waded into murky waters. The real reason was the fact he had only given her that cold peck on the cheek last evening, when he had kissed her genuinely before. She wasn't sure what it had meant and wanted to find out. Always one to be the leader, the one to take the initiative, she floundered on, saying she believed there was a blessing in keeping their distance.

"Susan, you surprise me. You are so different from the girl I remember. I was pretty nervous last night, and didn't want to rush things. You actually think we won't touch each other at all for the duration of our courtship?"

"Some couples do."

"I'm not some couples."

"Well."

"Well what?"

"Well, what did that mean last night?"

"I told you. I was nervous. I'm still nervous. I wasn't before we started to date. I figured I didn't have much of a chance anyway, so I relaxed and did my best to win you. Now, you're so different. Much sweeter and not nearly so rough around the edges, which makes me afraid this isn't real, and I get all befuddled."

"So what we need is simply more time, more conversation, more getting to know each other, right?" Susan asked, already rescuing herself from the awkwardness of her own well-hidden insecurities.

"Dating is different from hanging out with Mark and Beth," he said, shaking his head.

"Why is it, though?"

"I don't know. Could it be the insecurity we both have in ourselves, the pride we're so used to controlling it with?"

"It could very well be," she answered seriously.

"I do feel closer to you this evening than I did last night," he said suddenly, then gave a sudden laugh. "Scared. Absolutely scared. Quaking in my shoes."

She laughed with him.

"You want me to tell you the truth? I thought maybe you leaving at eleven and giving me that peck on the cheek meant you were going for the distant courtship idea, so I scratched myself into position really fast."

They really did laugh then, the pathetic humor in their situation seeming funny indeed. And at their age. Worse than sixteen-year-olds.

But a new closeness developed, a bonding of minds and hearts, a relaxing quiet of the soul, where they understood each other so completely, there was no need for words of affirmation or any fussy explanation. They were a couple now, the holy matrimony in mind, although it was not spoken of yet. And when he left that evening, well after midnight, both knew the strength of a shared heart and mind, both were convinced their union was God's will for the rest of their lives.

"You know you may as well plan your wedding now," Rose said, bending to lift a straggly pea vine with her left hand, grabbing at any peapod she could find with her right.

"James! Seriously, that boy's Pamper is falling off! Suzanne! Go get James. His Pamper is falling off. Oh, my word. Here comes the Schwan's man. Suzanne! Get James. Quick!"

Susan straightened her back, rubbed at the soreness, pitied the horrified Suzanne who shot toward the baby standing at the edge of the garden without the dignity of a well-placed diaper. When he howled at Suzanne, Susan went to help, listened to Rose place her order for pizza, french fries, and a huge variety of ice cream.

After the diaper was replaced, the Schwan's man had left, and order was restored, Rose chortled about the delicious lunch they would have if they ever got done with these never-ending peas.

"I don't know why Mam had to help Liz. She has all those nice in-laws. Unlike mine, who would never set foot in my sloppy garden."

"Oh, they would if you asked."

"Huh! No, they wouldn't. I'm an embarrassment to the family. I'm fat. I buy from the Schwanny man, and I read romance novels. All no-no's. All proving how low-classed I am. You know what? The next Princess House of Tupperware party any of them have, I'm not going. That stuff is overpriced, overrated, completely unnecessary for a good, frugal housewife like me."

"Uh, Schwan's man?" Susan asked, yanking at a pea vine.

"Anything delivered to your door is cheap."

Susan chose to let that go, but stood up and rubbed her back.

"Why doesn't Amos put up a pea fence?"

"Why doesn't he? Because he thinks I could. His mother always did her own. That's fine with me if she wants to stand in her garden whacking away at a stupid little stake. I ain't doing it. I told him so."

"So I get to pick peas in this mess."

"Quit complaining. Soon enough you'll have your own patch. Complete with a diaperless toddler."

She laughed obnoxiously at her own joke.

"Is this one for real now?" she asked.

"This is it."

"Never thought I'd hear you say those words."

"But it is different this time. Those months in Wyoming helped me to see the big mistake I made."

Rose straightened, rubbed her aching back, fixed a stare at her sister.

"You? Made a mistake? The first one of your life."

"Stop it, Rose."

Rose bent her back, went back to yanking pea vines, pulling off handfuls of the long, green pods. Susan eyed the brilliance of the orange fabric stretched across her wide backside, the absence of a modest black bib apron, and wondered if anyone really saw themselves in a true light.

Orange. Very fancy, but so typically Rose.

"Do I really come across as self-righteous?" she asked suddenly.

"Well, perhaps not that, but high and mighty, always having your act together, neat as a pin, managing your jobs well, always finished on time. You're just such a perfect person."

"You know I'm not."

"Oh yes. You watch. You'll marry Levi, live in a perfectly gorgeous house with a landscaped lawn and weedless garden, definitely a black-topped driveway. You'll only have a few children, and they'll be little angels, with the combined effort, the result of reading Christian child-rearing books. Even your horse and buggy will be spotless. You watch."

"That's not funny."

"Wasn't meant to be funny."

"Does it matter to you what I'm like?"

"Course not. I love you just the same. But you are like my in-laws. Amos's family. You should have married Amos instead of me. I mean, come on. Sarah stopped in unexpectedly and was so busy taking in the mess in my kitchen, she could barely say what she needed to say. It's awkward every time. I'm sure I'm the source of dinner conversations with all of them."

"But surely they accept you."

"No, they don't. They are nice to me on account of their upbringing. Plastered smile, proper words. It's fine, everything's fine, but if they were honest, they'd ask me what I do all day."

"Rose."

"Don't Rose me. I know what I'm talking about. And I am getting tired of it. I told Amos the other day, we should move to Indiana or Virginia or someplace far away from his snooty family. You know what Sarah said? She asked if I have a cultivator for my garden. Really? What does she care? I know my garden is green with weeds, but my vegetables grow just the same. I hate weeding my garden. If it was up to me I wouldn't have one. Just go to the Singing Spring Foods and buy vegetables in bags. They're just as good, but Amos would fall over backward. He's so much like his mother. It's disturbing."

What was there to say? The honest truth had been spoken, and for Susan to dispel it would never work, neither was the answer in her agreement, so she said nothing, allowing Rose to ramble on.

"Amos could run the cultivator. But would he? Never. That's my job, same as putting up the pea wire. See, the day he married me, he promised to care for me, and men don't take that serious. Not with a mother like his, who is a genuine workaholic, which he expects from his wife."

Rose stopped, caught her breath, then yelled at James to let that kitty go. James threw the poor kitten into the pea patch and ran bawling toward the house, and Rose shook her head.

"Suzanne!"

Thundering tones from her open mouth.

Eventually, she appeared, obviously used to her mother's bellows.

"Get James. He has to stop holding those kitties. The *grausich* (repulsive) little creatures. They all have sore eyes."

"They do not. Just one of them," Suzanne shouted, red-faced.

"Go get James. Go on. And stop being so mouthy, young lady."

And back to pea picking.

Susan counted three bushel baskets. Almost finished on the last row. The sun was climbing higher in the sky, the heat on her back becoming steadily more uncomfortable. She grabbed at tangled pea vines, snapped off pea pods in double quick time, looked forward to sitting on the porch for the remainder of the day, chatting with Rose, drinking iced tea and shelling peas. Rose was so easy to love, in spite of her chaotic lifestyle. She wasn't perfect, and knew it, but she didn't expect more from those around her, including everyone in her circle of acquaintances. If she was mad at her husband, she admitted it, bluntly stated the reason, and was over it a few hours later. She had a tremendous thorn in her flesh, the in-laws a constant chafing at her good humor, her conscience seared by the branding iron wielded by her mother-in-law especially.

The latest bone to pick with her was pea raising, without wire for the vines. She'd warned Amos this was the last year for peas if he didn't put up wire, which Susan knew would likely be the truth.

Enough was enough for Rose, and this pea picking meant she had reached the end of her rope, had no intention of tying a knot and hanging on, but had fully planned to fling the rope aside and go freely, arms outstretched, to the wonderful world of buying bags of frozen peas, and if Amos didn't like it, well, he could put up the pea wire.

It was time she stood her ground.

They lugged the bushels of peas to the porch, brought patio chairs, stainless steel bowls, plastic buckets, and sank gratefully to rest their tired backs, drink iced tea, and begin the tedious task of shelling. Rose leaned down to gather handfuls of pea pods, put them in her lap, and began popping the peas out of the pod with her thumb, listening to the tinkling sound as they hit the bottom of the bowl.

"I don't know, Susan. I say it every year, but I do love to sit and shell peas. Suzanne, put your chair over a bit. You're too close. Git. I'm so warm."

James set up an awful howl from the bottom of the slide. Rose watched, exasperated, before yelling to David, "Bring him here."

She held the crying child, consoled him, lifted his bangs to see if there was a bruise, then told Suzanne to fix him a bottle of apple juice.

"He doesn't like apple juice, Mom," Suzanne countered.

"Go."

And Suzanne went, sighing deeply and casting a look at Susan.

Susan smiled, told her she was so responsible for her age. And thought again of Titus, the awful heartache of her leaving, a heart wrenching goodbye. She had repeatedly told herself he was not her responsibility, but couldn't help the way he crowded into her thoughts.

"You should appreciate the fact that you and Amos are together, Rose. The pathetic situation in Wyoming. Motherless children. It's just . . ."

"Does it bother you?" Rose asked unexpectedly.

"No."

"Yes, it does."

"Well, maybe sometimes. Not for Sharon. She's so young. But that Titus. He's a mess. And that big galumph of a father. Honestly, Rose, he is the exact opposite of what a single father should be. All he thinks about is logging."

"Hmm. Doesn't sound good."

"It isn't."

"You lived with this guy. Didn't you ever wonder how it would feel to marry him and raise his children? Did you ever feel romantic toward him?"

"Of course not. I had Levi."

"You did? No, you didn't. He was here, and you were there."

"But I mean, I knew what I wanted then."

"Did you? Well, good. I hope you stick with it. But let me tell you, Susan, dating is a whole other ballgame. Once they know they have that knot secured and you are together for life, they can really turn down the charm dial. They don't shave or bathe, they complain about their food, they don't go where you want to go, and you quickly hit the real world after that first baby."

"So? Levi won't be like that."

"Mm-hmm. And the moon is made of green cheese."

Susan laughed.

"I think the long wait will pay off in the end."

CHAPTER 3

THE LETTER WAS WRITTEN ON YELLOWED NOTEBOOK PAPER, FROM a town in western Illinois. Kate's handwriting was as close to perfect as they all remembered, two sheets of positive news, a world filled with sunshine and happy days. They lived in a small double-wide trailer on a dirt road with woods around them, and the public school system was not a Christian environment, so she would be homeschooling kindergarten. Emily was a big help to her with Marie, who was chubby and becoming quite heavy for her to carry.

They were coming to Lancaster for a visit, would they be welcome on the twenty-fourth of the month?

Susan watched her mother's face for some sign of emotion, but her face remained unreadable, handing over the letter without comment.

Susan's eyes scanned the page, tears forming as she read between the lines. Another home, another chance for Dan to keep his job, this time as a truck driver for a feed company. Good wages, and he liked the driving. He had passed his test for the CDL.

As their visit approached, Susan found her mother's nervous energy reflected in herself. They finished the peas, cultivated the garden and planted late sweet corn, weeded flower beds, mowed and trimmed, raked the driveway and cleaned the house. Susan put clean sheets on the guest bed and Mam "fixed food," her way of staying busy as she worried about the first visit after the excommunication and expected shunning for those who had left the Amish church.

She made a rhubarb pudding, a chocolate cake, and cornstarch pudding with vanilla and Cool Whip. She grated cabbage and mixed it with a sweet and sour dressing, put a roast of beef in the oven, peeled potatoes, and watched the driveway. Her father's face was pale and stern, his words few. This was new. This was something other people experienced in their lives but never themselves.

Die ga-bahnty (the excommunicated).

His own precious daughter, having rid herself of past rules and regulations, lived a life contrary to all he had taught her, and it rankled.

Church rules required shunning, having nothing to do with them. Nothing? This was the question. Nothing at all, if it was your own daughter, who would be here in Lancaster County, dressed in the *ordnung*, driving a horse and buggy, were it not for the unstable Dan?

Dat wrestled with the unfairness, he wrestled with church rules and love for his daughter. He admitted to God the lack of conviction, prayed to stay strong in uncharted territory, when your heart told you one thing and the church another. He confided none of this to his wife, whose set face and frenetic energy spoke of her own struggles.

The purr of an engine, the appearance of an old blue minivan. Dat sat up in his recliner as Mam peered out the kitchen window. Susan smoothed her hair in the mirror, adjusted her covering, steeled herself for the sight of her beloved sister.

Before she could open the screen door, her eyes were swimming in tears, the sight of Kate's pretty face and dark hair cut short, the white T-shirt and skirt. She rushed across the porch, down the steps and into her arms. Kate's body remained rigid, her dark head on Susan's shoulder. There was her father, his arms around them both, their mother waiting, her face twisted with the effort to remain strong.

Dan stood nearby, his face grim, immobile, a figure cut in stone. He stretched out his hand.

"Dad."

"Dan."

They shook hands, one pump of expected politeness. Both hands fell away, dove into pockets as if seared. Kate wiped frantically at streaming eyes and nose, remembered children in car seats, turned away, her eyes going to Dan, begging.

Susan wiped her own streaming face and put on a smile for Emily, Nathan, and Micah. She held Marie, marveled at her size, the winsome face puffed with extra flesh, the little eyes squeezed almost shut with the wide smile.

"She's so cute, Kate," she said, her voice quivering.

Kate nodded, tried to smile, but couldn't quite accomplish it just yet.

The day was warm, so they settled on the back patio, Mam wiping tears, hurrying around providing chairs. The children were glad to be free of the restraints of the car and ran to the backyard to spend time in the remembered sandbox by the garden shed.

So many questions, so much catching up to do. But everyone was stilted, ill at ease, trying to appear normal when it was all so abnormal.

Kate repeatedly brushed at the loose hair, self-conscious, so guilty to see the reflection of sadness in her mother, the heartbreaking bravery of her father. Kate felt the disappointment, as uncomfortable as flung stones, disobedience the unspoken wall between them.

The parents felt the burden of failure, seeing the children living the *verboten* (forbidden) life of the *Englishy leit* (non-Amish people), driving a car, deserting the plain lifestyle, a slap in the face of expected obedience.

But this was here now, in plain sight, and what they could not change, they needed to accept.

And they found a foothold, a remnant of common ground. Until Dan started telling them about his spiritual conversion, having been delivered from hell by the blood of Jesus, the way of the cross.

When he was Amish, he'd lived in blindness, *ordnung* having stood in the way of Jesus, but now he was saved, a new person in Christ.

Wisely, Dat allowed him to say whatever was on his mind, watched Kate's impassive expression, then cleared his throat.

"And that be as it may, Dan, why did you have to leave the Amish to experience Christ's love?" he asked.

"Oh, it's not in the Amish church."

"I strongly disagree. But since you and I are obviously not of one mind, but both profess to be followers of Christ, then I think we had better not speak of these matters, since we will not be able to speak without argument, which is not what the Bible is for. If you can show enough obedience to respect my wishes, then we can be together in love. If not, I'll have to ask you to leave."

Dan sat forward, his eyes glaring, his nostrils flared.

"You can't do this. I have much to say."

"I don't doubt it. As I said before, if Mother and I were unbelievers it would be quite different, but we are believers who strive to live for Christ, and wish to remain in the church we were raised."

Kate placed a small hand on Dan's knee, said quietly, "Dan."

He gave her a withering look.

"I'm not staying here, listening to this blather. You know I'm right. You know the Amish are not saved."

Again, the gentle "Dan, please."

But his breathing became labored, a wild look appeared in his eyes, and he leaped to his feet. His hands clenched and unclenched.

Kate stood up; a hand went to his chest.

"Sit down, Dan. Please. It's okay."

"No, it's not okay, and you know it. We agreed to convert your family. Now you're already against me."

She pleaded, he pushed her roughly away, and she half fell sideways into a patio chair, quickly righted herself, gathered her composure as her husband stalked off the porch, tore open the door of the van, Kate on his heels, begging him to reconsider. Dat stood, opened his mouth, closed it again, his hands falling helplessly to his sides.

He left Kate standing in the middle of the driveway, joined the moving traffic on Route 340, and was gone.

Slowly, Kate turned, a small dejected figure, a woman defeated. Susan went down the steps, took her hand.

"Come, Kate. It's alright. He'll be back."

When Kate looked into her sister's eyes, Susan saw the deepest well of suffering, the unspeakable burden of self-blame, the heaviness of knowing she had failed to keep her husband on an even keel.

"It's my fault," she whispered.

"And how is this your fault?" Susan asked.

"I didn't help him talk to you. He really did have an experience where he felt saving grace. I believe him."

"So do I, Kate."

"Well, then . . ."

"Come, let's go inside. Mam is getting dinner. Dan will be back."

Slowly, as if in a dream, Kate walked toward the house, shaking her head.

"He won't be back."

"But he will. He's married to you. What about the children?"

Kate only shook her head.

As expected, her mother had hidden all her emotion, dealing with stressful situations by bustling, opening the refrigerator door, checking the roast in the oven, setting a stack of plates on the end of the kitchen counter. Knives and forks in a basket, napkins and plastic cups.

Kate, so thin, pale-faced, and sorry. Susan's eyes flashing with indignation, her father's sad eyes staring across the room from where he sat in the recliner.

"I'll mash potatoes," Susan offered.

Kate stepped up. "Mam, what about *bann* and *meidung* (shunning)?"

"Kate, it's alright. You and the children take the table. We'll eat here at the bar."

"Are you sure?"

"Yes."

And so they ate together, but not at the same table, which was the requirement for those who left the church. The children chattered as they ate, and conversation flowed easily, this being their Kate, their grandchildren, and they were happy to have them.

After dishes, they sat together and Mam asked Kate to be honest, open, to tell them about her life in Illinois. Kate's eyes went to the driveway, the back door, her hands knotting repeatedly in her lap. She struggled to maintain her composure, struggled to speak the truth.

Finally, Susan told her to stop holding back. No matter how bad it was, they needed to know in order to help.

"But . . ."

"No, Kate. We saw how he is."

Kate sighed.

"He was doing so good. He completely quit drinking."

Her father sat up. Her mother's eyes opened wide.

"Yes. Drinking. He has always . . . uh . . . done that in secret. But I don't think he can help it at all. He has troubles. It's only in the last year that he relapsed. He can't help it. Since I have a phone, I can google his behavior, and he is bipolar. Every symptom. Every single one.

"I can help him by obeying everything he wants. We go to another church now, and . . . other things. When he gets upset, he leaves for weeks at a time. I have no idea where he is, but he always comes back.

"He loves me. I know he does, and he says he needs time alone. I don't know where he is, but if I'm not patient, he says divorce is the only other option. And I don't believe in divorce."

Her voice was flat and barren as a desert, as hoarse and low as a person longing for an unreachable drink of water. Her beautiful face, framed by her dark hair, showed eyes large and black with suffering.

"Kate."

Her mother's voice was strangled with pain and disbelief. Her father got out of his chair, went to her, and as if she was still a young child, he lifted her gently from her chair and held her to his wide chest, his big calloused hand slowly smoothing her silky dark hair, as his tears fell on her head.

"Kate. Kate."

Susan watched through a blur of tears and knew in her heart her sister had reached a place beyond human emotion, a place bereft of hope, a place very similar to a description of suffering beyond words. Kate did not cry, her face a mask of contortion, the steel will coming to her aid whenever she needed it.

"Kate, does he hurt you?" her father asked, as he released her.

"No. Yes."

"Which one is it, Kate?"

She shook her head.

"Listen, we can't let you go back to Illinois if he's harming you, we can't do it," her mother pleaded.

Incredulous, Kate lifted her stunned eyes.

"But I have to, Mam. We're married. What about Marie? He loves Marie. I . . . I . . . He loves me."

All afternoon they listened as the floodgates of her emotional dam allowed the suffering to escape. Little by little, in bits and pieces, the tangled version of emotional and physical abuse flowed, though even then, only the tip of the iceberg was seen as she kept insisting his behavior was her fault, and the fact that he loved her did not allow her to leave.

"He's training me to be a Christian wife. When he leaves, he can depend on me to be there waiting, the true mark of Christian womanhood. That's real submission. In a marriage the man is the head, like the Lord, therefore he can do what he wishes."

Susan could see her father struggling for control of his anger.

Susan burst out, "Kate, why are you still putting up with this?"

"Because I love him. Because I thought I could help him. Some women can. I read so many books where Godly women actually changed their men."

"And how is it working for you?" her father ground out.

Her mother sat up, her eyes flashing behind her glasses.

"You are not going back. Ever. You are staying right here with us. You and the children. There is absolutely nothing to hold us back from protecting our daughter."

"But I am *im bann* (excommunicated)."

"So what? Your suffering is over," she said emphatically.

Slowly, Kate shook her head. "I can't."

Mark and Elmer came home from work, threw their lunches on the counter, greeted their sister shyly. Kate did her best to hide the deep heartache, joked and smiled, said they finally were turning into decent guys. Elmer wolfed his supper and was off to play ball, but Mark spent time with Kate and the children, playing a game of soccer with Nathan, Emily squealing and running with them.

Micah asked for his daddy and Kate assured him he would return, but they all had their baths, with borrowed pajamas and underwear from the neighbors, toothbrushes and combs produced from Mam's extra stash, a joke among the family, but coming in handy now.

Kate sat in Susan's room, wearing her night attire, one leg tucked beneath the other, looking so much the way she always had, except for the depth of hardship in her dark eyes. Repeatedly, she went to the window, watched the headlights snaking along on 340, listening for the sound of the blue minivan turning into the drive.

"Kate, sit down. You know he'll be gone for a while."

Kate nodded, obeyed. She lay her head on the back of the couch, sighed, shook her head from side to side, and said wearily, "That my life should come to this."

Susan swallowed the lump in her throat.

"You were so happy."

"We were. But you know, I should have seen the warning signs. I should have waited. I was so young and so in love."

"What if he comes back?"

"He will. Eventually. And I'll go back, no matter what Mam says. I'm married to him, till death do us part. I promised to love him, care for him in sickness and in health, and this is a sickness, this bipolar disorder. I think if I am patient, God will find a way."

"But, Kate . . ."

Kate put up a hand. "With prayer, all things are possible."

"You're not facing reality, Kate. You're in denial. He's dangerous."

Kate held a woven blanket to her face, hid her eyes as she rocked from side to side, moaning. So hard did she work to suppress her emotion.

Suddenly, the blanket was dropped, thrown with force.

"You know what he did? He beat me one night. With a broken chair leg. After he broke the chair. But he was terribly sorry. The next two weeks were the best weeks of our marriage. He was so loving and kind. And I did complain about not having any money, which is not the way God intended for a follower of him. Dan showed me that in the Bible. So it was for my own good."

Susan begged, she pleaded and cajoled, trying to get Kate to see the seriousness of the situation. She told her parents, and her father wasted no time getting her an appointment with a counselor at Green Pastures. After two weeks, with Susan living in constant worry of Dan's return, Kate began to weep softly, at any given time of day, a sound they had all been waiting on.

The sign of healing.

SUSAN WAS AWAKENED by the blue flashing lights on her ceiling. She gasped, leaped from her bed disoriented.

"Mam! Dat!" she called, stumbling blindly down the stairs, the blue lights illuminating the living room, the stairway, covering the house with alarming unreality. Her parents' bedroom was in back of the house, as was Kate's upstairs, but Mark and Elmer joined her as she awakened her parents.

She reached the door, her heart knocking loudly in her chest to find two dark-clad police officers. Quickly, she pressed the button on the battery lamp, opened the door to ask them inside. Her father appeared and took over as Susan stepped away. Her mother sat on the couch, a fluttering hand to her chest.

"Yes, Kate Stoltzfus is here," her father said, in a deep, steady voice, and Susan thanked God for the strength he possessed.

Kate, so small and thin, appeared like a wraith, no bigger than a child, a hand going to her mouth as photographs were shown.

Yes, it was Dan, her husband. His car had gone through a guardrail across the median strip and into a cattle truck. Dead at the scene. In Minnesota.

There were no tears, only shocked silence, the space of incredible minutes till Kate spoke.

"So, what is expected of me?" She sounded like a child, willing to do whatever anyone asked.

The week that followed was a dark, troubled fog of feeling their way through. Identification, arrangements made, the long trip, the eventual burial in Illinois, his family beside themselves with grief.

Since Dan was no longer a member of the Amish, the funeral was held at a large brick church in Illinois where Kate and Dan had attended, the congregation receiving the Amish people with grace and kindness, the sermon preached with hope, the minister speaking of Dan's illness, the often misunderstood and mistreated mental illness, with his family, dressed in black, receiving this hope, clinging to it in their time of crippling grief.

Susan sat in the beautiful nave of the church, the cool air-conditioned area with gleaming pews and thick carpeting muffling the sounds of footsteps, listening to the unaccustomed English language being preached by a minister, the message not unlike the German one often heard at funerals. She felt the power of his words and was comforted.

Kate stood by the opened coffin with her children around her, said her goodbye with grace and composure, her parents by her side.

They were received with so much love and caring in the church basement for the funeral meal, hugged and wished well by kind folks who felt like family by the time the afternoon was over.

Levi sat with Susan, his presence a calming pillar, her appreciation of him twice what it had ever been. When Kate came to say it was time to leave, her small face taut with exhaustion and grief, Levi rose quickly to go to her side, ask if she was alright, and she looked up at him, nodded, and said she was fine.

They returned to Lancaster the following evening, weary and saddled with grief for Kate, who would face her biggest hurdle, that of the debilitating self-blame. If only she had gone with him. If only she had tried harder to contact him. If only she had been a better wife.

"Kate, you need to listen to your counselor," Susan pleaded. "They know what you need most."

So much sadness, so great the need to be strong. The house in Illinois needed to be taken care of, her belongings brought back, the funeral paid for. Dat drained his savings account, paid every expense with an open heart.

Levi accompanied Mark, Elmer, and her father with the large truck to bring back Kate's pitiful furniture, the few items of clothing and belongings she had not sold to the consignment shop for a few dollars to buy groceries. The house had been a rental, so the back rent was paid, the owner happy to receive what he figured was lost, and they returned to the new home Dat had rented for her, a small Cape Cod only a short distance from their home.

"A scooter ride away," Dat said.

Kate felt she was not being true to the memory of him if she returned to the Amish, so they all had a family meeting, allowed Kate to express herself, listened to her view of the past few years, and decided to let her decide her life on her own. If she wanted to stay with the English in the honor of her husband, then so be it.

Susan was afraid Rose would literally have a stroke from steam buildup, but much to her credit, she remained silent. Liz sat beside her hefty husband with his trouser buttons winking over his round stomach and fell in love with him all over again. No matter that his father had the onset of dementia, at least her husband was kind and loving and in his right mind.

And Levi and Susan's bond deepened and became even more precious to them both, their weekends taking on a new dimension. Sometimes they were with Mark and Beth, but they enjoyed their time alone, driving along country roads, going out for supper. And not once did they feel the need to go on some big adventure, contentment settling in as their love grew.

As SUMMER DAYS came to an end, the cooling breezes drove out the cloying humidity and green leaves slowly turned from a faded green to astounding hues of red, orange, and yellow. There were whispers behind Susan's back, women wondering why Levi Yoder didn't ask Susan Lapp to marry him that fall.

Emma King, her gray hair pulled back from her forehead, her covering drawn forward, said you'd think he'd realize he wasn't getting any younger, and Becky Glick buttered her bread at the church table and said that was the way in the modern world, and it would leak into the church if they weren't careful, being older and older when they got married.

Sometimes, Susan wondered the same thing but hardly allowed herself to dwell on it, ashamed of her impatience, now that Levi had been so long suffering with her doubts and fears at times. And she was content, happy to return to her market job, falling back into the old routine beside Beth's sister Lydia.

Kate was back in her life, but only a former shadow of herself, thin and wan, harassed by indecision, afraid to make choices without Dan, afraid of being Amish for his sake. It was a hard time for the family, arguments breaking out easily as tension continued.

Rose said Kate knew better. Here she was being supported by the family, and she couldn't do what her parents wanted her to. Come on.

Liz told her to keep her mouth shut for once in her life, and Rose didn't call her for two weeks. Liz said she didn't care, everyone was afraid of Rose, and that was the whole trouble.

Through that summer, her father was a pillar of strength. Sometimes in church, Susan would see him, his eyes closed, his lips moving, and she knew he was praying, praying for Kate on this hallowed ground, the folding chair in the minister's row, close to the ones who preached God's Word every other Sunday.

And she was grateful for the strong men in her life who were steady, dependable, and true. Men like Levi, who gave her reason to believe the good men among them were worth their weight in gold.

CHAPTER 4

AND THEN, ON A CRISP SEPTEMBER DAY, THERE WAS A MESSAGE ON the answering machine in her father's office, the deep, hoarse voice of Isaac saying he was bringing the horse. He was on his way to some town in Maryland to purchase a mare, and he'd be there on a Saturday afternoon, the second of November. She could call him if it was okay on that date.

The message ended with, "Hope you're well."

She'd almost forgotten about Isaac with everything else going on, and she wasn't too sure about his horse. Dat wouldn't be happy, with the barn crowded like that, buying more horse feed.

But she called him, dismayed when he answered in a booming voice. She winced, held the receiver away from her ear, and said it was Susan.

"Susan who? Oh, that Susan. How's it going, Susan?"

She was laughing in spite of herself when she said fine, she was good.

"Good, good. Hey, is that okay to drop the horse off?"

"Yes. My dad isn't too thrilled, but . . ."

Before she could finish, he yelled, "He'll get over it. You need this horse. Titus says he misses you."

"How's Titus doing?"

"Good. Growing like a weed."

"Still running the roads with his dog?"

"Oh yeah."

That irked her so badly she almost hung up. The man would not listen to reason, wouldn't take advice at all. But she spoke in a level voice when she asked if Titus was coming with him, and he said yes he was.

"Did you get married yet?" he asked.

"I don't even feel like answering that question. How would you like it if I asked you that question?"

"Fire away. Tina? Boy, there's a piece of work. She went home to Geauga County. Good riddance."

"Seriously, Isaac."

"Wasn't serious to me."

"Well, what about the children?"

"They went to work with me for a couple of weeks, but since school started, Edna puts them on the bus and I pick them up in the evening. It works out pretty good."

"Mh-hm."

"What?"

"I just said, mm-hmm."

"Look, I gotta go. See you on the second."

Click.

Susan looked at the receiver, lifted her eyebrows, and laughed out loud. What a disaster. She had meant to have a meaningful conversation about Kate, hoped he would sympathize, but he had no time to listen. Likely he was off to the barn or stirring up trouble with the neighbors.

She could imagine the state of his house, the dust and mud and gruesome refrigerator. She wondered what Tina had done to deserve that label he gave her.

On Saturday evening, Levi suggested they pay Kate a visit. He'd met her at Giant in Lancaster and she'd asked them to come. Susan was happy to spend an evening with her sister, and especially with the children, so she was glad to walk the short distance to her house, the children clamoring at the door when they arrived.

Levi was like an old friend to the children, having spent time with Nathan and Micah on the trip to Illinois and through everything they'd been through. Kate greeted them warmly, a soft glow on her cheeks.

Susan noticed she was letting her hair grow, and hope sprang up. Why was it she hoped so fervently Kate would decide to come back? So the family circle would be united again, she supposed, and wasn't sure if one should think that at all. Kate was a believer, just not in their church, which was a highly controversial subject, tossed around with varied degrees of acceptance between liberals and conservatives.

And she let it go, knowing it was for the best.

But Susan noticed a new light, a certain radiance, emanating from her sister, and was grateful to see her gain confidence, to shed the crippling self-blame. Or didn't it have anything to do with it?

Levi entertained the children, playing Slap, with Emily giggling as she won one hand after another, Susan watching with pride. Kate commented on his way with children, saying he'd make a wonderful father.

She served a simple snack, soft pretzels hot from the oven, and mint tea. Levi complimented her, saying he'd never eaten better, and his mother made really good soft pretzels. Kate flushed slightly, but thanked him politely before going to put Marie to bed, leaving Susan to tell Levi she appreciated his kindness to Kate and the children so much.

That evening, after the children were in bed, Kate told them she'd finally reached a decision, after much deliberation. She was coming back to the Amish, not because it dishonored Dan's memory, but she, herself, felt she wanted to live the plain lifestyle, all she had ever known and cherished growing up at home.

"Please don't make a fuss. I don't want honor or praise. I have found my way, but it doesn't diminish the church in Illinois at all. I wish I could have the strong, unwavering faith some of those folks have. I simply need to return to my roots to have peace of mind."

"Oh, Kate. I am so happy for you. But I'll let you tell our parents."

"This is unusual, Kate," Levi said.

"I know. That is why I don't want to cause a stir. Just quietly return to my rightful place in life."

Levi watched her small face and tears sprang to his dark, brown eyes. Susan was so blessed to see him portray this strong emotion and decided she would forever be thankful for his warm and caring heart.

He seemed to take Kate's decision very seriously and was there with Susan and her parents when she told them the following weekend.

The news was received with quiet elation, her parents respecting Kate's wishes. And after six weeks, having received instruction and admonishing from the ministers she had always known, Kate was received back into the fold, her too-short hair coaxed and pinned into place with bobby pins and more than a few pumps of hair spray.

She was still so young, so petite and so pretty, her face glowing with an inner peace. Her family wept quiet tears of joy but remained true to Kate's wishes and did not create an undue fuss.

On November second, Susan was creating a fancy dish for one of her younger friends' wedding, when she heard a crashing knock on the screen door and lifted startled eyes to find none other than Isaac himself, standing like a giant on the back patio, no pickup or horse trailer in sight.

She flew to the door, wondered wildly at her appearance, but it was too late now. She'd forgotten all about this arrival.

So she greeted him with unkempt hair, an old black *dichly* (bandana), no bib apron, and an old navy blue dress with Clorox stains on it, not caring too much either way.

"Hello, Susan."

"Hi yourself. Where's Titus?"

"In the truck. I wasn't sure we could turn this thing around in here. I'm sorry to say. I have really bad news."

She looked up to find his dark eyes even darker with concern, and for once in his life, the bluster diminished.

"He, the horse, broke his front foreleg, and we had to put him down."

A hand went to her mouth, her eyes open wide.

"I feel so bad. He became frightened, carried on and caught his hoof, twisted it, and so quick, he was down. Titus is really upset. That's why he's in the truck."

"Of course. I'm sorry about the horse."

"I feel awful about it. I hate to see a horse suffer, anytime. So I'll be on my way, take him to a landfill, I guess."

He looked around, then said, "So this is where you live?"

Susan waved a hand, her arm extended.

"My home."

"It's great. Neat as a pin. Your parents home?"

"Actually, they aren't. November is wedding season, full swing. So they're out shopping. My brothers are at work."

"Oh. Well, look. I have to get going, take care of this horse. I can only apologize again. You know I meant well."

"Of course."

"Just sickening when something like that happens. Horses are beautiful creatures, it's almost like losing a person."

Susan lowered her eyes, thought of Dan, Kate's sorrow, the onslaught of grief following her from the time she woke up until her sleepless nights turned into restless, dream riddled slumber, the demon of self-blame keeping her awake.

"Yes, we . . . had a loss in the family. Kate's husband, Dan, was killed quite suddenly on the interstate highway."

"She the one who went with the English?"

"Yes."

"I'm sorry for your loss. Can't be easy. I'm well acquainted with grief. You know. Well, gotta go."

She said nothing.

"You want to see Titus?"

"I do."

"Come on."

She followed him out the door and down the drive to a huge dual-wheeled pickup truck hauling the fanciest horse trailer she'd ever seen. It was gray and black, with windows and doors spaced perfectly, detailing and lettering to perfection. She saw the driver behind the wheel and the small blond head, peering anxiously in their direction.

"You want to see the mare?"

She shrugged her shoulders. "Not really. I know how beautiful she was, and it's hard seeing a dead animal."

She met Titus's eyes, waved and smiled, then opened the door to greet him. The words barely left her mouth before he flung himself out of the truck and into her arms. He hid his face against her, and a strangled sob escaped the confines of his closed mouth. Speechless, Susan held him, awkwardly, before releasing him to step back, get down to his level, place both hands on his shoulders and look into the small face twisted with pain and the desperate resolve to regain the unwanted tears, the opening of his aching heart.

"Titus!" Susan said, trying to find a lighter note. With another choking sound, he threw himself back into the safety of her arms, and she held him and lost all her own reserve, tears running down her face and into his blond hair.

There were no words that could be spoken, no words to span the longing and pain, the truth of never being able to be there for him, so she held him, rubbed his back, and smoothed his hair. And when she looked up to question Isaac, she was shocked to see the craggy face wet with his own tears, his lower lip caught in his teeth.

Susan looked away, unable to subject herself to a glimpse of the immeasurable sadness of the parting of a wife and mother, a small boy having been wrenched out of a sweet secure existence into a life where another parting was too hard to be borne.

"Oh, Titus. Listen, I'll come visit."

He drew back, hope in his brown eyes, swiping furiously at his unwanted tears with the back of his hands.

"Will you be our teacher again?"

"I can't, Titus. I just can't."

"Why not?"

"Because I live here now. And . . . and I . . . just can't."

"Titus, come. We need to leave. We still have a few hours to go."

Titus stepped back, looked at his father, then to Susan. He shivered, sighed.

"Okay."

He lifted a hand. "Bye."

The acceptance was heart wrenching, the downward slope of his shoulders speaking of his giving in to hard circumstances, knowing at his young age things many older boys would never experience. When he climbed in and slid over to make room for his father, he lifted his hand again, a small tight smile erasing the worst of his pain.

She turned to Isaac.

"I'm sorry."

"Don't say that. We aren't your responsibility. We'll be fine. You have a good life, and I mean it. Maybe you can invite us to your wedding, which would help Titus understand."

Her eyes lit up. "I will. That's a great idea."

He extended a hand, and she shook it, looked into his eyes, and found only kindness.

"Goodbye."

"Goodbye, Isaac."

And he was in the truck, already eager to be in Maryland and getting the new equine acquisition. Always enthused about life, the hard work and never-ending challenges. She lifted a hand, watched the truck and trailer move off, blending with the traffic streaming past.

She turned, walked slowly up the drive, her sweater pulled tightly around her shivering form, the light of the day gone gray. Only for a moment guilt took away her security, her sense of well-being, of being on the road God meant for her. Isaac had assured her they would be fine, and she knew he spoke with conviction.

No, they were not her responsibility at all.

Somehow, though, a lingering malaise kept her staring into space, the cellophane wrap and brilliant ribbon she had taken so much pride in suddenly seeming frivolous, unnecessary. For a fleeting instant, she wondered how important her world really was, the constant shuffle of social life, the pettiness, the rush to attain, to acquire the next new thing, to wear the next new fabric in just the right color, to see and be seen at all the most popular functions.

And now, after the letdown, the pain and humiliation of Dan and Kate making their own way in the world, to have her return to the fold in her own quiet way, seeing her parents lifted up with so much admiration, praised and respected. It all seemed like so much hard work, this never-ending scramble to get married, to work hard and acquire so much, both materially and socially.

She felt weary now, a dark cloud hiding the sun, as if the day had been broken into shards of shattered glass. She shook herself mentally, picked up the corners of the cellophane, and brought it expertly up over the wicker basket filled with rolled-up Ralph Lauren towels.

Had to be name brand for Melissa. This would be some wedding, no doubt. And she felt the same gray weariness fold its wings over her usual happy outlook, shook it off, gathered the ends of the ribbon around the bunched cellophane and shook her head.

The dead horse.

She shivered. Had it been an omen? She had not been meant to accept Isaac's gift. Perhaps if she'd had the horse, a part of her would always remember Wyoming, the great open spaces, the life-changing scenery, a whole world so unlike her own. She was meant to be here with Levi. The thought of him brought up a great swelling tune of love, like an orchestra of the heart, the cadence dashing all her doubts and wondering.

He only had to propose, and her future would be sealed with the sacred vows.

SHE WAS WHIRLED away on the winds of November, conveyed to weddings in the gleaming new carriage drawn by the finest horse, her companion the love of her life, blessed beyond measure. She sewed and wore the colors required of friends and cousins, giggled and shared secrets with Beth, or SaranAnn, or Betty, or Ruthie. She listened to an array of sermons, always with the same text, the same story of Tobias found in the Apocrypha, a touching story even if it was not from the

Bible itself. She admired bridal tables, set her gifts with the vast array of other wedding gifts, ate the chicken filling called "*roacsht*," mashed potatoes, gravy, creamed celery, and pepper slaw, dipped a cookie in her coffee before leaving the table to help sing hymns as the bride and groom opened their gifts. Each wedding lasted till late in the evening, and each one served the purpose of making her more eager for her own special day. Levi had not spoken of an engagement so far, so she knew her wedding would likely wait till the following year, but perhaps, just perhaps, she could be married in spring, before council meeting and communion.

Levi remained the perfect boyfriend, always considering her needs, always asking what she wanted to do on Saturday night, on Sunday, a fact she never overlooked. She often told him how grateful she was.

Sometimes they would visit Kate, who lived a simple life in her rented house, received cash in envelopes with no signature, the true alms of the Amish. "Let not your right hand know what your left hand does, let all your giving be done only to the glory of God and not your own."

Kate learned to applique and quilt, but on that money alone she could never have supplied for her and the children's needs.

Kate was sad, without appetite. She missed Dan, the Dan she had married, the first rosy year when love was spontaneous, exuberant, her whole existence alive with dazzling Cupid's arrows.

Her face held a pale vulnerability, almost childlike, her thin form always moving, caring for her children's needs.

She refused all wedding invitations, saying it was too hard to sit alone, knowing Dan would never again be seated on the opposite side of the huge building, told Susan to go and enjoy herself, she'd go to her wedding when the time came.

They were seated around her kitchen table on the Wednesday after David Esh's Nancy's wedding. Mam was at the stove, stirring the chipped beef gravy, checking the biscuits in the oven, with Rose saying she was absolutely not hungry this morning, with that new keto diet she was on. She already lost four pounds and she'd started on Saturday.

"It's the greatest plan yet," she chortled, drinking black coffee and eyeing the homemade pancakes in the casserole dish.

"Four pounds! Wow," her loyal sister Liz commented.

"Yep. I feel so skinny."

Rose smoothed her bib apron over her well-rounded stomach, her tight sleeves accentuating the heaviness of her arms, although today she wore a somber shade of olive green, which went well with her smooth, golden complexion. Rose was very pretty, only a bit larger than any of her sisters, which was fine, Mam assured her repeatedly.

"I would gladly accept twenty of the pounds you're losing," Kate said wryly.

Liz hooked an arm across her shoulders, leaned her cheek against her shoulder and said, "Ach. Kate. I pity you so much."

"Don't. I am okay, for real. Everything just happened so fast. The last year of my life has been a rollercoaster, and sometimes it feels so terribly unreal. He was so young, so troubled, and should have gotten help. If only . . ."

Rose lifted a hand.

"Nope, Kate. You're not going there. That's why you can't eat. You're going to end up with a stomach ulcer. Whoa, Ray. Whoa. Liz, get your little boy. He's literally beating up on James. *Komm*, James."

She lifted her howling one-year-old, glaring at the hapless Ray while Liz rushed to the rescue, apologizing as she gathered him up.

Always the queen, that Rose, Susan thought.

Mam served the brunch, a delicious assortment of breakfast foods and pastries, everyone exclaiming over this dish or that one.

Rose was allowed the egg casserole, but none of the biscuits or pancakes. Her resolve steadily decreased as she watched Susan enjoy the fluffy biscuits with a generous helping of chipped beef gravy, brown and rich.

"You know, I think I'm going to make a new rule for myself and cheat on days we have sisters' day. I can't always deprive myself. They say that's the wrong thing to do. If you get too *fer-late* (despondent), you're not going to keep it up."

With that, she helped herself to two biscuits and a generous ladle of gravy, put a forkful to her mouth, and closed her eyes.

"Mmm. Dear carbs. I love you always."

"Ach my, Rose. Just be happy. You'll never be thin," Mam said.

Susan knew she felt sorry for Rose, the only one who had a weight problem, the other girls never having to worry about the caloric intake.

"Did you see Susie King's tight dress, though? She should not be wearing those dresses in her condition," Liz remarked.

"Tell her," Rose said.

"I don't have the nerve."

"Me, either."

The conversation turned to Kate's past, her deceased husband's slow slide into an unhealthy emotional state, his refusal to address the diagnosis, with Kate always by his side, trying to make his life better.

Sometimes she cried, recounting moments of fear, times when she was more afraid for him than herself.

"After I consented to leave the Amish, he became increasingly unhinged. His highs were so out of control, his lows so menacing, I was often afraid for all of us. The only thing I had to hang onto was my faith in God, and being thrust into such a new and different way of worship, it was just difficult. I mean, all my life I wore a dress, cape, and apron."

She stopped, touched her covering.

"Do you have any idea how naked my head felt? I always had these moments of panic, as if I forgot something. You totally have to reinvent yourself, to decide how you're going to look and act and be. You don't really know how. All my life, I was used to *Englishy leit* (non-Amish people), but if you really have to go out there and fit in . . ."

Her voice drifted off.

"You don't know how. My hair wasn't right. I wore dresses, of course, and only from yard sales and thrift shops, all I could afford. The people in our church were so nice, though. The only thing that got me through."

Mam watched Kate's face attentively, her eyes limpid with emotion, one hand going to her chest as if to quiet her pounding heart.

Kate went on, "I do believe if this would not have happened . . ."

Her voice drifted into a whisper; she waved a hand as if to dispel the terrible accident, the bewildering aftermath, and now, the days ridged and hollowed with cloying, clinging grief.

"I know I would have adjusted. I already had, in part. I just had to tell myself I was no longer required to dress a certain way, that anything was okay. Colors, patterns. It's just so hard to wrap your mind around this freedom of choice, which was a poor kind of freedom, with you and Dat living in my head."

She gave a small laugh, her eyes going to her mother's.

"Are we ever free of trying to honor our parents as best we can?"

"Absolutely not," Rose said forcefully.

Susan picked up on the righteous tone, opened her mouth, and closed it again, before reminding Rose of the fact she didn't always abide by her mother's wishes either, dressing so far out of the *ordnung*.

"Whatever!" Rose shot back. "As if you're perfect yourself."

"Let it go, Rose. You know Susan's right. We can't judge Kate by doing what her husband required of her. God is on His throne, the only true righteous judge, so everyone drop it," Mam said.

There was a space of time when contention hung in the air as thick as pudding, till Kate began softly weeping.

"I'd give anything to have my old life back, with Dan, in our little brick ranch house. We were poor, and he wasn't easy to get along with . . . all that depression . . . but we had our good times, too. I'm glad to be back here with all of you, but sometimes I feel old and battered and wise."

"You are wise," Liz said. "Wise beyond your years. And I imagine God has a reward all ready for you. If anyone ever deserved happiness, it's you."

And Susan felt almost greedy, the blessings heaped on her, one right after another, week after week.

CHAPTER 5

SUSAN WAS THOROUGHLY DISENCHANTED BY EVERY WEDDING BY the time the end of November finally arrived. She knew the whole Tobias story by heart, the only difference the various ways in which each minister portrayed it. She was tired of roast and mashed potatoes and gravy, had never seen so many wedding gifts and decorated rooms. But every couple was glowing with happiness, glad to have their special day finally arrive, eager to begin their new lives together.

Susan realized early in November how much she longed to be engaged to Levi, to plan her own wedding day, live in their own home. She wasn't getting any younger, she told herself, and living with her parents was not the ideal arrangement. They were no longer young, had both put on weight, wore dentures and slurped coffee, chewed food a bit sloppily, ate cold fruit soup and fried squash sandwiches in summer, that disgusting combination loaded with white bread. The torn pieces soaked in the milk with strawberries or bananas or peaches, heavily sugared, mayonnaise on more bread to support the fried zucchini. They still ate fried cornmeal mush for breakfast and shoofly pie with their coffee.

Dat took off his shoes and sat on the back patio, his hairy white toes spread to the cool evening breeze, then got out the clippers and worked on his ingrown toenail. Mam's dentures were loosening, so she often took them out over the kitchen sink, rinsed her mouth, the teeth, and flipped them back in without blinking an eye, while Susan swallowed and looked away. She told herself she loved them both, of course she did, it was the fact she wanted her own home, her own life with Levi.

Her brothers were noisy, clopped up and down the stairs like buffalo, left green toothpaste smeared all over the bathroom sink, wet towels on the floor, reeking socks draped over the hamper with the lid open.

Elmer came in at all hours of the night, sniffled and coughed, banged his shoes and his closet door, then rolled into bed and forgot to turn off the battery lamp in the bathroom. Mark was more respectful, but he had some bad habits in the bathroom as well, like hooking one shower curtain over the other, so you had to untangle that before you could close the curtain and get on with your shower.

She'd often told him about it, but he claimed he didn't know what she was talking about, and the situation continued.

But, of course she was aware of the fact she needed to be patient, which was not one of her virtues. Levi was merely taking his time, making sure she was one hundred percent ready and willing, given how she'd been so standoffish in the beginning. When it was their turn to go to the supper table at a wedding, she always felt proud, knew everyone eyed them with appreciation, this older couple who had found each other later in life, and such an attractive couple.

He was the perfect companion, kind and attentive, but when the weddings were over and he still had not mentioned marriage, never opened the subject in a lighthearted way, never teased or wished it was him getting married that day, she became unusually quiet on the way home, while he whistled under his breath and drove along without a thought in his head about engagement or marriage evidently.

One blustery November evening, when Susan shrank back against the side of the buggy and didn't have much to say, he took her hand and asked why she was so quiet. He laced his fingers in hers, his thumb massaging the back of her hand.

"I'm just a bit tired of weddings, is all."

"Yeah, me, too."

There was a space of silence, not uncomfortable, before he sighed, pulled back on the reins at a stop sign. Approaching headlights sent slivers of light across his face, the clean cut planes in sharp relief against the dark interior of the buggy. She saw the tenseness in his jaw, the set of his eyes, and wondered. As he turned left on Hill Road, he sighed again, and she looked out the window and felt an arrow of concern, a stab of fear she had never felt before with anyone.

"Susan."

Her breath seemed clogged in her throat, the oxygen in the carriage depleted.

"What?"

"I'm not dumb."

There was nothing to say to that, so she stayed quiet.

"I know you must be wondering why I don't ask you to be my wife. To let the world know we are engaged."

He stopped, and Susan's heart banged so loudly she honestly thought he would hear it.

"But now that I'm sure you are willing to . . . to go ahead with the relationship, I'm becoming restless, wondering if this is all I want out of life. Get married, go to work, come home, have children, live here in crowded Lancaster County, look and do and say everything I'm supposed to, fit in like a herd of cattle."

There was sarcasm, which stung painfully.

"This is not to dishonor the plain way of life, or to disappoint you in any way at all, Susan."

He stopped as they approached Route 340, then turned right before flipping the turn signal again, turning into her driveway, and bringing the horse to rest by the hitching rack in front of the barn.

"Say something, Susan, please," he said.

She shook her head, could not find her voice.

"But I have to go on. I cannot enter into marriage without honesty. I . . . well, you know how I always planned adventurous weekends before we dated. I have a restless spirit, I guess. There's so much to see and do, and I'm not quite ready to give up traveling. Experiencing new things."

"I can travel with you," she said in a very small voice.

"Ach, Susan. I do love you so much."

He reached for her, held her in his arms. She felt the fabric of his *mutza* (suit coat) against her cheek, heard the beating of his heart, and knew her dreams would evaporate like a vapor, a wind-blown fog always ahead, just a bit out of her reach.

She pulled back.

"You don't love me, Levi."

"But I do. I truly do."

"I'm not eighteen years old. If you loved me in the true way a man loves a woman, you would not even consider an alternative. I would be your top priority, and by all appearances, I am certainly not."

"But I don't want you to take it this way. Your words hurt me."

"Really? And yours don't hurt me?"

"All I'm saying is, I need to find out who I am. My coworker and I are planning a trip to the Yukon in spring. It's the chance of a lifetime. If you would be willing to wait through the summer, perhaps longer, I'll know which direction my life is headed."

Would she even be able to describe the hot rage sweeping through her body? She swallowed the quick retort, sat like a stone.

"I know, Susan. I know how this must disappoint you. But I think if we go through with this, our love will be stronger in the end. We are both mature, as you said earlier, and this time apart will only bring us closer."

"You think? Sorry, Levi, but no. I'm not waiting, going ahead with my single life harboring dreams that will never happen. If you do this now, no matter if you marry me, I'll always know I'm second best, not your first priority."

"No, no. That's not true. That's not what I'm saying."

She took a deep breath, steadied herself.

"That is exactly what you're saying."

"Please, Susan."

"Please what? You don't know what you're asking. To wait around for another year, all my friends knowing how patiently I stay single, while my 'boyfriend' . . ." She raised her hands, wiggled two fingers, mimicking quotation marks. "While my boyfriend goes off gallivanting into the wilds. No. It's one or the other."

"Susan, you're making this very difficult."

"I think you're the one who brought up the difficulty."

"Look, why don't we think about this for a week, finish the conversation on Saturday night?"

"Oh, you're planning on seeing me next weekend? Why?"

"To . . . well, to see you. You're my girlfriend."

The silence was so thick with unspoken words, the dark sky seemed like a sulfurous black vapor, the horrifying knowledge seeping through the night.

It was over. Susan knew, then, with wrenching accuracy, if she married him, her life would be a constant seeking for something that had never been there in the first place. He wanted her desperately when he thought he might not be able to have her. She was an almost unattainable adventure, exactly like the Yukon. After she consented to being his girlfriend, he grew bored, the Amish way of life depressing.

"I'm not your girlfriend. I'm your dream, and dreams end."

"But this is not what I want. I want you."

"No, you don't. You want me when you can barely have me. After I give you my love, you're bored. So go. Go on your trip, but don't expect me to be your girlfriend, because I'm done."

"You are actually saying it's over?"

"I am."

The horse tossed his head, asking to have the neck rein loosened. He stamped his front hoof, swished his tail, asking to get back on the road. Traffic moved along, a long car, then another, the clopping of hooves as more folks wended their way home from a wedding.

"So I can't come see you on Saturday night?"

"Of course not, Levi. I'm not taking a risk by staying here waiting. I will miss you, of course, and I'm not looking forward to the future, but it is what it is."

"Won't you give me another chance when I come back?"

"No."

And with that, Susan was out of the buggy and on her way to the house, his voice calling her name echoing in her head. She lay in bed, sleepless, dry-eyed, waves of irritation at all men rippling through her.

She allowed herself to feel the anger and shame, the disappointment. She was never, ever risking another relationship. She'd become a bitter old maid.

It was only when she prayed that the tears seeped from her closed eyes, and she wept softly, beseeching God to give her the strength to take this fresh hot anger and replace it with a godly love and forbearance.

And still she did not sleep, sometimes reveling in her fury and the fact she had surprised him and ended the relationship. As the night wore on, she found herself increasingly unstable, wavering between sadness, a deepening heartache, the sense of unfairness, to a raw outrage at the unbelievable self-superiority of men. As if they had the right to meander off, gaily pursuing selfish whims, expecting the weaker vessel to go about every day of life admiring and respecting the happy wanderer.

It was maddening.

Was she being unfair? After all, he had waited for her when she went to Wyoming. But she hadn't asked him to, hadn't assumed he would put his life on hold for the possibility that she'd decide to date him eventually. She'd been honest from the start of their friendship that she wasn't committing to a relationship. Whereas he'd led her to believe they were moving toward marriage when apparently he had no idea what he wanted. "I need to find out who I am," he'd said. What did that even mean?

And she was so weary of it all. Ashamed of being subject to this humiliation. If only she'd stuck to her original plan of staying single. She had known that romantic relationships just led to hardship, and still she had fallen for Levi like an idiot.

Well, she would make sure everyone knew she had broken up with him, not the other way around. She was the one who had taken matters into her own hands, and she was the one who would hold her head high.

Yes.

And she told no one until her mother asked on Sunday morning why Levi had not come to see her last evening. In clipped words, she told her they had broken up, and she would rather not talk about it just yet.

She ate Honey Nut Cheerios in her room, only on account of her stomach being in an uproar, lifted the bowl and drained the milk like a child, then read a few chapters in Psalms before weeping at her own sad life, exactly like King David's. At least she had not done a grievous sin by taking another man's wife the way he'd taken Bathsheba, then put her husband on the front line of war so he'd be killed. That was pretty awful, really. And God had forgiven him. Almost unreal. A man after God's heart, and he'd done that?

Her mother called anxiously up the stairs in the late afternoon.

"Susan?"

"What?"

"Aren't you hungry? Aren't you going to the supper?"

"No, and no."

"Susan."

She heard footsteps coming up the steps and resigned herself to her mother's itching curiosity, the zealous questioning that drove her emotionally up a wall. Why didn't mothers get it, really? There was absolutely nothing to be done. Go mind your own business and allow the poor loser some space to lick her wounds.

Rebellion sprang up and blossomed, so when her mother came into her room, sat down on the small sofa, pushed a pillow away, and stuck her stockinged feet out in front of her, she refused to give her the courtesy of meeting her anxious eyes.

"Susan. What happened? I was so sure."

"Yeah, well. I was, too."

"Do you care to talk about it?"

"No. I told you last evening."

"But who was it, you or him?"

"Mam, stop."

"Susan, this is hard for me, too. When my children hurt, I hurt with them."

Her lower lip wobbled unattractively, her eyes swimming as she began to weep.

"I'll be okay. When I'm ready, we'll talk about it."

"You're alright?"

"Of course."

With a sigh of resignation, her mother heaved herself off the sofa and down the stairs, leaving Susan with a large helping of self-loathing and a deeper sense of loss.

WHITE-FACED, TENSE, NURSING a burning rebellion, Susan drove her mother to sisters' day at Kate's house to bake Christmas cookies, swap them, and try to have a jolly old time. Halfway to her house, she wished she had not consented to drive her mother, with her senseless chatter meant to cheer her up, which did exactly the opposite.

"Rose says the keto diet doesn't work for her, with headaches popping up every day. Too much protein. I told her, but you know Rose, you can't tell her anything. Now she's taking some pill called Orange Tiger."

"Purple Tiger," Susan growled.

"Oh right. Anyway, it does wonders for her energy. She flies around and is always happy. I hope she stays on them. She's so heavy again."

Susan didn't answer, the knowledge of her own bubbling cauldron of irritation helpful. She couldn't be unkind to her mother. It was unfair to think any of this was her fault, so it was best to keep her prattling on.

"I wish we'd have a white Christmas for a change."

No answer.

Susan was lost in thought, the previous Sunday evening the worst she could remember, with Levi sitting almost directly opposite her at the singing table. His eyes pleaded, hers sizzled. Huh-uh, she thought, taking clean satisfaction in his handsome face with the normally bright eyes, an enthusiasm for life, emotion flickering through like wind-driven leaf shadows on water. His best feature, so dark and quiet, begging.

How she would have loved to say, "Levi, let's talk," but she knew all too well it would buy her a few months' time, a span of falling even deeper in love, until she foolishly promised to wait till he returned. And then he'd go to the Yukon and wind up meeting someone else or, in the process of figuring out "who he was," he'd realize he wasn't meant to be her husband.

Her sisters knew, but she had steadfastly refused to speak to anyone about it, even Kate. They all took one look at her strong silent face and didn't dare approach her or bring up the subject at all.

There were chocolate cutouts, snickerdoodles, molasses creme, chocolate chip, gingerbread, sugar cookies, chocolate crinkles, cranberry walnut, all waiting to be baked, sprinkled, and frosted. The kitchen was small and increasingly uncomfortable, so Susan picked up Marie, who was almost asleep on a child's rocker, and took her to the glider rocker to put her to sleep. The soft molding of the chubby little girl to her own pliant body relaxed and softened her mood. What an innocent angel, this young soul who was truly a gift of God with her good humor and sweet smile.

Kate came to sit beside her on the La-Z-Boy, reaching for Marie.

"You want me to take her?"

Susan shook her head.

"How are you, Susan?" she whispered.

She shook her head again, swallowed hard. Kate put a hand on her arm, rubbed her thumb across the sleeve in wordless empathy. This proved to have the same effect as opening a faucet, and Susan's mouth turned soft as her eyes closed and tears seeped from between them.

"Susan."

Her name was spoken in pure love and understanding. Sorrow was no stranger to Kate, and she understood so well the need for comfort and loving care. The kitchen turned strangely quiet, and quickly the living room was filled with wide-eyed sisters. Cookies burned in the oven, children scrambled on table and countertops, shoved forefingers in cookie dough and ate gobs of it. Susan talked quietly, brokenly, and they all wept together. Boxes of Kleenex, honking noses, the smell of smoke pouring from the oven, Rose shrieking and galumphing, Liz admonishing the children.

After order was restored, Susan's story was told in fits and starts, with prompting from alternating sisters.

"You did the right thing," Kate said soft and low.

"Absolutely!" Rose shouted. "If he thinks he can get away with leaving you on a string while he goes off to Alaska, he's crazy. I tell you, the end of the world is coming. Men nowadays have no idea whatsoever what it means to give their life to their wife."

"As young women don't know how to submit," Mam said.

"Really?" Rose shot back. "How do you respect a man like that? How? What an ignorant . . ." She let her sentence drift off before saying something inappropriate.

Liz nodded emphatically, lifted James, and sniffed at his backside.

"Rose. He's messy."

"Go change him."

"He's yours, not mine. So, Susan, have you prayed? You know God is the one who will guide you. There has to be a reason for this. Somewhere in your life I think you're missing something. Is there another road God wants you to try and you can't see?"

"Oh stop!" This from Rose, changing James's diaper. "You make my head spin. What are you? Some kind of evangelist?"

Mam said very seriously, "Liz has a point. You know the old saying, 'God closes one door but opens another.'"

"There will never be another," Susan said wearily. "I was happy with my life before I met Levi. It was stupid to think a man could make things better. I don't know how I got sucked into thinking he was God's will for me."

Kate wept softly.

"Bitterness eats away at your emotional health, Susan. It sours your soul and makes you spiritually ill. You have to recognize it, put up a guard."

"I'm not bitter, Kate. Just finished. Done. Flat out. Ka-put."

"I don't blame you," Rose said, grabbing a chocolate crinkle cookie, breaking it in half and eating both pieces.

The cookie baking went on, but the day had been sweetened by Susan's confession, the sincerity of everyone's understanding and empathy, so each cookie turned out to be special, flavored with love. Mam hummed as she drizzled snickerdoodles with white chocolate, smiled at the grandchildren, laughed at Rose when she claimed she'd eaten six cranberry walnut cookies with brown butter icing. And Susan felt her life returning, the winds of hope bringing a fresh rain, seeding wildflowers along the way. She laughed, she ate snickerdoodles and drank hot chocolate, and color rose in her face. She washed dishes, made tuna melts for lunch, opened a bag of pretzels and dipped them in ranch dressing. She smiled, she wept, and she talked.

That day there were hugs, a new closeness brought on by even more sorrow after Kate's harrowing time of losing Dan.

"It isn't like a death, Kate," Susan said. "I'll get over it."

"You will, and so will I," she answered. "I can't tell you how much I appreciate you, my dear family. You just don't understand the priceless gift of unity, of love and closeness in a family, until you don't have it anymore. And to be able to be a part of it again is so wonderful."

But who was to say things would be easy from that day forward?

They weren't.

It was hard to be back in the same old groove, making hoagies at Harrisburg Market, cleaning Carol's house, helping her sisters with various jobs, and worst of all, going to the youth gatherings, the senseless volleyball games, standing in line as the crowd snaked past tables laden with hot food, an assortment of desserts. Balance a plate, find a place to sit, over and over.

There was Christmas, New Years, Mark and Beth's wedding in the early spring, when winter still dueled with spring's tentative approach. The winds were as trustworthy as boyfriends, blowing viciously one day, bringing rain and bits of snow, then settling into soothing breezes and warm light from the sun, until it began its fury again.

She was a *nāva sitza*, literally a "beside sitter," a member of the bridal party, dressed in a white cape and apron, the dress a deep plum color matching the bride's. Her companion was Beth's cousin from Indiana, a tall, pimply faced youth of eighteen who smoked and made crude jokes, made fun of all the fancy dishes that were served, and in general, was bored out of his skin. It would have been deliciously satisfying to slap him.

And, of course, there was Levi. So achingly handsome in his white shirt and black mutza, his hair wavy, perfect, his eyes containing the same old light.

Her heart sank but she held her head high, smiled and laughed, and hoped he thought about the fact this could easily be their wedding day.

Mark and Beth made a striking couple, and the sermon was especially touching, with Mam's brother, a bishop with the ability to speak from the heart to young people, preaching an unforgettable amount of advice for newlyweds, but especially to the husband, to take seriously this new responsibility of caring for his wife. Susan wiped a few tears, hoped Levi was squirming uncomfortably.

And she went home alone. She was still happy for Mark, and so proud of him and sweet Beth, the glow helping her fall into a dreamless sleep. And she woke up to the fact that things seemed to be going a bit easier, for now. She lay in bed, stretched, then asked the Lord to be with her that day, to guide her steps and cover her with His love.

And please, dear Lord, help me to understand why this has happened. Help me to see the pitfalls, the wrong direction. Or am I simply missing something here?

That day she cleaned Carol's house again, answered questions about the wedding, said nothing when Carol asked Susan when her turn was coming. Carol lifted her eyebrows and gave a probing look, and Susan knew she'd have to say something.

"We broke up."

"What? You broke up? I thought Amish people didn't do that. Like, if you're dating, you're one hundred percent getting married."

"Not always."

"So you still have the freedom to choose?"

"Yes."

"Hmm. Well, good for you."

The subject was closed, and the work began after the car hummed into the garage. Susan felt the weight of her arms, the heaviness of her eyelids, and dragged herself from room to room upstairs, opening windows to allow the spring air to rush through the cleaned areas. She thought of the visible humiliation, friends and family and acquaintances watching poor Susan, stuck with that boy, the love of her life on the bench with the row of single boys. Wasn't that boy, Amos, a piece of work, though? She couldn't help laughing out loud at his description of cooked celery. He literally shivered at the sight of it, and Susan loved it, took a second helping as he leaned away from her.

She'd caught Mark's eyes and smiled, the softening of her heart full of love for her brother on this special day. He was truly marrying his best friend, and she was a treasure, a rare jewel, so in love with him she couldn't see straight.

Ah well. That state of bliss had been yanked away from her, and she was left in the dust once again. If only she could go back to being happily single, before she'd foolishly let herself fall in love or dream of marriage.

CHAPTER 6

T RUE TO HIS WORD, LEVI WENT TO THE FARTHEST REACHES OF THE United States, the beloved Alaskan territory called the Yukon. Susan got out an encyclopedia, her fingers tracing the thin lines portraying rivers and mountains, highways and forest. She knew enough to realize he was likely putting himself in danger, but what was it to her, really?

He was no longer a part of her life, in spite of his beseeching looks, the letter he had written, asking her to allow him an evening to explain himself better. Guilt had driven the masculine penmanship, the senseless explanation of why he was doing this, with Susan slowly shredding the letter into a hundred pieces, scraping them back into the envelope and stuffing it in the waste can.

Words on paper were even more hurtful than spoken ones—there on paper, taunting for many years. She did not need to read them twice, the message still the same as it had always been.

He did not want her, took the Yukon as a shield against her. Where had she missed the signs? He was so genuine. And she had taken her time, allowing commitment after a fairly long period of time, and he was so grateful for her acceptance.

Why was romance so elusive for her, and so simple, so joyful for Beth? Had she brought this all on herself?

Needless to say, another season, another spring finding her with her mother deliberating about the rows of peas, a serious contemplation, left Susan with enough irritation to want to howl.

"Mam, really, what does it matter where the peas go?" she said, sounding more terse than she'd meant.

Mam said nothing, her eyes going from one side of the garden to another. Serious business, the growing of peas. There was no comparing the taste of homegrown peas to store bought ones, no matter how much work was involved. Gardening was imprinted on every Amish housewife's mind, an important undertaking. Vegetables were a large part of the evening meal, the time spent around the table a gathering, with a healthy variety of food for growing children.

A garden was essential, as necessary as a refrigerator or stove.

Mam lamented the state of some liberal newlyweds who bought their peas already frozen, no longer wanting the backbreaking labor, or the small amount of peas from so much fuss. In her view, anyone who didn't grow peas was lazy, lacking the skills of an accomplished housewife. That poor husband, eating those large, overripe, bought peas in a bag. It was awful.

What was better than new spring peas with *raum salaut* (creamed lettuce)?

Likely, these young women didn't grow lettuce, either.

She lectured as she ran a string from one wooden stake to another, made a perfectly straight row with the edge of her hoe, moved the stakes and on to the next one. Susan followed with the bag of pea seeds, dropping them at a steady, measured length apart.

The air was chilly, the wind had a bite to it, but Susan wore a sweatshirt, and her mother didn't mind at all, her cheeks red from exertion.

She was always happy in her garden, and especially early in the season, when she was delivered from being cooped up in the house, quilting, crocheting or doing housework.

"Hey!"

They both looked up to find the neighbor lady, Barb, parting the arborvitae and stepping through it, her black scarf tied beneath her chin, a sweater buttoned from top to bottom, giving her the appearance of a well-stuffed sausage.

"Good morning, Barb."

Her mother stopped hoeing and turned to face her neighbor, a wide smile hiding what Susan knew was impatience, being stopped from her work. Pea planting time was serious business, with a short window of time between rain showers.

"Already? Planting peas already? My garden isn't dry enough," Barb said, crossing the yard to stand at the edge of the garden. "Looks plenty wet."

"I think we'll be alright," her mother answered, gripping the hoe handle and tamping the steel part up and down a few times, not unlike a horse pawing the gravel at a hitching rack.

"You think?" Barb asked, doubtful. "Well, hi there, Susan," she added.

"Hello, Barb. How are you?"

"Good, good. My back has been bothering me, but that seems to be normal for fat, old women. Too much gardening in my lifetime. I say good for these young women who don't grow peas anymore. They're a hassle."

Clearly bristling, Mam replied, "We're losing the old ways, Barb."

"Old ways my eye," Barb countered expertly. "Some things in the name of progress are plain smart."

She pursed her lips, shoved her hands in the pockets of her sweater, her wide backside even more pronounced, and sniffed self-righteously.

"If it would be up to me, I'd quit raising them, but hubby thinks he can't live without peas."

Susan cringed at the term "hubby." She never liked that irreverent description of a husband, and it was so like Barb, thinking it was modern and would impress Susan. When no reply was forthcoming, she raised one eyebrow and said she'd just pulled a pan of sticky buns from the oven, ready to spread with caramel icing. Would they come over for a cup of coffee?

Mam sighed, clearly struggling, on a mission with the pea planting.

"Sure," Susan chirped, and her mother carried the hoe out of the garden and laid it down on the grass, wiped her hands on her apron, and said curtly, "Go," lifting her chin in the direction of Barb's house and then following Susan.

They went through the cluttered mudroom to a kitchen filled with the heavenly aroma of fresh baked cinnamon rolls, a bowl of caramel frosting beside it. Shoes, banana boxes, magazines, newspapers, an odd assortment of glass jars, dried tea leaves littering the floor, the oilcloth-covered table hosting a greasy lazy Susan with at least two dozen plastic bottles filled with herbal pills and capsules. A white square of fabric was pinched between two wooden embroidery hoops, the cross stitching begun but laid aside, in grave danger of being food splattered.

A parakeet in the corner shouted, "*Goota marya. Goota marya,*" the floor beneath his cage an interesting assortment of feathers and bird seed, dust and bits of paper.

The coffee was fresh and hot, with real cream *fon die koo* (from the cow) and cinnamon rolls as warm and delicious as Susan knew they would be.

Cluttery housekeepers were often wonderful cooks, a nod to their slow and easy lifestyle.

"There you go. Here, Susan, sit here," Barb chattered.

And Susan enjoyed the company of the older woman, found herself shaking and laughing inside about the differing views, her mother as uptight and restricted as Barb was relaxed and easygoing.

"Another thing. We were talking about the younger women changing some things—well, it's not just the young ones. I heard Eli sie Mary say she found the best peas at Giant in Lancaster. Hanover brand. Petite peas."

She pronounced it "pa-teet," and Susan found herself visualizing a very tiny pea shell dressed in a tank top and shorts.

"Well, good for her," Mam said in clipped tones.

"Yes, I know how you are, Erma. You would never buy peas. But let me tell you, it's tempting. I don't get a kick out of working so hard for a bowl of peas."

She glanced at Susan, her small eyes twinkling.

Susan smiled, complimented the cinnamon rolls, completely decadent and off the charts with their calorie count.

"Come over sometime, and I'll teach you," she said.

Her voice lowered to a sympathetic tone.

"Although you might not need to bake them for your husband anytime soon. I'm sorry to hear about your breakup."

Mam eyed her sharply.

Susan cut in quickly. "It's alright. He wanted Alaska. Adventure."

"Yeah, well there's more to it than that. Are you sure he actually went to Alaska?"

"What are you talking about?" Susan asked, her mouth gone dry.

"I shouldn't be saying this, but Sam's Levi's Amos told Elam that Levi Yoder . . . That's his name, right?"

Susan nodded.

"Levi Yoder was seen almost every morning at a diner out along Route 30. Said he was popular with this one waitress out there."

She lifted a finger.

"Now, I'm not saying this is so, but where there's smoke, there's fire. I think he had an eye for the English girls. And how much better to have this heartache now then after you're married. I couldn't help but think of Check's Choe's Hannah. That poor woman, left to fend for herself and her four children. Her brother took over the farm, but she helps him with the milking, won't sell out, says he'll come back to her. Imagine her life."

Barb chomped down on a cinnamon roll, chewed vigorously, and shook her head. "God is not mocked. That man will reap his wild oats, and it won't be nice. And that Hannah, so patient, so sweet."

"Every story has two sides, Barb. We never know what goes on behind closed doors. It takes two."

"Well, it wasn't her fault he left."

"I'm not saying that."

"Well, say what you mean, then."

The awkwardness dissipated after a few minutes of coffee slurping, and Barb lifted the ever-ready forefinger, a harbinger of forthcoming wisdom.

"I have someone for you."

"Oh come on, Barb. I'm done. I won't date again."

"You mean you'll be single? Whatever! A girl like you?"

"Why does everyone have to be married? What's wrong with being single? It's only in our culture that every young girl has to be married."

"Now listen to me. I have just the young man for you. My aunt Anna's boy. They live way down below Coatesville. He's even older than you. Would you want to meet him sometime?"

Susan shook her head.

"Oh, come on, Susie."

"No. Absolutely not."

But Barb pursed her lips, gathered her determination, carried it around for a few weeks before they attended church services at Leon and Anna's place, driving their horse twenty-one miles on a crisp, early morning. She planned her strategy and approached Anna after lunch dishes were washed and packed into Rubbermaid totes, which Anna did not take to kindly. She told her she was a busybody, trying to run God's affairs, and Barb smarted with raw humiliation.

Barb was the beginning of many more attempts at finding Susan a husband, all of them a sound flop.

Pea plants poked through the soil, the rain watered them, and the warm sun drew them from the soil. Susan went through her daily routine and felt the old lethargy creeping in. Ashamed of her bouts of irritation, she talked to her sister Kate, who was always ready to lend a sympathetic ear.

The rain beat down on them as they dashed from the small barn to the house, slammed the door, and shook out their sweaters and laughed.

"You had to pick the worst downspout to arrive in," Kate giggled.

Emily and Nathan were in school, which left only Micah to play with the wooden barn and plastic farm animals, with Marie taking her morning nap. They understood each other so well there was no dancing around the main topic, which was Susan's ever-increasing speed into the vortex of depression.

"I know I'm selfish, Kate. I know my lack of joy stems from thinking only of myself. I need a goal, I need new life breathed into me. I feel like a balloon with a tiny pinprick, slowly leaking air."

Kate's warm brown eyes filled with tenderness.

Susan felt a break in the pent-up tears and wept softly as Kate merely sat, waiting for the tears to subside, before asking, "Did you ever think of returning West?"

"What? No, of course not. I hated it out there."

"Did you?"

Her eyes penetrated, gouged out the truth.

"Well. Not really hated it, but . . . No."

"Did you ever imagine doing something for someone else, even if you sincerely resist the idea?"

"Kate! Really? What are you trying to say?"

Kate took a deep breath.

"It's just that I wonder if you're not missing something here. There's a need for you, I believe. And until you find that need, happiness will elude you."

"There are plenty of needs here in Lancaster County. You know that. Teachers, market workers, house cleaners. I do that. Well, not teach, but . . ."

"What about that little boy, Titus? Did you ever think about his life? For some reason, I can't seem to put him aside when I think of you and your disappointment with Levi. Susan, listen now. If our eyes are focused on our own wants and desires, we can't successfully see what God wants of us. Let me tell you something I have never told a living soul."

She stopped, got up, and went to check on Marie, then came back to sit at the table, a hand going tentatively to her cold coffee cup, then restlessly to Marie's pacifier holder, clipping and unclipping it.

"Before I dated Dan, Samuel Stoltzfus asked me for a date, and I said no. He was not my idea of a husband."

"Samuel? You mean Ike's John's Samuel?"

"Yes."

"Wow. I would have said no, too."

"I'm sure you would have. But for months, I was under serious conviction. I thought I should discuss it with our parents, but was so resistant to their answer. I dropped it. In plain words, I knew the answer to something I didn't want to know."

"God doesn't require that of us!" Susan said forcefully.

"Of course He doesn't. He doesn't make us do anything. He tries to gently prod us in the right direction, and if he sees we're only going to resist, He's like, okay, you go, girl. And I went. Straight into Dan's arms. And you know the rest."

"But Kate, none of Dan's miserable life is your fault."

"I know. I'm not blaming myself. I'm just saying. Look at Samuel and Mary now." She swallowed hard. "And look at me."

"But . . ."

Susan's forefinger traced the marbled pattern of the oilcloth on her scratched tabletop. No. Every fiber of her being resisted Kate's words.

"I mean. Samuel is the best example of a Christian husband and father I have ever seen. Did you ever notice how he looks at Mary and their son when she hands him to his daddy in church? And his business? Seriously, who would have thought. Rose told me they just bought a hundred acres in Perry County, to build a cabin."

Susan shook her head.

"But you can't look back, Kate. You just can't. What is that verse in the Bible? 'Whoever places his hand on the plow handle and looks back is not worthy of the Kingdom of God.' What's done is done. And Dan needed you."

"Dan never loved me."

"Yes, he did, Kate. You were the perfect couple."

"He put on a good show for my benefit. He was irretrievably incapable of true, sacrificial love, the kind where a man gives his life for his wife. He told me from time to time, how he wishes he never would have married me."

There was nothing at all to say to this.

But Wyoming? Her whole being resisted, a deep ebony cloud on the horizon drew closer, her chest heavy with the weight of her sister's revealing words. And yet, what was the alternative?

"I know how this makes you feel, Susan. The choice is yours entirely. I'm just trying to show you how we miss the beauty of God's calling so often, our blessing half recognized."

And still Susan shook her head no.

She threw herself into her work, found renewed energy and another job at a different market in Hagerstown, Maryland. She learned the art of cutting fruits and vegetables into tempting trays, the fresh organic produce a popular seller, a different crowd of people to please. The harder she worked, the easier it became to push back the troubling thought Kate had brought up, in her own gentle, loving style.

And her trademark rebellion kicked in once more, her thoughts on a constant merry-go-round of self-justification, propelled by her manic energy. Depression? What depression? She was fine.

She took a renewed interest in *rumschpringa*, bought new fabric in fancy shades of color, acquired a new friend named Laura from over by New Holland, a sweet, tall girl with a shock of dark red hair and a splattering of freckles across her pert nose.

Sitting in her room on a gorgeous Sunday afternoon, a thunderstorm having dispelled the heat and humidity, the sheer curtains blowing on the clean breeze, Susan shared her life's story with Laura, who listened attentively.

"You're going to flip out if I tell you this," she said, in her low husky voice.

"What?"

Instantly alert, Susan sat up straight, threw the cushion off her lap, put both feet on the floor.

"I dated Levi Yoder when I was seventeen years old."

"You didn't."

Nodding, Laura told her of the perfect boyfriend, the insanity of her happiness and trust, and the quick, unexpected end.

Susan was incredulous.

"But why would he do this?"

"Guess we weren't good enough. Like flawed towels or dishes with an 'irregular' sticker on them."

Laura grinned ruefully, shook her head, then continued. "Sometimes I can't really wrap my head around it. He was so perfect for me. The charm, the . . . I don't know what it was. He had this mesmerizing effect, or something. After Levi, no one was good enough, no one came close to him. Everyone was second best."

Susan could only nod her head.

Well, life took some interesting turns, no doubt. But she felt accompanied in her journey, as if Laura stepped into her small craft and took a turn rowing, allowing her a bit of respite. Laura, bless her heart, was exactly what she needed to take a renewed interest in life, to bolster her low self-esteem and keep going. Who knew what new adventure was around the corner? And at least she was home in Lancaster.

AND SO BEGAN a new whirl of social life. Laura and Susan were everywhere, trying new groups of youth, meeting guys, playing volleyball, baseball, cornhole, croquet. If there was any sport, they were involved, fiercely competitive, the life of the party. And in the evening, when Susan dropped wearily into bed, exhausted by the constant round of social life, the emptiness presented itself in the form of sleeplessness, a wide-awake half anxiety she could not understand.

One Monday morning, with temperatures in the eighties when she finally appeared downstairs, Mam eyed her over her cup of coffee, and thought she might as well face reality. Her daughter was officially an older girl, on her way to being single for life, and she would have to accept this, hold her head high, smile, and tell folks she'd simply never married.

"Morning."

"Mh-hmm."

"Want coffee?"

"Do I look like I want coffee?"

Susan went to the counter, poured a cup from the Lifetime drip coffee maker, bent to retrieve hazelnut creamer, and poured a generous amount. She brought the cup to the table and sighed.

"Tired?" Mam asked.

"A little."

"So . . . you had a good weekend?"

"I did. Volleyball was awesome."

Mam raised her eyebrows, broke a piece from a blueberry muffin.

"Quite sporty, you and Laura."

"Yeah, we are."

Mam pushed a blueberry muffin in her direction. "Taste this."

Susan nodded, bit off a generous portion, chewed, and nodded.

"Good, aren't they? To think I bought them at Giant."

"You actually bought these? You're slipping, Mam."

She grinned, shrugged her shoulders. "Too hot to bake. Besides, I'm getting chunky."

Susan laughed. "Do you care? Grandmothers are meant to be a bit fluffy."

A comfortable silence followed, the tepid air coming through the kitchen window doing nothing to cool the trapped air in the house.

Without air conditioning, the Amish had to accept the weather and deal with it as best they could. Battery-powered fans were more and more common, the aging couples appreciating them even as they reminisced about the good old days, before fans were necessary.

Church services held in packed basements and steel-sided sheds were a misery on days the mercury crept to ninety-five degrees. Seated on wooden benches, the sun heating the poorly insulated buildings like an oven, folks swiped at streaming perspiration.

"Did you go to Laura's church?"

"We did, actually. I wasn't planning on it, in this heat, but she insisted. She can really boss me around."

"Huh. That's rare."

"Her parents are still fairly young. They live on a farm, which isn't as common nowadays as it used to be, is it?"

"No, sadly."

"Dogs help."

"Right. So many families supplement their income by raising puppies."

"Why don't you?"

"Me? I don't particularly care for dogs. They lick my ankles, the little ones, and I'm flat out scared of big ones. No dogs for me."

"I know. So what are we doing today?"

"I'm doing pickles. I don't need your help—there's only a bucket full. But Rose is swamped today, her red beets still in the ground. Sometimes I wonder about her. She is never really done with her work."

"She was always like that. A bit unconcerned. And I do believe she often doesn't tackle a job if she doesn't feel like it. Unlike you, Mam."

Mom grinned, got to her feet to empty her coffee cup, and called over her shoulder, "I like to work. Doesn't matter what it is."

"How well I know."

Mam rinsed her cup, wiped the coffeemaker, then took off her white covering before tying a *dichly* (a small bandana) on her head, the usual covering when she worked in the garden. Amish housewives always had their head covered, taking the verse in the Bible seriously about wearing a covering, raised by a mother who wore one, and her mother before her, way back into history. It was a way of life, never questioned, except for those who followed different teachings and left the Amish way of life entirely, adopting a new way of dress and never looking back.

"Should I help Rose? Ugh. It's so hot. And you know exactly how it's going to go. I'll be the one pulling red beets, and if her cucumbers are ready, the red beets will be way overgrown. She'll have a bushel. And that James is a mess. Into everything. He drives me nuts."

"If you help me real quick, we'll go together. She left a message this morning, said she was overwhelmed."

"Alright."

Susan knew Mam was proud and wanted her daughters' homes to reflect their good upbringing, though she'd never tell her girls how important that was to her.

Mam was a good mother, but she wasn't above caring what other people thought of her and her family. Appearances mattered, whether they should or not.

CHAPTER 7

A THICK LAYER OF WHITE FOAM COVERED THE HORSE'S HAUNCHES where leather britchment rubbed against them as he trotted. The sun shone mercilessly, the temperature climbing, which made the dark horse sweat profusely.

Mam fussed, wished she'd hosed him off. She hated driving through town with a *schaumicha gual* (foaming horse).

"You know tourists think we're cruel, driving horses until they sweat like this. I should have washed him off. Your dat could have done it, but then, I'm not sure I told him we were using Sam."

Susan drove steadily, ignoring the gasping tourists, the cell phones held out of car windows, the grinding gears of a truck loaded with gravel. At a red light, Sam held perfectly still, then moved off when the light turned green along with the flow of cars, trained without a flaw. This was all a part of life in Lancaster County, horses and residents adapting as the flow of tourists increased, parking lots filled to over-flowing, making it difficult to access the hitching posts at local stores.

But on the rural road to Rose's house, the corn grew thick and tall, the fields divided by alfalfa hay fields or a neat row of trees, a meandering stream through a pasture dotted with black and white Holsteins. White barns stood like beacons of agriculture.

Teams of Belgians plodded along in unison, drawing hay wagons or rakes, produce fields thick with pumpkin vines and staked tomato plants.

Children on scooters lifted their hands in a friendly wave.

And Susan was glad to have found her way, to be part of this blessed land of her forefathers, a partaker of the gift of dark soil and outstanding crops, where business and trade flourished, a reward of hard work and ingenuity. She had come back from Wyoming with some regrets about leaving Titus behind, but now it all seemed like an old dream, one she barely remembered, and she felt no qualms about her decision to come home.

Here was her home, her life. And God had given her the gift of a bubbly, fun-loving friend in Laura, to lift her above the threatening depression and bewilderment. Eventually, she'd feel like her own self-assured self, a hard worker who could provide for herself, capable in every way and content to be single.

Mam's mouth looked pinched as she climbed down, drew the reins after her, and attached them to the ring on the harness. Plastic sand buckets, trikes, a wagon, candy wrappers, and a red and blue Pepsi can in the driveway greeted them. As Mam surveyed the weedy garden and unmowed grass, her mouth clamped even tighter. Almost, she felt a kinship to the picky in-laws Rose constantly complained about. Little James and Rosie were in the sandbox, with James still in his pajamas, snot running from his nose. Rosie was in a Cinderella nightie, her hair uncombed. Flies darted from screen doors and a host of baby kittens ran out from the playhouse.

"Mommy!" Rosie shouted, dropped her dump truck, and ran toward them, her arms opened wide, followed by James, whose diaper was so full he could only waddle.

The corner of Mam's apron was put to good use as she bent to swipe at his nose, then hugged him. She kissed his cheek and turned to greet Rose as the screen door was flung open.

Rose shrieked, saying no sight had ever been more welcome. Susan pulled red beets, Mam bent her back and lifted prickly cucumber vines, snapping off oversized cucumbers that should have been picked a week ago.

"You'll have to do banana pickles, Rose. These things are way past their prime," Mam said, unsuccessfully hiding the note of irritation.

"I don't care. I hate doing pickles. The only reason I do any is for church. We don't eat pickles. Same with red beets. Does anyone actually eat pickled beets?"

She lifted her skirt, wiped her sweaty face with the hem, and said no one in their right mind should be in a garden on a day like this.

Mam looked tight-lipped again.

"Well, your kitchen won't be any cooler."

"I'm not cooking these red beets in the kitchen. I have a stove in the warehouse."

"Still hot," Mam said, still tight-lipped.

Susan washed the red beets with the hose, directing the jet spray at the mound of dark red orbs, the tops cut to an inch or so, and prepared them for the two kettles Rose brought. They added clean water and set the kettles on the stove to boil until the beets were soft, ready to be peeled and cut into bite-sized pieces and put in jars with a syrup of red beet juice, sugar, vinegar, and a tablespoon of salt.

The cucumbers were peeled at the kitchen sink, cut into strips, and put into jars. The kitchen became steadily hotter as steam rose from the kettles. The pickle syrup sent an acrid odor of boiling vinegar through the house. Rose opened the refrigerator door, sighed loudly, and banged it shut.

"These stupid refrigerators don't work in hot weather. There's water all over the top shelf again. I'm not putting up with this."

She was yelling, her face red, her dress straining at the seams.

"I told Amos my refrigerator isn't working, but does he want to do something? Huh. Never."

She looked at the clock.

"Twelve-thirty! Wow! It's too hot to make lunch. I'm ordering from Pizza Hut."

And out the door she went, heading to the shed where the phone was.

Amos came in a few minutes later, his shirt drenched in perspiration.

"Well, hi!" he said, cheerful as always, happy to see them. "Hey, Susan. How's it going?"

She stopped ladling syrup over the slender white lengths of peeled cucumber, turned, and said, "Hi, Amos. Good. Going good."

"Where's Rose?"

"Went to order pizza," Mam said, swallowing the word so it didn't sound as worldly. Really. Pizza delivered if you had perfectly palatable food in your refrigerator. Times certainly did change, and not always for the better. What a waste of money. But she was wise, knowing when to be quiet, when feathers would be ruffled by an unwise word, and besides, she did love Pizza Hut's pizza.

They enjoyed the steaming, cheesy pizza and the cold Diet Pepsi, with a side order of wings for Amos, who smiled agreeably, going along with whatever kept his wife happy.

The reward of the day was a long row of pickled beets and one of sweet and pungent banana pickles (which were called that because the pickles looked like small bananas). Mam gloated, proud of her work. Here was a beloved tradition, her daughters doing red beets and pickles for church, a necessary part of traditional Sunday after-services lunch. This was good and right for the Amish, in spite of Rose yelling about her refrigerator and ordering pizza.

They sat in the yard under the generous shade of the spreading maple, Rose and Susan's dresses pulled to their knees, flies annoying them by perching on bare arms and legs. Honeybees droned in the clover, and the smell of fresh cut hay hung thickly.

"Well, thanks, guys. I don't know when I would have gotten to this on my own."

Mam's eyes narrowed, but Susan knew the words would remain unsaid. It would be on the way home that she would hear the usual account of Davey's mother having been so much like Rose. Easygoing. Nothing bothered her much. And yes, she'd been plenty fashionable, for her time.

"So Susan, the next time you have a date, bring him around," Rose said, teasing.

Susan slanted her a look.

"You know what I said."

"I don't care what you said. There won't be another time."

"We'll see, honey pie."

Susan swatted and Rose dodged.

"It's too hot to drive your horse home. Stay here till evening."

"No, I have to get on home. But we'll wash Sam off this time," Mam answered. "Embarrassing, driving through Ronks with a foaming horse."

"I know what you mean. I get a driver, Mam. It's too hot for a horse."

"Oh, come on. It's only five or six miles. That's what horses are for."

"You come from the nineteenth century," Rose snorted.

"I like it back there," Mam laughed.

The day ended on a fond note, Rose so genuinely appreciative, Susan with a sense of accomplishment, and Mam feeling happy that her girls were happy.

It was close to suppertime by the time they reached home, so Mam decided a quick meal of garden salad and fish would be plenty after that pizza. Dat came home from his work at the woodworking shop, his thin hair stuck to his head beneath the stained old straw hat, his eyes drooping with weariness. The hot summer weather was increasingly hard on his endurance, the fans doing little to spare them the ninety-plus temperatures.

He sat on the back patio, grunted as he unlaced his work shoes, then pulled off his wet socks. He spread his toes, rolled up his trouser legs, and leaned back, clasping his hands behind his head. A hummingbird hovered at the red feeder.

The screen door creaked open as Mam brought him a tall plastic tumbler of *vissa tay* (meadow tea), the sweet mint tea made from a variety of herbs grown in the garden. He smiled up at her as he reached for it, then asked what she did today. Susan joined them with a glass of tea, listened as Dat said the day had been a test to his good humor with the heat and the sawdust, and that Leroy was on his worst behavior.

"He's the boss's son, so what can we do? An unhandy little character. At sixteen, he's old enough to show a bit of obedience."

He shook his head.

They all listened as the white diesel truck pulled in, deposited a grimy Elmer, then backed out the drive.

"Hey."

"Sup, Elmer?" Dat asked, grinning.

"C'mon, Dat."

But they laughed, Dat's imitation of the teenage greeting always funny between the two.

"When's supper? I have a ball game."

"Oh yes. Right. I'll be ready by five-thirty."

And Mam bustled off.

"Hot," Elmer remarked.

"It's summer."

"Not always this hot. I gotta get in the shower."

And he was off.

Dat grinned at Susan. "We're only young once."

She smiled. "Yeah."

"You're doing okay, Susan?"

"I'm fine."

"Don't you ever think about going back to Wyoming? I'd think that teaching job must have been very fulfilling. Did you ever think about teaching here in Lancaster County?"

"I have my jobs. And no, Wyoming was a wild shot in the dark. I was homesick, and I'm happy here."

She looked off across the backyard, the glut of trees, well-manicured garden, trimmed hedges, neighboring houses, the sound of engines, and remembered the unbelievable amount of unused space, the towering Bighorns, the purity of the air. And only for a fleeting moment, the beauty of Isaac's home, so different, so unique from anything here in Pennsylvania.

"I'd like to see it sometime," Dat said suddenly.

"I'd go visit with you sometime. But not on Amtrak. If I ever go again, I'd rather go in a van."

"Four, five thousand miles round trip at a dollar a mile."

"Yeah."

They sat in comfortable silence till Mam called them to supper, the kitchen stifling, appetites lagging.

"Why don't we eat outside?" Susan asked.

"It's even hotter out there."

But after dishes were done, they did move to the porch, a slight breeze ruffling the petunias on the railing boxes. They were content to rest, no one saying much of anything.

Susan went upstairs for her current book, then settled herself on the lounge chair. A shrill voice made her put the book on her lap, as neighbor Barb came through the hedge.

"Did you have supper?"

"Yes, dishes are done," Mam said, resigned to her fate.

"Good. Mind if I visit? Hubby had to go to a township meeting. Something about zoning. I don't know why he has to stick his nose in all the English people's business. Him and Henner Stoltzfus. They won't change anything anyhow. So, Erma, what were you doing today?"

"Helping Rose."

"Oh, were you? Such a blessing, helping the girls. Well, if they want you. Mine don't. They always have their work done. They take after Elam's side. His mother. She almost worked herself to death. Well, she did. She wore out at seventy-five. Her organs simply gave out, and that's the truth. I don't believe anyone should overdo themselves, especially in this weather."

Mam eyed her neighbor with a wise look, and Susan read her thoughts, smiled to herself, felt a fondness for her mother and neighbor Barb.

This was home, literally where her heart was, and she hoped to stay for the rest of her life. Eventually, as she approached thirty years of age, she would want her own home, a small rental house, perhaps, or if she saved enough money, she might be able to put a down payment on some very small property.

Or, if her parents' health failed, she might have to be their caregiver, which would be a bit of a sacrifice, but still.

AND SO THE summer days went by, her weekends filled to overflowing with the enthusiastic Laura going full speed, from Saturday evening volleyball games, to visiting churches, youth gathering and singings. She met a dizzying array of young men who were attractive enough, but she always managed to keep them at arm's length, put up a wall of reserve, and they all respected that eventually.

Levi wrote to her, the letter arriving in late August on a steamy day when the humidity was so high a cold glass of tea shed water on the outside. Her mother handed the letter to her silently. With no return address, Mam imagined it was from some old-fashioned suitor who would be the one. Finally, Susan's time to meet the one God had for her had come.

Susan's eyes questioned her mother, but there was only a question in return. She shrugged her shoulders, and Susan sat in a chair, tore the end of the envelope, and shook out a single page, her eyes going to the signature.

Levi Yoder.

Her mouth went dry.

The handwriting was neat enough, but the message was quite disturbing.

She gasped, her eyes wide. A hand to her mouth, she read on. Her tanned face turned white as she silently handed the letter to her mother.

The grandfather's clock in the living room was the only sound in the kitchen as her mother's eyes scanned the page.

"What? Susan!"

"I know."

The letter was a confession. He tried to make things right with her, but there was no such thing, she realized quickly. He'd had an affair with a nurse from a doctor's office in Quarryville for many years, including while he was dating her. He said he'd been too weak to withstand her advances. But there in the wilderness, he'd found God. Jesus had forgiven him, but he had to make things right with her.

"My soul is finally at rest. I can't tell you the relief, the great unbelievable mercy I have experienced here in the solitude of God's creation. I know you will never take me back, but I am fulfilled by Jesus alone. I plan on making Alaska my home permanently, for here is where my destiny lies."

For a long moment, Susan felt sick to her stomach. Her head pounded as she reached for the letter again. She read and reread the words.

Almost, she still wanted him. She could still conjure up the scent of his cologne, visualize the lemon yellow polo shirt, the set of his shoulders.

But then came a river of anger and betrayal as she considered the smoothness of his deception. Like a flow of lava from a volcano, every thought of him was smothered in raw disdain.

Forgive him? It would take a while.

And the thought of ever giving her heart to anyone was completely out of the question. She'd made a resolve before, but never like this.

Her mother watched the expression on her face, then sat down and expelled a whooshing breath.

"Susan."

"Mam, don't. I know what you want to say. I need some time to work through this, okay?"

As usual, Kate was the one who listened quietly, making no comment as Susan told her story, the desperation to overcome her heartbreak, and now this.

Kate read the letter, her eyes swimming with unshed tears. She laid the letter on the tabletop, patted it a few times, then turned to Susan.

"I'm so sorry," she said softly.

"Looking back, there were signs. Sometimes he left immediately after the drive home from the singing, other times he seemed preoccupied, as if he wasn't there. I know the old cliché, 'love is blind.' It's a bit overused, but there's a lot of truth there. I'm mad at myself for being so gullible."

She stopped, shook her head.

"You know, God is always faithful," said Kate. "He is with us every step of the way. Our stories are not the usual boy meets girl, date, get married happily ever after kind of thing. But it's real life. Life gets messy."

"Does it ever!"

"And so we go on," Kate said wryly.

No one could prepare Susan for the following months of soul searching, the mental and emotional anguish she waded through. A thick sludge pulled her down, made her journey impossible. She went through her days without hope, her strength depleted, a constant swarm of doubt and fears like angry bees.

Why? Why had she allowed herself to love him? Why had he even bothered pursuing her? The letter was a brush fire, destroying her faith, burning up every aspect of trust in humanity.

Her prayers were without words, mere groanings of despair. Her faith shattered, she waded on, blindly. Gone was the quick wit, the ready smile, the saucy replies. She went to and from her jobs mechanically, robot-like, obeyed orders without questions. She made excuses for herself, refused Laura's company, stayed away from any social event, endured church services with a softball-sized lump in her throat, the kind words from the loving old bishop threatening to break her resolve.

She read and reread the letter.

Oh, Levi. Could it be he would be a new person, completely changed by a visitation from the Holy Spirit in the blink of an eye? It happened. He could come back to Lancaster, be a good husband to her, cleansed from any inclination to be unfaithful. The Bible made it so clear, how a person who was born again was purified from the inside out, and the new life that followed sprouted fruit, good things like love and kindness and patience.

Should she write to him, suggesting another stab at a relationship? How could he be so certain Alaska was his destiny? She swung between detesting the thought of him and wondering if she was underestimating God's power in his life.

Her thoughts revolved around this question of whether he was truly changed, and she could not let it go, convinced it was God's way of speaking to her. All these things were hidden then, hidden away from her mother and sisters, who finally stopped asking questions, shrugged their shoulders and agreed, Susan was going through a rough time. If she chose to keep her struggles to herself, then so be it.

One evening, when sleep eluded her yet again, she threw back the covers, grabbed a pen and lined stationery, and began a long letter to Levi. She told him of her anger, her unwillingness to accept his apology, and finally, her hope of redeeming their relationship, with his change of heart as evidence that it could work.

She wrote, "I know our Amish culture looks to the born again thing as a process, starting out with the milk of the word, but I believe it is different for many people. If you have been cleansed, forgiven, and ready to live for Jesus, why can't we begin again, start over? I still love you and find it hard to imagine a future without you. Can you imagine the amount of pride I have lain down to tell you this? Why can't I forget about you? God's will is sometimes hard to decipher, I know, but surely this conviction of trying again is directly from Him."

She sent the letter in secret, dropping it into the mail slot at the post office and walked away like a guilty thief, glancing over her shoulder, from left to right. As she placed a foot on the base of her scooter, she wondered why she felt guilty, being a grown person capable of making her own decisions. She was allowed to send a letter to Alaska, free to speak her mind and make her own decisions. For a brief moment, she blamed the Amish culture for dangling all that guilt in front of her.

Guilty for this, guilty for that, all her life.

If she wanted to give Levi another chance, it was no one's business but her own.

As she pushed her scooter away from the post office and moved out on the shoulder of the road, she held her head high.

Yes. Wasn't it amazing how God's will was revealed to her? Suddenly, the hopelessness, the sludge on her pathway evaporated, swept away by the courage of having written that letter.

The fog had lifted, the light brilliant. Yes. There was a clear path ahead of her, winding over green rolling meadows alive with birdsong, wildflowers blooming in happy profusion. It was wonderful to be free of the fetters of indecision. She threw herself into the joy of awaiting a letter in return, with the firm conviction of having done the right thing.

IN THE FALL, customers flooded the market in Harrisburg, the crisp days waking up everyone's appetite, women's minds full of the creations they would assemble in the kitchen, purchasing fresh produce, new potatoes, and always a sandwich for lunch. Susan's hands flew as she sliced the crusty rolls, folded meat and cheese, layered tomato slices and shredded lettuce, slathered mayonnaise and whatever other condiment anyone could think of, completed the sandwich, wrapped it deftly in paper, and moved on to the next one. She laughed when Anna Mary said the line was ridiculous, she had a notion to flip every order into the air and run away.

Anna Mary was Beth's younger sister, a petite version of Beth herself, blond haired and blue eyed, as sweet as she was pretty. Many glances were cast in her direction, largely unnoticed or ignored. She loved her first year of *rumschpringa*, had many friends and admirers, her life a canvas of yet uncolored possibilities. Susan envied her from time to time, exhausted from the twists and turns in her own life, but bolstered her mood by reminding herself of Levi's reply, an eagerly awaited event.

She cleaned Carol's house with a song on her lips, told herself it could easily take a week for the letter to reach its destination.

She wiped windows, fluffed pillows, sprayed Pledge on a microfiber cloth, and dusted with her usual energy, thankful to have a renewed interest in the jobs that so obviously bored her before her stay in

Montana. That, too, had been a part of God's plan for her life, to direct her back to Lancaster and teach her appreciation.

She had been spoiled, bored, and now the adversities in her life had taught her even more gratitude. Here was a blessed land, and she was grateful to be part of that blessing.

But still.

As she took a cold ginger ale from the Sub-Zero refrigerator, popped the top, and gazed absentmindedly out the kitchen window, she wondered what she would do if Levi never wrote back, or if he was serious about this destiny. Was life like a bowl of hard candies, and you could pick only the ones that you loved?

Here she was, downplaying serious defects in his character, still waiting. With that thought, the neighbor's yard lost its brilliant green hue, turned to a dull withered brown, the shrubs and flowers looking like drought-stricken hopelessness.

Lord, you know my thoughts. Take away my questioning and replace it with stepping stones for my feet.

CHAPTER 8

SUSAN WALKED QUICKLY, HER WHITE CAPE AND APRON STARCHED and ironed, her royal blue dress setting off the purity of the white fabric. It was too chilly to be without a light coat, but she did not like to wear the traditional black shawl and bonnet, a Sunday morning requirement hard to meet. Elmer was supposed to walk with her, but he had never made it home during the night, an event that happened far too often of late.

Dat had not been happy at the breakfast table, buttering his toast with hard stabs of his knife, his eyebrows drawn.

Without a curfew, during *rumschpringa* kids were free to spend the night at a friend's house and the parents didn't worry, knowing the friends and parents most of their life. But to skip church twice in a row was bringing Dat's firm disapproval on Elmer's hapless head.

She found herself with the usual group of girls, made small talk, greeted latecomers with handshakes and smiles, before being seated on long, hard benches for three hours of service. Today, she was awake and alert, having declined Laura's invitation to yet another volleyball game the day before and instead had stayed home and slept deeply, dreaming of Levi, which was very likely a good omen. She enjoyed the first sermon, but dozed off for a few minutes after the second one began with an unusually soft, timid voice of a visiting minister she did not know. She was seated too far away to fully understand his words, so a sneaking lethargy lulled her to sleep. She was jerked awake by an elbow in her ribs and found Lydia Ann's eyes on hers, a giggle making its way past her lips.

Susan elbowed her back, and they both bent their heads to keep from laughing out loud.

After the last hymn was sung, the slow rise and fall of the plainsong still in her mind, she helped set the tables, carrying bowls of cheese spread, red beets, pickles, and fresh dried apple pie.

A hand on her shoulder stopped her on the way for more forks.

"Susan."

It was her friend Mary.

"Hey, my husband listens to some kind of hot line, plain community news from all over the US, and he told me last night there's a boy missing somewhere in Wyoming. I can't remember the name of the town, but I figured there's only one settlement out there and maybe it's one of your old students. The kid was eight or nine. Unfortunately, he couldn't remember the name, but he said he thought it was Timothy or something like that."

Susan stared, openmouthed, uncomprehending. Black circles cavorted her eyesight as her breathing accelerated, her heart hammering.

She looked behind herself, found a padded folding chair, and folded weakly into it.

"Could it have been Titus?"

"Maybe. He honestly couldn't remember what the guy said, but he did think it started with T."

"No. No. Please no," she whispered.

"Susan, you're as white as a sheet."

A hand went to her mouth. She looked up at Mary with terrified eyes.

"He's lost," she hissed. "I told him over and over. He wouldn't listen."

Susan looked around, told Mary she had to leave.

"Please tell my mother I left."

"I will. Take care, Susan. I can tell you're deeply affected by this. I'm sorry to upset you."

"No, no."

And Susan made her way through the crowded basement, up the steps and out the door. She took deep gulps of chilled air as she hurried away, her mind set on finding Roy and Edna's telephone number.

Surely, she had it somewhere.

She burst into her room, her breath coming in gasps, tore open the drawer of her nightstand, and grabbed the striped blue and white address book.

"W. Weaver," she whispered, her forefinger tracing the letter.

"Here. Here it is."

She tore back down the stairs, to her father's office, lifted the receiver, and dialed the nine-digit number. One ring, two, then three.

"Hello?"

Oh, thank God.

"Hello? This . . . this is Susan. Susan Lapp."

"Oh. Oh yes. Roy here. You heard?"

"Yes. Well, a little. Is it Titus?"

"Since Thursday afternoon."

"This is Sunday, Roy. How long could he survive on his own?"

"Better for that little chap to be lost in the woods than be taken by some crackpot. You never know. Search parties are combing the area."

"Is the dog gone too?"

"Of course. That dog is the only reason we think he may not be kidnapped. He wouldn't let anyone near."

"So, they think Wolf is with him?"

"We do."

"And Isaac?"

"He's a wreck."

"I'm coming out there."

"Be nice of you."

They talked of details, the closest airport, numbers to call, drivers. Edna got on the phone, crying hysterically, hardly able to speak coherently.

"Little Sharon cries, her dad can barely keep it together. Family is here from Ohio, Indiana . . . it's a mess. They have no trail, nothing to go by."

"Look, I have phone calls to make, okay? I'll see you soon."

By late afternoon a flight was booked and a driver was scheduled. Her parents' protests rang in her ears, but she pleaded her case. This was an emergency. This was beyond normal *ordnung*. She had been his teacher, lived in his house. She probably understood him far better than anyone, including his father.

"I just don't see the need to fly. Why can't you hire a driver and go the way that is honored by our people?" her mother moaned, a hand to her forehead in typical martyred fashion.

"He could be dead," Susan shouted.

"Susan."

Her father's quiet voice broke through her outrage.

"I'm sorry. But I have to go."

"Which airport?"

"Baltimore. BWI."

"Oh, come on." Her mother began weeping softly.

Susan threw clothes in the large black duffle bag, showered, changed, and was ready and waiting when Carson Rolls came to a stop at the doorstep. She hugged her mother, told her father she would be very careful, but could never forgive herself if she didn't go. Her eyes were alight with purpose; she bristled with ambition, something her father had not expected to see anytime soon.

Carson eyed her doubtfully, gathered an empty McDonald's sweet tea cup, a Dunkin Donuts cup, and a few French fries off the passenger seat, and handed her a wad of brown napkins, telling her to stick them in the glove compartment.

An old friend of the family, Carson had been hauling the Dave Lapp family for thirty years. They were the nicest people anyone could ever hope to meet, usually handing him an extra five dollars, or even twenty if he waited too long at Lowes or Walmart. This Susan was a feisty one, though, and he was half scared of her.

"Never thought I'd haul one of Dave Lapp's girls off to the airport. What gives?" he asked, picking up his current cup of McDonald's tea.

"You know I was in Wyoming for a while, right?"

"Yeah."

"One of my former pupils is missing."

She explained quickly, conscious of the fact he had a tendency to slow down if he tried to digest too much information.

"So, you know this kid?"

Susan nodded.

"I hope you know you're not going to be much help finding him. Leave it up to the professionals."

"I'm going so I can be there for his sister. And father."

He made no comment as he hoisted his sweet tea, then picked up a Mounds bar, held it with the same hand he gripped the steering wheel with, and began picking at the paper with his opposite hand. Susan watched oncoming traffic, thinking unwrapping candy bars should be right up there with texting while driving.

"A missing kid. Really." Carson shook his head.

Susan nodded grimly, her eyes burning with unshed tears. Surely, Wolf would have protected him from evil men. Surely, he was still alive. Perhaps fallen and injured, but alive. If something happened to Titus, she hardly knew how Isaac would continue on.

She appreciated Carson's help as he parked and then led her from one wide, crowded area to another. Her heart was pounding, her ears pulsing as the stress built.

He made sure she got checked in OK and then walked her to security, where he told her how to find the gate and then said goodbye. She found her way just fine and sat on a hard chair, her legs tucked underneath, her sweater caught tightly around her waist by her folded arms.

She prayed to be kept safe, prayed to be able to recognize the driver Roy would send.

She visualized Jesus in his calming white robe, his kind eyes and dusty sandals, keeping her out of harm's way.

Be with me now, she whispered as her flight was called.

And He was with her the entire way. Of this there was no doubt.

The takeoff was breathtaking, the smooth ascent up above the clouds almost unbelievable. She had a short layover in Chicago, and then she was off again, feeling more confident for the second flight. And finally they landed and she exited into the befuddling crowd of boots, Stetson hats, and strangers. She followed signs to the exit as she'd been instructed and was relieved when she heard her name called by a red-faced woman who looked as if she had been fried like bacon in the heat of the sun.

"Hi, honey. Audrey Campbell."

"Hi. It's so good to see you."

Her hand was gripped in a vise-like clench of hard calloused fingers; a set of yellowed teeth flashed between her wide lips.

"Yeah, it's good of you to come, honey. The whole community up there by Crazy Woman Creek is in an uproar. Isaac fit to be tied. I hope you're brave, cause it ain't for the light a heart."

"I can imagine."

And she could. Isaac on a calm day was still a force to be reckoned with. She could not fathom what he'd be like under these circumstances.

They found the vehicle, the expected old Dodge pickup, once green, now a rust-tinged shade of olive, the seats torn and stuffing exposed, the floor littered with rusted chains and cigarette butts, holes burned in the rubber floor mats. Beer cans and used paper towels fought for limited space on the floor. Susan merely gave up and placed her feet tentatively on top of the whole dump.

"One thing they got going for 'em," Audrey said, placing an elbow on the steering wheel as she twisted her lean form to peer out the dusty back window, put the truck in reverse, and slowly pulled away from her parking spot.

"The weather's been mild, for October. So if he's a little guy used to being in the woods, we might be surprised. And if the dog's still with him, that's something. But I dunno."

Susan allowed her eyes to take in the sheer height and tremendous power of the Bighorn Mountains. The word "awesome" was inadequate, didn't even begin to describe what she felt, the worship-fulness that began as a song in her heart. How could she ever have thought Lancaster County a place of beauty after experiencing this towering, amazing work of God, the air around her as crisp and clean as freshly picked apples on a cold morning? The sky seemed a different version, even if she knew it was the same blue dome seen over her home county. It was larger, with clouds more pronounced, thick fluffy ones that seemed close enough to touch. It was autumn, and she took in the brilliance of yellow against a backdrop of fir green, the windblown grass bleached by summer winds, the dusty, rocky roads winding along between.

Well, I'm here, she thought. And yet she could not quite shake the memory of homesickness, the winter storms keeping her in Isaac's house when her entire being longed for home with a physical ache. Her heart pounded, remembering.

They passed Roy and Edna's place, the guest house she had made her home. The road was the same, a cloud of dust billowing behind them, the truck bouncing over rocks the size of a fist, spewing small stones.

Susan kicked at the rolling cans and kept her eyes on the road, suddenly wishing she was anywhere but here. Would Isaac even want her here?

She cast a sidelong look at her driver, bony knuckles gripping the wheel, thumbnails like small spoons, leathery skin the color of an acorn.

Silence was her normal rider, so she was relaxed, finding no need for conversation. She glanced at Susan, looked away. Here was an uptight one. Properly straitlaced, no doubt. Uppity, too. She'd never make a westerner, this one.

But she said nothing.

As they rounded the final curve and came down the gradual incline, the buildings came into view, the walnut brown house blending so well with the trees in the background, the great stone patio eye-catching, drawing in the viewer to a place of rest and enjoyment.

She had loved that porch, imagined the flowers and arrangement of furniture if she was the one who owned it.

A band of vehicles, two sheriff cars. She caught her lower lip in her teeth, drew a steadying breath.

"Do you think he's there?"

"Who?"

"Isaac."

"Dunno. If he is, he's crazy. That man needs to be out there looking for his son. He shouldn't of let him wander off like he did."

There wasn't much to say to that, so she bent down for her wallet, asked how much she owed her, and was pierced by a diamond-edged, icy stare.

"If they find this kid, it'll be a miracle. So don't go prancing in there thinking this is a ball of fluff, cause it ain't."

"Uh, yes, of course."

A hand was jutted in her direction. "Hundred bucks."

"Are you sure that's enough?"

"Well, yeah."

Susan handed her six twenty-dollar bills, and one was thrown back.

"I said a hundred. Good luck to ya. Here's my number."

Susan took it, unsure why it was offered, but thanking her just the same.

She grabbed the black duffle bag, her purse slung over one shoulder, and stood, facing the house, half listening as Audrey put the truck in reverse. There was no sign of life from the house, so she took a few hesitant steps before deciding to meet whatever or whoever head on. She walked the length of the stone sidewalk and up on the porch, knocked lightly on the closed oak door.

The length of time before she knocked again seemed like an hour, and she was relieved to hear footsteps shortly after.

An older lady, with white hair tucked into a covering drawn forward over her ears in the way of those who were mature, opened the door and peered out.

"Yes?"

"I'm Susan Lapp. I was Titus's teacher last year."

"Oh? Is Isaac expecting you? Come in."

She stepped back with a small welcoming gesture.

Susan found herself in the company of acquaintances, some of the men whose children she had taught, a few strangers introducing themselves as Isaac's relatives, a police officer and a sheriff. The mood was somber, the hope of finding the boy becoming slimmer as day turned into night yet again.

There were maps of the region, radios crackling, an air of rigid urgency.

Susan found herself the center of attention, questions following a brief outline of her year as his teacher.

"He loves being alone. Nothing bothers him. I mean, nothing that would normally bother a child his age. He loved hearing coyotes howl. If he heard a rustling in a bush, he'd run toward it instead of away. He's different. I've thought about this a lot, at home after hearing about it, and on my trip here. I may be wrong, but I think he and Wolf just wandered too far along a trail and got lost."

"It's what his father thinks. But two and a half days? Nights are freezing."

It was the sheriff's sober voice that stood in the way of any fresh hope, but still Susan clung to the daring belief that Titus would know what to do. For a while, at least.

People came and went, strangers for the most part, although she believed she recognized the burly, tattooed man as one of Isaac's logging friends. She roamed the house, noticing the dirt and dust that she had worked so hard to rid the place of when she'd first moved in.

Two women brought casseroles, covered containers of food for the returning searchers as night fell. Abe Louise, her face pale and grim, wrapped her in arms so full of love and welcome, tears came quickly.

James Miller's wife, Frieda, a staunch supporter of Isaac, simply shook her head, squeezed her eyes shut, and hugged them both.

"It just can't be. I can't believe Isaac will have to suffer another parting," she wailed quietly.

As twilight turned to dusk and the gray light turned increasingly darker, the group returned, on foot, on the back of pickup trucks, and in Jeeps. Helicopters were heard in the distance, the throbbing heartbeat keeping the search alive. There were voices, shouts, the revving of engines, the sound of men on the patio.

Susan stayed in the living room, wishing she could become invisible. How would he react to her being there? Would he take offense, become angry at her intrusion? For a minute, she was afraid.

She watched for him, but he never appeared, the remaining searchers finding their plates, speaking in low tones. Susan slipped past everyone and out to the laundry room, intending to check the patio, to explain her being here.

He was bent over the sink, the sheer size of him dwarfing the countertop, his denim shirt wrinkled, stuffed haphazardly in trousers stiff with filth.

A three-cornered rip in the fabric of his shirt exposed a patch of skin, making him appear vulnerable, uncared for.

"Isaac."

He stopped, reached for the hand towel, and buried his face in it. He turned, drying his hands as he did so. His eyes were dull, burning with pain, sunken into shallow cheekbones, a face ravaged by loss and pain. For a moment, he could not comprehend who had spoken, the light in the kitchen casting her in a dark silhouette.

"Isaac?"

"It isn't you, is it?"

His voice was hoarse with weariness, the words choked with emotion.

"It's Susan."

Two great strides and she was in his arms, crushed against him. He released her as quickly, and she reached for the doorway to keep from staggering.

"Come."

He caught her hand, and she was propelled out the door, down the steps of the patio, across the flagstone and through a door. He switched on a battery lamp, waved a hand to the opposite office chair, fell into his own and ran a massive hand through the tangle of his unwashed hair.

His odor was rank, the smell of damp earth, old ashes and smoke, stress and perspiration without a shower for days. His face was wretched, the color gone, the plates beneath his skin almost visible.

"Susan."

She said nothing, tried to fathom the unreasonable havoc this had wrought, the desperate search, the guilt and self-blame.

"You came to tell me 'I told you so.'"

Bitterness tinged his hard words, took away the vulnerability.

"No."

"Don't tell me you didn't think it."

"We don't always say what we think."

"No doubt." He sighed. "Well, you're here, and I'm glad."

"You are?"

"Yes. Are you planning to stay at the house?"

"If you'll have me."

"Please."

She began to weep, very quietly, then blinked furiously, ashamed of the strong wave of emotion. One troubled little boy alone and frightened out of his wits. Or lying somewhere, injured, crying, hungry and thirsty. Calling for someone. Anyone. Or a still, cold form, the angels carrying him to his mother, already in heaven, eagerly awaiting her son.

"Susan, I should have listened to you. I was arrogant."

She shook her head.

"How did you arrive so soon?"

"Flew. An emergency."

"I can't believe you're here. It's almost like a mirage. A dying man, and there you are. I guess you're real."

She smiled.

"Are you okay?" She knew it was a silly question.

"No. I'm not okay at all. I range from anger to hysterical weeping to life-sucking self-blame, doubt that God cares about me at all. I'm a mess."

"Where's Sharon?"

"With Darryl and Marianne."

"There are so many questions," Susan said.

"Look, I'm exhausted, okay? I haven't had a shower in three days. Let's do what needs to be done, get something to eat, and we'll send 'em all home. I don't sleep, so we can talk."

He paused. "Thank you for thinking of Titus."

They rose to their feet and he raised his eyebrows, held the door for her. Everyone looked up as they came to the kitchen, but few words were said. The food was good and still hot, the cups of coffee plentiful.

Susan listened to the women's version of Titus's disappearance, the trouble he'd caused at school, followed by being expelled, and now this. Isaac wolfed down his food, then disappeared with curt words thrown behind him.

It was time for everyone to leave.

There were a few hurried glances from Louise and Frieda as they gathered up their belongings, casserole dishes and potholders stacked in large totes.

"You sure you want to stay here?" Louise asked.

Susan nodded, but said she had her misgivings.

"They say he's a lion. He roars, swears, breaks things. Then he cries. We're all afraid this will get the best of him."

Susan bit the inside of her cheek, swallowed hard.

She was here for Titus, and if he wanted to behave like some lunatic, that was up to him. She was certainly not afraid of him. She hoped he was mature enough to realize his raving only made matters worse.

But why did she feel as if she was here to embrace the worst? Nothing was perfect, nothing was promised to come up roses every time.

She had a keen sense of focus, of knowing her feet were on solid ground. If not solid ground, then firm stepping stones leading to a place she had never known, could not understand, and didn't need to.

She carried her duffle bag upstairs, showered, changed into a clean navy blue dress, the color matching the somber atmosphere.

She couldn't allow herself to think of wearing the black suit she had folded gravely in the bottom of her bag.

Just in case.

Chapter 9

It was late by the time he returned from the barn. Susan was dozing off on the recliner, her wet hair in a ponytail holder, her feet in woolen stockings. How well she remembered the pervading chill of these Wyoming winters.

She sat up, a hand to her hair.

He put the coffee pot on, turned, and said brusquely, "You can go to bed."

"I won't sleep."

"Neither will I."

"Tell me what happened."

"So you can go back to Lancaster and tell everyone what an incompetent oaf lives in Wyoming? You're probably snickering behind my back already."

Susan sat up straight.

"If this is how you're going to be, I'm taking the first flight home. I mean it. You're only making a horrible situation worse."

"You haven't changed."

"Neither have you. You were so glad to see me, now what gives?"

He sat on the couch, put his elbows on his knees, buried his face in his oversized hands, then threw himself against the back of the couch and ran his fingers through his hair. He expelled a deep breath that caught in the back of his throat, which he tried to stop by shifting into the former position, but his shoulders heaved as raw, hoarse sobs shook his frame.

Susan was frightened at first, afraid for his mental stability, but the sight of a grown man, one of gigantic proportions especially, weeping like a child, triggered the womanly empathy, the need to comfort, and she went to him, laid her head on his shoulder, an arm across the wide, muscular back.

There were no words necessary. When he lifted his face, she handed him a box of Kleenex, waited till he wiped his nose and streaming red eyes. He refused to look at her, however, so she moved away.

He reached over and laid an arm across her lap, tugged slightly.

"Stay, Susan."

And she did, for a long quiet moment.

"School started, and right away there was trouble. Teacher picked on him, I know she did, they all do. It's his constant nervousness, the jitters. He does anything for attention, negative or otherwise."

He stopped, wiped his face.

"So I was called to school to have a meeting with the school board, and they all decided the best procedure was to expel him. He needs to learn there will be serious consequences to his actions, and since I am an absentee father, discipline is lacking. So . . ."

He took a deep breath, spread his hands. Susan edged away.

"All that time on his hands. Flew through his lessons and was off with Wolf."

"Who kept the children?" Susan asked.

"Roy Edna sometimes. Sometimes Trisha. It was . . ."

He pressed his lips together, shook his head.

"Roy Edna tried, but he drove her batty. Didn't listen. Anyway, on . . . what is this? Friday? Wednesday afternoon, he never came home. I have been through more than I can say. My wife's cancer was awful, but this is beyond description. The mental anguish, the not knowing. The thing hardest to bear is the fact that he might be alone, in pain, crying out for me, and I'm not able to help. He's so little and so scared."

Susan touched his shoulder.

"Where is God in all this?"

"God?" Isaac snorted. "I'm not very close to God. He hasn't been dealing fairly these past years."

Susan stared at him.

"Don't look at me like that. Did your husband die? Did you lose a son?"

"No, neither of them. No. Some heartache in the romance category, but it doesn't compare to this."

He turned to her sharply.

"What are you saying?"

"Levi took off for the Yukon when I thought we were soon to be engaged. I broke up with him, and then he told me he'd been having an affair the whole time we were together."

"Hmm."

"Is that all you can say?"

"I would say more, but you don't want to hear it."

He got up suddenly and walked to the kitchen, the slump of his shoulders giving away the inner despair he carried on his strong back. His denim trousers rode low on his hips, and in his stocking feet he almost reached the doorframe. He opened the cabinet door, got down two cups, turned the gas burner on with a hand on one hip. He half turned, stared at her as if he had never seen her before.

"Black? Cream?" he called softly.

"You know I never drink black coffee."

"Couldn't say. It's been a while."

He brought the oversized mugs to the table, pulled out a chair.

"Sit."

She sat. Silence hung between them, an uncomfortable divider. The tension was as thick as pudding, the clocks ticking as loud as a gong.

"So you were going to marry Levi?"

"I was planning on it. He wasn't. He wanted to find himself, had a trip planned. The Yukon in Alaska. The thought of being married, living the traditional Lancaster Amish life, was boring, depressing."

"Hmm."

"So, a few months ago, I received a letter. A confession. While he was dating me he was seeing an English girl. 'Seeing.' I'm sure it was much more than that. But I wrote him back now, saying I will forgive him."

His eyes pierced through the barrier of her pretense.

"You're not taking him back." It was a statement more than a question.

"I don't know yet."

He got off his chair. She heard him reach for his coat and hat, the door slam solidly, and then the house was empty, save for the sound of her own breathing. She stood for a long time, her hand on the back of a chair, exhausted in every sense of the word.

She had no idea what she should do about his departure, if she should go on up to bed or stay on the couch or recliner. What had she said to bring on that reaction?

She finally went upstairs, brushed her teeth, got into her warm flannel pajamas, and climbed into bed. She guessed he'd figure it out sometime, and what did it matter if she went back to Levi or not?

IN THE MORNING, before reality faced her, she couldn't remember where she was, or why, until the harsh truth struck her full force, a blow both emotional and spiritual. She felt a deep disappointment in Isaac's lack of faith, his disappearance last night. *He is still so strange*, she thought wearily, before dragging herself from bed, still feeling like an imposter, wishing she had not come.

To be alone in the house, to wonder and pray and panic by spurts, was a form of torture all its own. Why had she come? Now Titus was still missing, and obviously, so was Isaac.

She faced the searchers bravely, told them Isaac had left during the night, so perhaps they could search for him as well. Grim faced, she was informed of the fact this was not unusual, some parents simply unable to hold it together, attempting foolish but heroic maneuvers. They asked her to stay. With her inexperience and lack of knowledge of the area, they felt it unwise for her to go out searching.

More women of the Amish community arrived, like old friends, greeting her with warm hugs and questioning eyes, but no one was bold enough to come right out and ask why she was here. They cooked, baked, made huge meals for anyone who wanted to join in the search. Susan felt at home with these women, glad to be part of this close-knit community, asked if it was okay to clean the house, which was met with cheers of approval.

She started upstairs, wiping floors, polishing furniture, changing sheets, a satisfying job, one that took care of the ever-increasing worry about Isaac. She prayed constantly. With every breath she gave him and Titus to God, to protect them, bring them home alive and well. She always added, "Thy will be done, if You want Titus with his mother, it's okay." But for Isaac, she stumbled.

Why couldn't she shake this heavy weight of knowing it was something she said?

Searchers came and went. Susan greeted well-wishers in a haze of worry and incomprehension. If only she would have stayed away from Isaac, kept from upsetting him, but there was no use now trying to reverse what had been done.

He came walking down the drive in the late afternoon, disheveled, his hat low on his forehead, his clothes torn. Susan was cleaning the great stone patio, a sturdy broom in her hand, bent to her task, when she looked up and spied his unmistakable form. As he neared the house, Susan's heartbeats sped up, seeing the spring in his step, the light in his eyes.

Without thinking, she dropped the broom, took a few hesitant steps to greet him. The group in the yard dispersed, drifted toward him, so she found herself last as eager men surrounded him.

Isaac nodded, then began to talk.

"I think I may have a clue, small as it is. He traveled farther than we think, and he's always been fascinated with the creatures, as he calls them. North of here, toward the mountains, there are lots of washouts, ravines, dry creek beds, and forests of older pine, just a mess of brush, rocky cliffs, and well, it's crazy. I found . . ."

And here he choked up, his face working, the battered face, too smooth where the titanium plate held the cheekbones in place, craggy, scarred, the lips lifted on one side by skin grafting and a permanent scar.

His eyes squinted, seeing nothing. When he lifted his straw hat and ran a hand through his hair, Susan felt a keen sense of sympathy. He was so oversized, so loud and blustery, so confident, but this small son's disappearance had brought him to his knees.

He lowered his face after replacing the hat, scuffed the toe of his work shoe in the dirt. When he lifted his face again, there was a semblance of control, but his voice was heavy with emotion.

"I found a paper towel, where he went to the bathroom. I knew there was a den of badgers somewhere, because he talked to me about hanging on to Wolf. He watched them, he said, all evening, till he had to come on home. What I think happened to him is this. He got carried away, traveled too far, and he's either lost or injured. Likely, he fell somewhere, as I can't imagine Wolf wouldn't find his way home. I have to believe he's out there yet."

Nods, murmured assents, the crowd shifting, making eye contact. Yes, this was the father, and he knew the ways of his son.

That day, a vein of adrenaline throbbed through the searchers as they drove the high flat country, binoculars trained on the beige-colored grasses of October, every incline, every ditch and creek bed explored. Where the flat land gave way to cliffs and paths snaked between rocks, scrubs of droughty bushes concealing ledges and caves, eager searchers combed the area with renewed vigor. Voices called his name from bullhorns, dogs scrambled for toeholds, their twitching noses to the ground.

And still there was nothing.

Susan walked with Isaac. She couldn't stand another hour at the house waiting for news and as long as she stayed with the others, she wouldn't risk being more of a burden than a help. Her hiking boots hit the powder-dry dust between rolling sagebrush and bleached grass. Her feet hit the earth twice to Isaac's once, the long strides moving him with efficient speed. ATVs crawled the countryside like giant black bugs, the drivers swinging into ditches and swaths of sandstone, sending up huge clouds of dust.

Overhead, the sky was a white gray with only intermittent patches of blue, a huge porcelain bowl of swirled colors. The air was crisp and cold.

Isaac pointed a finger wordlessly, shook his head. Susan saw the reason for his concern, a long bank of milling black clouds to the north.

"Snow?" she asked, lifting her face.

"I dunno. Afraid so."

His face was gray with weariness, his mouth a thin, sharp line.

"If it snows . . . I don't know how I can go on," he rasped.

Susan didn't know how to answer, so she merely watched the clouds. Like a giant sleeping animal, the dark gray clouds loomed across the outline of the snow-capped mountains, heavy with portent. The land seemed helpless, devoid of defense, dry, bleached by the harsh summer elements, and now awaited the prevailing storms of winter. Everything was so raw, so elemental, exposed to whatever God chose to send in the form of wind, cold, heat, dust, an unlimited supply of nature's tomfoolery.

And little angry Titus, somewhere.

She caught a quick intake of breath, felt the panic rise.

"If only we can find him before the weather turns bad," she said weakly, it feeling more like a prayer than a statement.

He said nothing, striding ahead with his shoulders held erect, and Susan had to quicken her steps. She shivered, thinking of this unforgiving terrain, the wild creatures roaming the base of the Bighorn, the hunger and thirst.

How long could a boy his age keep himself alive, if he still was alive, and hadn't fallen or become wedged between rocks, or attacked by a mountain lion? Her imagination ran wild, bringing an almost unbearable sense of urgency.

She realized the need for mental and emotional clarity, to stay calm when the forces around you pressed inward like hot irons. The only way to stay calm was to give it over to God, the great and omnipotent Master of the universe, but that in itself was a hard job, switching from your own control to the One you knew, but was never visible, and His will was not always aligned with your own.

She glanced at Isaac as they reached the rocks, the bleached grass like a fringe along its base. He hesitated, glanced at her with a doubtful eye.

"You better not come along," he said. "It's too dangerous."

"If you're going, so am I," she said, and meant it.

He stopped, looked down at her, then at the expanse of sheer walls, tortured paths winding between sharp ledges. He looked at her boots.

"Susan, I really wish you wouldn't."

"I want to go. This is what I came for."

He shook his head no. She nodded yes. After which they stood together at a dissimilar crossroad. The air fairly crackled with the approaching clouds, the swirled pattern giving way to the heavy layer now even more visible. Isaac lifted his face to search the sky, then looked down at her, the determination in her green eyes, the way the smattering of freckles stood out against her pale face, the distended nostrils giving away her emotion.

He shook his head again.

"I can't let you go down there. It's simply not safe for an inexperienced person. Will you please listen to me?"

She stood still, undecided, weighing her own capability against his idea of her. She'd gone hiking with Levi, but that hardly compared to this terrain. But she had no intention of going back alone and had just opened her mouth to tell him so when he turned as still as stone.

He held up one finger. "Shh."

Yes, there it was again.

A distant gunshot, then another. Another.

"Dear God," Isaac breathed, his eyes squinting.

"What? What is it?"

Only then, it registered in her mind. A gunshot meant he'd been found.

"Isaac?"

Chills washed over her back, along her arms as quick tears sprang to her eyes. She watched his face, which remained inscrutable, his body as if it contained no life.

"I don't know if I'm strong enough," he whispered.

And she realized a gunshot meant he'd been found, dead or alive.

Susan felt as if the strength left her own body, her knees like water, unable to support her. They heard the distant grinding sound of a four-wheeler coming closer, so Isaac stepped out, waved a hand, then cried out, waving both arms.

The rider was young, hatless, had only room for one, but his cell phone was brought to his ear, instructions given, before contacting another person with the means of transporting them both home. Susan felt awkward, shy, her skirts bunched around the leggings she'd donned at the last minute. He showed her where to put her feet, how to grasp the bar behind her, and they were off in a roar of dust and choking wind.

Ahead of her was Isaac's hulking form, hatless, the ATV bouncing and roaring along at top speed as the continued echo of gunshots reverberated in his ear.

How could she bear the sight of a lifeless Titus?

She put the thought out of her head, tried to give her own will to God and say, *it's okay, but please, please for Isaac's sake, let him be alive.*

As they neared the homestead there was a huddle of tan, navy, gray and black coats, an old beat-up pickup truck, completely colorless, with one white door and patches of rust fringing the edges. The ATV ahead of them skidded to a stop, and Isaac flung himself from the seat and ran toward the house. The crowd parted, made way for him as he fell to his knees.

Susan remained seated after the four-wheeler came to a stop, allowed Isaac this time alone. There was no sound, only the group dispersing, hardened old ranchers wiping their eyes, turning away.

And still Susan didn't know.

Isaac was on his knees. She caught her breath as he gently lifted the small form, ruined trousers and filthy shoes dangling. He turned, searching for someone, his face lit by a thousand stars.

And she knew.

"Susan!" he yelled in a hoarse voice.

She slid off the seat, ran to Isaac as if it were all a dream, found the pale face of Titus, his brown eyes dull with weariness but alive with recognition. Her arms went around him, her face to his scratched and filthy one, and she whispered, "Hello there, Titus."

His one arm encircled her neck and he held on with the bit of strength remaining. Susan was weeping softly, aware only of his soft and pliable, thin and battered body, of the heartbeat steadily thumping beneath the denim coat.

He was alive.

And there was Wolf, blinking his eyes as he waited, seeming to say, "What took you so long?"

A broken limb, a dangling leg. Questions, then. Who? Where?

A man stepped forward, his appearance unlike Susan had ever seen. He seemed to have hair sprouting everywhere and wore a filthy coat, slick with grease, shoes held together with duct tape, frayed and flapping.

"Wrench Vark, here."

Mouths open, eyes staring, the crowd stepped back.

The man jutted his jaw in Titus's direction.

"Best get the boy some help. He's hurtin'."

Isaac nodded, his eyes squinting, his mouth working. Titus moaned softly. Susan stepped up, laid a comforting hand on his shoulder.

"I found 'im with his dog, lyin' at the bottom of a cliff. Could easy tell what happened. Creepin' along the ledge, crumbly sandstone, one mismove an' he was down. Down hard. Stayed put I'd say a day, maybe a couple. He was a fighter."

Nods all around, voices erupting in amazement.

"Give the little guy some space here."

He stepped forward, spread his arms.

Isaac asked how he'd stumbled on him, how it was possible in the untraveled, unknown area.

"As you kin see, I'm a mountain man. Cabin a few miles away. No electricity, no running water, just me and the cat and dog. My truck, which don't get used hardly. I was on an elk trail, lost the blood, think he headed into the brush. I heard a growlin' low like, scared the bee-jeebies out a me. Thought a rabid wolf, but he started a slight waggin' a his tail. Looked an' there was this big-eyed kid. No biggern' a fawn. Spunky little booger, big eyes lookin' at me mad like. Told me to be careful a the dog, and did I have any water on me."

He stopped, pleased to have an audience, pushed back his hat and scratched his beard.

"Little guy knows a lot about these here mountains and all the areas in between. Though mebbe he don't go to school, the way it seems as if he's always out with his dog."

"He is," Isaac said, shamefaced.

"So I packed him to the cabin, plenty a cryin' loud, lotsa pain. Loaded him in the truck as best I could and here we are."

"Did he know where he lived? How to get home?" Isaac asked, clearly amazed.

"Yeah, he did."

After that, he was carried to a waiting car and a pillow and blankets brought to make him comfortable. With Isaac in the front seat, they were off to the hospital in Sheridan. Susan stood, hoping to catch Isaac's eye, a wave, anything, but he'd forgotten all about her, already eager to hit the main road to town.

She turned away, listened to the milling crowd, most talking excitedly, the man named Wrench obviously enjoying his moment of fame.

She stayed on the outskirts, but took in every word.

"Lotsa kids wouldn'ta done what he done. Don't know where he got his learning. Inched himself around, had sticks and leaves gathered, a kind of hollow where he lay, covered himself as best he could. Guess he's been gone two nights?"

Someone held up three fingers, another four, but together decided it was four days and three nights. Loud murmuring followed by exclamations of how it could be possible.

Wrench told them all he owed his life to the dog, no doubt about that. There was more than one mountain lion in those foothills and more than a few bears, too. Plus wolves, now that they'd been introduced again. Anything could have happened without the dog.

Susan turned to look at Wolf, who was being fed a large bowl of dry dog food, Roy Edna carrying a bucket of water, Louise bringing up the rear with two cooked hamburgers on a plate.

She declared he winked at her, before lowering his face and lapping at the water.

The crowd dispersed, cell phones were put to use, calling off the search, faces relaxing into smiles of gratitude and relief. Slowly, vehicles made their dusty way out the winding drive, under lowering skies, the wind picking up as Susan made her way back to the house with Louise and Edna to sit in the large kitchen and enjoy a cup of steaming coffee, and the uplifting addition of female conversation.

She talked, she wept, she laughed, joining the women in the flow of rejoicing in the fact he had been found. Both agreed, they didn't know what would have become of Isaac, going through another loss, another funeral.

"The thing is," Edna said, spearing a dill pickle with her fork and placing it in the center of a piece of ham, eyeing the Swiss cheese before sending her fork in that direction. "The thing is, he looks so big and burly, so in charge of everything, but he's not that strong mentally at all. He literally went to pieces when his wife died. I pitied those children so bad."

She stopped, looked around.

"Do I hear Sharon?"

They stayed quiet, but the child must have gone on sleeping, as there was no further noise. Edna had brought her that morning, knowing she spoke of missing her father, and him gone when they arrived.

After washing up the dishes, Susan told them she'd be here with Sharon, everything would be fine when Isaac returned. They both offered to stay, but both were glad to take their leave and get back to their normal lives after three days of doing all they could for Isaac.

And she found herself wandering aimlessly, arranging a cushion here, draping a throw on the arm of the couch, staring out the window as the clouds took away the bright light of the day. *Menacing*, she thought.

These cloud banks looked full of menace. Ice, wind, snow driven by gusts up to fifty miles an hour, according to the weather station on his desk. She would be here alone with Sharon, and the injured Titus, plus one very busy, very cranky father to them both.

She would have to book her flight home, miraculously enter the world she truly belonged to, the neatness and predictable order of Lancaster County, where she knew everyone in her church district and people were polite and respectful and kind. They didn't talk in a blunt, loud voice saying exactly what they wanted, when they wanted, and how they wanted to say it.

Like Isaac.

But why did she feel so let down, so deprived of energy, thinking of returning to Pennsylvania? What was there, other than the fruitless waiting and watching for a letter that would never arrive?

CHAPTER 10

He left a voicemail on the phone in his office. Curt and to the point. A broken femur, between hip and knee. Hypothermia, so he was kept for the night. He was okay. Feed the horses. Thanks.

As usual, she held the phone away from her ear, the decibels much too high. His voice was rough, gravelly with exhaustion. She sighed as she punched the seven to discard the message, replaced the receiver and, after lifting it again, dialed her parents' number. She gave them a brief message with the good news, then said she'd call when she expected to be home. Almost, she asked if she'd received a letter, but decided against it.

He came home the following afternoon through the whirling snow of October. There were dark circles under his eyes, his hair greasy and matted, his face pale. He was only civil to her, said very little, with Titus sporting a cast from hip to ankle and a new pair of aluminum child-size crutches.

Titus and Sharon shared a quiet, joy-filled reunion, chattering away as if nothing had ever happened. At one point, Susan heard the little girl exclaim, "*Doo vawysht so lang falowda* (you were lost so long)."

Titus said he was after a badger, still knew where the den was. He laughed about Wolf, how he would snap at the hissing animal, then turn tail to run. Sharon told him in a serious voice that he should not be laughing about that at all, he almost died.

Titus hooted.

"I wasn't near dead. Not even close. I was actually in pretty good shape. Except for nights. Freezin' cold."

Sharon nodded, her large dark eyes alight with sympathy.

"I would have brought you a blanket if I could," she said sweetly.

"I know you would have, Sharon. But you didn't know where I was."

She shook her head solemnly.

This exchange brought tears to Susan's eyes. No matter what came their way, these two children would always have the solid foundation of trust in each other. Perhaps she was the one who would always keep him centered, without being aware of it.

There were visitors from the Amish community as well as townspeople and logging buddies, acquaintances and friends from all over. Of course, the daily paper carried a big article, with Wrench Vark on the front page, but no photos of Titus. Wrench was quite the celebrity in the area and lived it up for a few days before returning to his cabin for some much needed solitude.

Susan spoke to her parents, booked her flight home.

On the last evening before her departure in the morning, she found herself hoping Isaac would shake his mood, or at least communicate with her. She resented him, not showing more appreciation at all the cost and trouble she'd put into supporting him at this troubling time. She'd reconnected with Titus, listened and laughed, gave him motherly warnings, put her arms around him often, kissed the top of his head, felt the wiriness of his not quite clean hair and wished she could be his mother to give him a real shampoo.

She sighed, got up from the comfortable recliner, laid her book aside, and went upstairs for her shower. *So be it*, she thought. He was a man of a thousand puzzling ways, so if he was not friendly in the morning, she would have to live with it. The least he could have done was thank her for being there. Then again, he'd been through so much. Perhaps it was selfish of her to expect more from him.

As she padded back to her bedroom from the long hot shower, she peered down the open staircase and found there was a light on in the kitchen. Eating something, likely.

She was drifting off to sleep, half awake, half dreaming, when a soft rap on her door awakened here, then another.

"Susan?"

"Coming."

She grabbed her robe, belted it, and opened the door, only part way.

"Susan, I'm sorry to wake you. But I need to talk."

"Um . . . here? Now?"

"Come down to the kitchen, if you don't mind."

She drew a dress, any dress, from the closet, adjusted the ponytail holder in her hair, and went quietly downstairs. As she drew closer to Isaac, she could tell something was different. His mood had shifted.

"Coffee?"

Her mouth had gone strangely dry, so she shook her head.

"Not this time of the night."

He lowered himself into a chair, his wide chest dwarfing the substantial back, laid a hand on the table, then used the opposite one to rake his fingers through his hair, a nervous habit annoying her to no end.

"Susan, I'm going to come out and say what's on my mind."

She blinked twice, caught her lower lip, placed her hands in her lap before clenching one set of fingers with the other. Her bewildered eyes found his, looked away quickly.

"Are you ready for this?"

"I . . . I guess."

He took a deep steadying breath.

"This isn't easy for me, either, but here it goes. I don't want you to go home. I'm asking you to stay."

He lifted a hand as she opened her mouth to speak.

"Let me finish. I don't want you to be our *maud*, or our school teacher, but as my wife. I can't live in this house with you under any other circumstances. I know you don't love me, and you don't have to.

It would be a legitimate union, for the sake of the children. For Titus. I love you, Susan. Actually, I'm completely obsessed with you. You're in my dreams, my house, my logging, my whole existence is centered around you. That horse dying was a flop, so I tried to forget about you, but it doesn't work. I want you, Susan, in every way a man wants a woman."

"But . . . there's Levi."

"No, there isn't Levi."

"Yes, there is."

"Listen. Please just listen to me."

"I love him, Isaac. I can never love you as long as I love him. He's the perfect man for me."

"No, Susan. He is not. He proved what you mean to him by being unfaithful, then running off to get away from his self-inflicted trouble. He's not a man you need or deserve; you're simply sticking your head in the sand, in total denial. He doesn't want you."

"But he might."

"Believe me, Susan, he doesn't. I guarantee if you do go home to Lancaster and wait, you will be disappointed."

"But . . . you're not my type."

He gave a short sardonic laugh.

"No, I guess not. I'm probably nobody's type. But don't you think we're sort of beyond picking our type? There's so much hype, so much worldliness attached to choosing a partner. They have to look a certain way, act a certain way, or we don't even consider it."

"But I don't even like you," she faltered.

"You don't have to like me. Just marry me. You can stay in your upstairs bedroom, get away from Levi, thrill your mother and sisters, and be a mother to my children. It's a good plan."

"But it will be forever."

"Sure. It surely will. I can hardly wait."

"Well . . . can I go home tomorrow? I have to think this through."

"Sure, you can go. I expected you to. Think about it. And Susan, please don't say no, okay? I'll make you a good husband. You already love my kids, right?"

"I don't know. Do I? I probably wouldn't make a good stepmother at all. But . . . oh, I don't know."

She put her face in her hands.

And he was on his feet, closing the space between them. Down on his knees, his big hands gently removing hers, his eyes taking in her face. He released her hands, one of his traced the outline of her cheekbone, slowly lifted the thick hair on her shoulder.

She swallowed.

"You're so beautiful, Susan. And so terribly mixed up and unstable. You'll send me to my grave if you even think about Levi again. He's not even worth your time, and I know how you're thinking you could change him. Men don't change. I won't change. I'll always be loud and obnoxious, I'll have my moods, I eat too much, am way too outsized for someone as perfect as you. But I know what love is, and I feel exactly the way I did the first time, but even more so. You're an amazing person, and I'm hoping I can spare you more heartache in the future."

Susan felt a smile beginning to form, but it was caught halfway by an unexpected sob. When the first glistening tear appeared on her cheek, he touched it with the tip of his finger, then brought his face to hers and kissed the spot very gently. He put both hands to her face, looked deep into her eyes, and whispered, "I love you so much."

And Susan's mouth trembled, her nose burned, and no matter how hard she tried, she could not stop the tears.

"I don't know what to do," she whispered.

"That's okay. I figured you wouldn't."

He straightened, got to his feet, then reached for her hands to pull her up with him. His eyes never left hers as he took her gently into his arms, and she felt the length and breadth of him, and for one startling unexplainable moment, she could outline every nuance of the word "home."

"May I?" he asked.

She nodded, lifted her face, and his lips found hers. He drew away after the first soft touch, and she knew she wanted more.

But he only held her, stroked her still wet hair, then placed her at arms length, his eyes taking in every feature of her face.

"This is your decision now, and I'll be waiting."

"But Isaac, what about Titus? Who's going to stay with him till that leg heals?"

"You could. You can always cancel your flight."

He almost fainted when she stepped back into his arms. He felt her arms close over his waist, felt her head on his shoulder, felt the beginning of another sob, before she said, "Can I stay till he's healed?"

"Oh, Susan," was all he could say.

"I don't want to go home and think of a letter that will never arrive."

Her voice was so soft and low he could barely hear, but his heart swelled in his chest, and he knew he could never let her go.

Far into the night, they talked. Old hurts, too much pride, the mistakes made along the winding path of seeking a life companion. Love or romance, call it whatever you like, it was the same thing.

"You know I get terribly homesick out here," Susan said.

"I know. And that's an awful thing for a man to inflict on his wife. Roy Edna gets into this bizarre mood."

He laughed, then turned dead serious.

"Should I move to Lancaster if we get married?"

She eyed him doubtfully. "That overcrowded place is not big enough to hold you."

"You mean me, or my voice?"

"Both."

She looked at him, openly and honestly.

"You belong out here in the West. Lancaster County would cripple you, like a bird in too small a cage. Titus would suffer. No, if I do consent to be your wife, Wyoming comes with it, in all its terrible beauty. The weather is like a grouchy old bachelor, never knowing what's going to happen next."

"Grouchy old maid," he corrected her.

"Us?" she asked, and laughed.

And he loved her until he could scarcely draw another breath.

DURING THE NIGHT, the snow stopped falling, the wind picked up until the logs groaned, the eaves whistled, and a leftover hanging basket was hurled into the outdoor fireplace and broken into dozens of pieces. The dead fern and the black potting soil were flung all over the stone patio. Wolf snuggled down in the soft hay, lifted his ears as he heard the crash of a chair being flung off the porch, then sighed, rested his chin on his paws, and closed his eyes.

Susan lay awake, feeling as if a solid foundation had been ripped away, leaving her faith to crumple in its wake. How did one go about processing this turn of events? Her feeble resistance was cringeworthy. "You're not my type." No, he wasn't at all. That battered face, that loud voice and obnoxious manner. Rude, arrogant even, going around thinking everyone loved him. Truth was, they did. The number of people who helped search for Titus, and most of them knew him.

She allowed a soft groan to escape.

So, he thought Levi was nothing but trouble. Well, he certainly made a good boyfriend. But the moment that thought entered her mind, she knew he had been a champion deceiver. So what had possessed her to literally skate on thin ice, blindly gliding along to the deceptive plunge into polar water? And then continued to try changing the freezing water into a balmy blue of a tropical island.

No, it could not be done. He had done everything Isaac said he had done, and only he would be blunt enough to tell her so.

He spoke the unvarnished truth, and was that such an awful thing? But marriage to him? The word held so many unfamiliar pitfalls. For one, there were the children. Two, living thousands of miles away from her beloved family. How was a person expected to survive?

Till death do us part. A long time to be with someone you didn't love, with their odor permeating the air, the loud voice jangling her nerves.

Could love creep up on someone? Sort of like receiving a nice golden tan by repeatedly spending time in the sun, until one day you are quite pleased with the results? She blushed, thinking of his tenderness, and had no reason to believe his words were not true.

She'd believed every one of Levi's flowery speeches, so this was something that needed to be addressed. By the time the hands of her alarm clock reached somewhere between three and six, she felt exhausted, defeated, too bone weary to have any reasonable thoughts pertaining to romance, marriage, or any of the repercussions.

SHE AWOKE LATER than usual, astounded to find light creeping into her room, bringing into clarity the event of the night before.

Embarrassed at having overslept, not wanting to greet him at all, she was torn between hurrying to brush her teeth and comb her hair, or take her time, which would allow her to miss him entirely. She realized she wanted to take the first flight home, wanted it so badly she could feel the plane lifting off. It had been a new, first-time experience, one she would likely never repeat, flying *verboten* by the Amish except for emergencies.

But when she thought of Titus, she knew she would stay, knew it was for him she had come in the first place. She hadn't bargained for this, but if she was needed, she'd stay.

As she came out into the hallway and headed downstairs, she heard a low whimper, then a soft cry, "Susan?"

Titus.

She ran down the stairs and to the small form on the couch, reached out to him and asked if he needed anything.

"Yeah, it hurts."

"I'll get your pain meds."

She returned with the prescription pills, water, and a few graham crackers, and tried to persuade him to take them with the food. He glowered, his eyebrows drawn down, said he didn't want crackers, he wasn't hungry.

"But your stomach might hurt if you don't."

"Don't want them."

She heard the door open, a rustling in the laundry room, and Isaac's large form moved into the living room, where Susan was holding the crackers and Titus was pouting.

"Good morning, Susan."

"Oh. Good morning."

She did not meet his gaze, suddenly shy.

"You awake?" he said to Titus.

Titus didn't answer, merely kept his mouth in a pout.

"He doesn't want to take these crackers, and I'm afraid the pills will hurt his stomach. It says here, 'To be taken with food.'"

A vehement shake of his head, a glare piercing the air, Titus remained rooted in his opinion.

Isaac shrugged. "You don't have to, Titus."

Nothing to do but comply, and she found herself stuffing the crackers back in the box, furious at Isaac, upset that he allowed himself to be so manipulated by one small boy.

She felt him close behind her, waited for him to pass.

"Susan."

She turned, her green eyes flashing.

"See, Isaac? You haven't changed. You let that boy get away with anything. He should be made to obey."

Isaac raised his eyebrows.

"You know what? If his stomach hurts, he'll eat the crackers next time. He's that kind of kid. You can't force him to do anything."

Her temper flared.

"So you let him do what he wants and a three-day course of torture is endured by the whole community? Really?"

She saw the anger in his face, knew she'd pressed the wrong button, and didn't care. This man was so set in his ways, so terribly sure of himself, there was no way on earth she would marry him.

And when Titus groaned with an empty stomach filled with the acidic pills, she let him howl before bringing a dish of cereal.

HER MOTHER CALLED. A letter had arrived from Alaska. Susan's voice became light and breathless as she begged her mother to send it that day, gave her the address with a shaking tone.

He had finally replied. Perhaps her dreams would still come true and she wouldn't have to consider Isaac and all his baggage.

Isaac noticed the heightened color in her cheeks, the light of antic-ipation in her eye, took it as a good sign, went to work with the confi-dence he felt, and had a terrific day with a record number of loads pull-ing out of the logging year. He wanted to ask her about her good mood, but thought better of it after she seemed distressed, anxious. He heard her at night, shifting in bed, walking the floor, and realized something else entirely might be in the works.

She ran to the mailbox, ripped the letter open with shaking hands and bated breath, her eyes darting back and forth as she read. When she finished, she laid the letter on the table, crossed her arms tightly over her waist, and stared into space. Sharon was rocking her doll in the living room, singing a sweet children's song in German. Susan began to cry. She cried all afternoon, discreetly, in corners of rooms, blowing her nose softly so the children wouldn't hear. Humiliation was heaped on her head, ran over her face, her clothes, and puddled on the floor.

He wanted her sister Kate. Her sister! She was the sweet one, the one he admired and had come to love. She was the reason he had had the affair, the reason he ran to Alaska, the reason for his existence.

He thanked her again for all the good times, and hoped she could yet find a true and abiding love.

Oh, I will, I will, she thought bitterly. *But it won't be in Lancaster County where you will be the perfect husband with the perfect sweet sub-missive wife.* No. She would never return.

They stayed up late, Susan handing him the letter silently. Isaac read it slowly, then read it again. He put the letter back in the envelope and gave a low whistle, his eyes on his shoe tops. He shook his head.

"So, this means your sister will take him?"

"Of course she will. Looking back, he loved going to her house, loved doing things for her. She's the opposite of me, never speaks her mind, goes along with whatever. She went through Dan's depression, moved to Virginia, his alcoholism, his abuse, left the Amish, and he died on the highway. Through all that, she remained steadfast. She loved him, can you imagine? Said it was God's will that she married him, helped him through. She genuinely grieved for that loser."

Isaac's mouth twitched. He coughed, then gave in and laughed his deep, rumbling laugh.

"I take it you didn't."

"I'm not going to answer that."

And then Isaac talked. He told Susan surely she could see God's hand in both of their lives, said he knew she thought he wasn't close to God, which he hadn't been for too long. Overcome with gratitude at Titus being found, he felt God's presence strongly while he knelt by his bed that night.

Susan pictured that big, bold Isaac kneeling, his head bowed, and she felt an unexplained stirring of emotion.

"You were here. I felt every ounce of gratitude for that. I still feel God is using one circumstance after another to bring us together, and this . . ."

He tapped the letter.

"That is the final answer for me. If you don't feel the same, we'll give it time, and hopefully soon, you will."

Susan asked if he really was convinced she was God's will for his life, and he told her yes. He had loved her now, for how long? When did she arrive at Roy and Edna's?

"I thought you were the most beautiful girl I had ever seen. But I'm not much, so of course I let it go. Widower with two kids, a fancy, prissy Lancaster girl, a real greenhorn from the East. Nope, she'd never look at me."

Susan smiled.

"Who could help looking at you? You almost crashed into the porch there at Roy and Edna's, on that uncontrollable horse. Of course I looked at you."

"And?"

She shrugged.

"Don't say it," he laughed.

"No, you certainly were not unattractive. Just so big and loud and, well, sort of scary."

"So now what do you think we should do about us?" he asked.

"I don't know. I need to think, to pray, to process all of this. I don't feel the same about Levi after reading that letter, but I don't understand my own feelings about you."

He nodded, smiled, then got to his feet.

"Okay, that's fine. We'll give it time."

He stretched, yawned, abruptly said good night and disappeared into the bathroom, where she heard water running, the sound of teeth being brushed. What? Why did he do that? He could at least have held her hand. She allowed that thought of how much she had liked to be held in his arms, those big, burly logger's arms dragging a massive chainsaw all day. His chest. And he actually had no smell like diesel fuel, only the scent of laundry detergent on his shirt.

She guaranteed he wasn't tired. He just wanted her to think he was bored with her. She had half a notion to knock on the bathroom door and tell him she didn't care whether he held her or not. Go right ahead and brush your teeth.

Whatever.

As she got into bed, she realized if she consented to be his wife, it would never be a perfect union. More like the meeting of two minds.

They never thought alike, and often, he made her so mad, with his overconfident ways, his straight honest talk, bouncing opinions all over the place, thinking he was never wrong. It rankled her now, thinking about Titus taking those pills. That was how it would be. He'd take up for his children, knowing they were pitifully motherless, and she would struggle to love them the way a mother should. She wasn't their biological mother, no blood ties, so she would always try to love them, and never accomplish it truly.

And he felt God was leading them together. She sighed. He was smart enough to give her time, while she could practice being a mother to Titus and Sharon.

Sharon was no problem, as winsome and sweet as any child she had ever met, but that Titus. And with Isaac always on his side, was she really smart even considering entering a union of marriage?

Till death do us part was a very long time.

CHAPTER 11

THEY WENT RIDING IN THE SNOW ON SUNDAY, TITUS STATIONED AT
the low living room windows to watch. The air was crisp, frosty, but
not uncomfortably cold, the snow layer less than six inches. The sun
was blinding, the reflection off the snow causing them both to squint
against it.

His horse was acting up as usual, pawing the snow, snorting, side
stepping, rattling his bit as he tossed his head. He saddled a large, black
gelding for her, a sensible horse with a smooth gait, but with Isaac's
mount throwing a fit, the black gelding seemed unsure, ears flicking,
shifting his weight from foot to foot. He helped her mount by holding the stirrup with one hand, the bridle with the other. She thought
the stirrup was way too high, considered asking for a stepstool, even a
five-gallon bucket, but her pride would not allow this, so she stepped
back, made an effort, and missed.

He said nothing, and she glared at him, the color in her cheeks
brightening.

"I'm not used to this, you know."

"I didn't say anything."

She hopped around, made a heroic attempt, and shoved the toe of
her boot into the stirrup, then stood there almost split in two, one hand
on the saddle horn and the other dangling clumsily. She tried pulling
herself up, but the saddle tilted sideways, and she thought the whole
works would slide down beneath his stomach, saddle blanket included.

"Go. Heave yourself up," Isaac instructed.

"Well, the saddle isn't tight."

"Yes it is. Go for it."

And she did, putting most of her weight on the stirrup, swinging the other leg across, hanging desperately to the saddle horn, which seemed to be as high as an eight-foot ceiling.

But she was up. She looked down at Isaac, who seemed way too far below her, and grinned. He smiled back, patted her leg.

"Good job."

"Huh," was all she could think to say.

Hadn't they been through this before? He could easily tell she had never mounted a horse in the time in between. Embarrassment welled up, but her pride took its place. If she fell off this horse, it would be all his fault for persuading her to go riding in the snow in the first place.

She was just so far off the ground. To sit on horseback was like being in a tree without branches. And she wished that snorting monstrosity he was riding would calm himself down, the way he stirred up her own horse.

"Ready?" Isaac called out.

"Ready for what?"

He waved an arm. "To go."

"Where are we going?"

"Just . . . come on."

He started out on a walk, which was more like a clownish dance, his horse tipping from front to back, sidestepping, chomping at the bit, wanting to run. Susan's horse walked steadily, with a smooth, rocking gait, so that she became increasingly comfortable, more assured as a rider.

She allowed her gaze to wander, taking in the immense expanse of snow, the aspens with their few remaining leaves like nuggets of gold on a clean canvas of snow, the fir trees starkly outlined against the majesty of the Bighorns. The air was pure and clean and crisp, the sun as if magnified by the unspoiled expanse of snowfall. She couldn't help comparing this to an early snowfall back home, the township's monsters, those feared yellow trucks with angled blades sending curtains of wet, salted slush off the busy roads, car tires hissing on the wet pavement as they rushed through as fast as they possibly could, appointments to meet, shopping to do, homes to arrive to on time, impatient horns honking.

The mad rush.

But she didn't think she could survive here. Too much solitude. Too extremely the opposite.

The wind sprang up, sending a swath of fresh snow in their path, sending Isaac's horse into a tailspin, up on his hind legs, around and around, and with Isaac hauling back on the reins, he got in a few good leaps before he was brought under control.

The black gelding took off unexpectedly, allowing Susan no time to gather the reins, grab for the saddlehorn, or any other means of keeping her seat. She was neatly deposited, landing with a teeth-jarring *phwomp* in the snow, her teeth clacking like castanets, her backside taking the worst of the fall. The horse ran on and Susan sat in the snow seeing stars from the sharp knifing pain in her lower spine. She gasped, she heaved, bent sideways, then lay on her side. Grimacing, she watched the disappearance of the black gelding and Isaac. She tried to deal with the terrible pain, the cold wet snow, but worst of all, her humiliation at being unseated.

She decided then and there she was going home. She wasn't cut out for this kind of life. Stupid horses, cold wet snow long before it was actually time for the first snowfall, children getting lost, the eternal never ending wind that jarred your nerves.

No, she was going home.

Isaac returned, the gelding in tow, dismounted, got down on one knee, his big hands reaching for her, his face the perfect picture of care and concern.

"Are you hurt, Susan? I'm sorry I couldn't control my horse better."

"Yes, I'm hurt. I *sotzed* right down on my tailbone, and it hurts."

"I'm sorry. Where does it hurt?"

Her temper flared, fueled by abject misery and blistered pride.

"Where do you think?"

His mouth worked, his eyes squinted, he sputtered, tried to cough, but failed, then completely stopped trying to squelch the humor and burst out laughing. He roared, slapped his knee, finishing up with a drawn out, "Hooo!"

Susan glared at him, would gladly have punched his nose. Without thinking, she sat up and yelled, "You're so ignorant. If you think I'm going to live out West, you have another guess coming. And good luck finding someone to marry you, cause it won't be me."

She was furious, didn't care if her words hurt.

He looked at her, still smiling.

"Here, give me your hands."

"No."

"Come on, Susan. I'll help you walk."

Her backside seemed to support her weight quite handily, her steps as easily accomplished as before. He grabbed the reins, put one arm around her waist to support her, and together, they moved toward home. He took his time, measured his steps with hers, and she found herself liking the idea of walking in the snow with him, so close she could hear his breathing, feel the strength of him as he walked effortlessly. Her spine ached, but only a mild, dull pain, the kind where you knew everything would be alright.

She saw the homestead nestled against the side of the ridge where the aspen trees were grouped with the pines and thought she had never seen anything quite as picturesque. It was surreal. The atmosphere was so quiet, she heard only the dull shuffling of the horses' feet, Isaac breathing, an occasional shrill call of a hawk, the chirp of a cardinal.

She was happy to see the end of the road, to turn into the drive leading to the house. Suddenly she was very aware of the big arm around her waist and wanted it gone.

"I can walk by myself," she said, twisting her body to be free of him.

His arm dropped immediately, and she was left on her own, experiencing an excruciating shot of pain in her lower back and down one leg. She grimaced slightly, stifling the cry of anguish.

"You're not okay," he said, stopping the horses.

"Yes, I am," she said forcefully, glaring at him.

He shrugged his shoulders and walked off, the horses being led obediently.

The moment he was out of her way, she stood still, took stock of her situation, and could see no exit out of this agonizing pain.

Gritting her teeth, she walked on, placing one lead foot in front of the other, carried along by pride and determination.

SHE TRIED ICE, ibuprofen, heat, Tylenol, spent near sleepless nights, let the laundry pile up and the housework go.

It was a few days of this, snapping at Titus and yelling at Sharon, before Isaac stopped her on a painful walk to the bathroom.

"Susan, I got you an appointment at my chiropractor's office."

"What for?"

"To fix your back."

"Nobody's touching this thing."

"You can't go on like this. Doctor Woods is great. He knows back injuries and will be very careful."

Susan felt drained, miserable, exhausted by the inability to sleep, her stomach in an uproar with the regularity of painkillers dumped into it every four hours. She looked up and found his brown eyes intently on hers, a look of so much caring, and something else.

She found herself getting used to that unusual face. Too smooth where the titanium plates held his cheekbone in place, the upper lip pulled into a perpetual lopsided mini-sneer, the nose a bit crooked, the deep cleft in his chin, just above the line of his neatly trimmed beard. She compared him with Levi's smooth good looks, his flawless skin and impeccable manners, and for one moment of reckoning, she realized this face was the face of a man, a man who had lived and suffered and risen above circumstances that drove him to his knees.

Was she merely woozy with painkillers addling her brain?

She thought this might be the case, so she clasped her hands tightly to keep from reaching up and tracing the crooked part of his mouth with her fingertips.

"Okay," she whispered, her eyes on his.

He put his hand on her shoulder. "Good. Two o'clock. Your appointment's at three fifteen."

They took Sharon as well as Titus with them as a distraction from his long day in the house, banging around in crutches, fighting with his sister, and getting on Susan's nerves.

The roads were clear, the sun melting the snow on the trees and southern slopes. The driver was the proud owner of a newly purchased twelve-passenger van, a 2001, he informed them. No rust, only a little over fifteen thousand miles on it. A retired rancher, he could talk endlessly about the history of ranches, local folklore, true or untrue, but all very interesting.

About ten miles down the road he pointed out the McCade ranch, the Bar XL, where Ernest McCabe, the old man, froze to death in a blizzard, back in the seventies, only twenty feet from the corner of the shed. His son Hugo still lived there, had married his third wife after the second one ran off with the vet.

"The first wife got measles and died in the hospital from complications. They say his dog never ate another morsel of food, crawled away and died a few weeks later, but then, likely she was the only living soul who showed him a bit of kindness."

He chuckled, lifted his bottle of Sprite, held it against the steering wheel with one hand, twisted the cap with the other, took a long swig, and replaced it, the van taking a sudden curve, gravel splitting like hailstones.

Titus picked a fight with Sharon, putting his leg too far over on the seat, tapping his stockinged toe against the side of her leg.

"Stop it, Titus."

A bit of silence, except for more history from the next ranch, the driver spinning a yarn about his Red Angus herd, skinny as rails and not cut out for the West. He'd be going under in the next five years, give or take a few.

"Titus!"

Susan turned around, her eyebrows raised.

"What?"

An insolent stare, a look of total disregard.

"Don't touch her with your foot, okay, Titus?"

"I'm not hurting her."

"But she doesn't want you to do it, so please don't."

"You're always taking her side."

She looked to Isaac, but he was in the middle of a spirited conversation about Simmental cattle, his profile beneath the narrow brimmed black hat unexpectedly appealing.

"Isaac."

He stopped talking, turned in his seat. No seat belt, she noticed, not on him or the driver.

"Titus is teasing Sharon."

"Titus, I told you before we left. Now straighten up."

Titus faced his father with guileless, big brown eyes, a half-smile on his mischievous face.

"You heard me, right?"

He nodded.

Another twenty miles, a different road, macadam this time, a few pickup trucks appearing in the distance, passing with friendly waves, Stetson hats pulled low.

"Daddy!"

Sharon's voice was plaintive, impatient.

Isaac turned. "What, Sharon?"

"Titus is poking at me with his toe again."

"Okay." He looked at the driver. "Would you pull over, please?"

When the van rolled to a stop, he got out, came around to the side, opened the door and reached for Sharon, placed her in the front seat with Susan.

"Now settle down, Titus."

"I wasn't doing anything."

Isaac chose to ignore this, and they were on their way.

Susan shifted her weight, winced, put a hand behind her back, wished she'd brought a pillow. This was an awfully long way to travel for a chiropractic adjustment, and she was not at all confident it would be worth it.

Really, everything was so different here. The edge of town was a few lumber and corrugated brick buildings, rusting fifty-gallon drums, truck tires, tired, bleached weeds poking up out of the melting snow. The wide street straight down the center was lined with slanted parking spaces like the bones of a fish spine. Some buildings had wooden false fronts, others were somber-looking brick buildings stacked in rows like packing crates. Obviously not much urban planning. The word "cheerless" came to mind. Drab.

"There's Leo!" the driver shouted, lowering his window.

"Hey, buddy!" he shouted, his arm out, waving furiously.

The object of his attention turned, looked, his eyes opening wide. A flick of the wrist, two fingers in the air and they were past.

Susan guessed folks were elated at the sight of any acquaintance, living out in the middle of nowhere, human beings a rare sight. Everything was so elongated and so far apart, as if you stretched Lancaster County like a rubber band until it snapped and all the little pieces flew in different directions. A ranch here, a cabin there, an old rusty trailer a few miles after that.

The chiropractor was a presentable man in his mid-fifties or sixties. It was hard to tell, with his weathered face and lean physique.

He was knowledgeable enough, took X-rays, poked and prodded, asked questions, then worked on her back, cracked vertebrae, manipulated and kneaded.

She hated going out to the waiting room to Isaac and the children, her face reddened by being stuck face down on the table, her hair disheveled, and still in pain. She made no eye contact, mumbled about being ready to go, got her coat off the rack and got into it, noticing how he never thought of helping her.

She wrote a check, pocketed the receipt, and walked out ahead of him, her head held high. She heard the thump of the crutches, sniffed, and found the van parked where he'd pulled in, opened the door, and climbed in without saying a word to anyone. Isaac's form appeared at the side door, said he was going across the street to Culpepper's.

"Burgers for the kids."

"Stop called them kids," she snapped, wishing he'd use the more accepted term among the Amish, "children."

"Sorry. Are you hungry?"

She wasn't in the mood for greasy food. She didn't like the idea of eating at any of these low-class establishments, thought of cow hair stuck on bloody raw meat, a filthy grill. But the children were clapping their hands, yelling about French fries, so she nodded her head. She hoped the talkative driver wouldn't sit with them.

The interior was dark with only weak hanging lamps over the wooden tables and booths. The odor of frying oil, grease, and a sharp scent she could not place was overwhelming, like a dense fog. They seated themselves, Titus with his father facing her and little Sharon, shy and big-eyed as a fawn, her white bowl-shaped covering in sharp contrast to the stained wood.

"Okay, Susan, so how are you feeling?"

"Still in pain."

"Too bad. Did he help at all?"

"Some."

"This is Culpepper's. The best steaks in Wyoming. But there's plenty to choose off the menu, so you don't have to eat steak."

"I can take care of myself."

He didn't answer, a flicker of irritation in his eyes. She didn't like sitting here with her red face and swollen eyes from being stuck in the space between two upholstered cushions on that table, her hair sticking out like a disheveled poodle. She felt out of place, not in control of the situation, and to top it off, she found herself repeatedly liking Isaac's craggy, mature face. Liking the way his mouth was imperfect, the set of his shoulders.

The waitress was heavyset, in a too tight pair of jeans and western shirt, the space between the pearl snaps bulging.

"Hi, guys!"

"Hello."

Susan said nothing. Sharon was too shy, but Titus waved at the waitress.

"My name is Chessie, and I'll be your server. What can I get you to drink?"

Still uncomfortable, Susan shifted her weight, ordered a lemonade, waited as Isaac asked the children what they wanted. Mountain Dew for everyone. Right. How could he let them drink that sugary stuff?

The food was undeniably delicious, her smoked barbeque absolutely wonderful, with a perfect mound of mashed potatoes and spicy pepper slaw, thick beef gravy and dinner rolls as big as a cereal bowl.

The children ate mostly French fries and ketchup, giggled and played with the straws in their drinks. Isaac kept the conversation going easily, pointing out people he knew, who lived close to them, who was still ranching, until she forgot about her appearance and became interested in the lives of these rural Wyoming people.

"They didn't take to the Amish very good at first. We were like immigrants crossing the border. But after a couple of years most of them decided we were doing a good job of building, restoring some of this acreage and so on. They're suspicious of anything new, just the way we Amish are, sort of. They think Wyoming is fine just the way it always was, and most of them don't want change."

She buttered a small section of her dinner roll.

"They'll live in near poverty as long as they can hang on to the land. Land is everything. A few cows, an old pickup truck, the house in disrepair, but they still own a thousand acres, so in their mind, they're wealthy landowners. They'll die happy, proud owners of good Wyoming acreage."

"Is that what you think?" she asked.

"About myself? No. I have to work. I'm not built with the same blood lines. I love my job. Logging. It's a thrill, even if I have to travel and leave you and the kids."

He caught his error. "Children."

She smiled, a small lifting of her mouth that didn't reach her eyes.

"The children and me. I don't know why you're worrying about leaving me. I'm not your *maud* or your housekeeper anymore. What is the community saying? I mean, definitely not normal, is it? Just dropping by because of Titus and staying."

"I need you."

"For the children."

"You know better."

Titus's keen eyes went from one face to the other, missing nothing.

"Yeah, Susan. You know we need you. I want you to stay as much as Daddy does. You could marry him."

Her eyebrows shot up. She picked at her dinner roll, would not look at Titus.

He pressed on. "Why not? You could marry my dad as good as anyone else, then I wouldn't have to run around with Wolf. I hate our house when Dad isn't there. Except when you're there. Hey, you know when I broke my leg, when I fell? I found some arrowheads. We should go back there. Actually, me and Wolf will go as soon as I can."

"I thought you said you're not going to do that anymore," Susan said, shaking a finger at him.

"If you stay, I won't."

Sharon clapped her hands. "Yes, yes!"

Susan watched Isaac finishing the last of his steak, an unbelievable amount of beef having been devoured, the red greasy juice mopped up with a dinner roll, mashed potatoes inhaled, gravy slurped. Could she live with those table manners for the rest of her life? Did men change, ever? And that booming voice, the sheer volume of it.

Could a person merely mix the good and not so good qualities in a man, pick out whatever suited, and come up with a winning combination?

How did one go about falling in love with one who would always love you back? She wasn't sure it was possible for her. Starting a relationship, feeling independent, in control, allowing herself to fall bit by bit, finally taking the plunge, and hitting her head on the rocks, literally hitting rock bottom.

The thing was, she wasn't sure this was possible, achieving the level of admiration she'd had for Levi. Isaac was so complicated, so rough around the edges, no social graces. A man didn't just ask a girl to marry him for the sake of convenience, as a kind of mother-housekeeper mixture.

Or did he?

She had no clue, so she folded her napkin in half, then fourths, smoothed it against the tabletop, over and over, her thoughts in turmoil.

One thing she knew for sure, she could not make up her mind yet, and with her staying at Isaac's house indefinitely, eyebrows would be raised, whispers exchanged. She had her own integrity, needed to keep her pride intact.

She looked up to find his eyes on her face, a smile creating crow's feet around his brown eyes. He held her gaze.

"You about done ironing that napkin?"

She blushed, put a hand to her hair, and straightened her covering.

"Let's go," she said, needing fresh air, feeling the need to get away from this dim lighting and throbbing music, Isaac's face just a bit too attractive.

"I want some of their apple pie and ice cream. You want something else?"

She drank coffee in small sips, trying not to watch him attack the mountain of ice cream and pie, coming away with a huge bite, edging it sideways into his mouth and chewing enthusiastically.

"I love this stuff," he chortled.

She didn't say anything, reached over and picked up a cold French fry from Sharon's plate.

Sharon looked up and smiled. "You may have it. Do you want more?"

She drew the plate closer to Susan, and her thoughts were like a blender with the puree button pressed.

CHAPTER 12

It was three days before Christmas when Kate's letter arrived. The letter sealing her destiny.

Dear Susan,

I miss you, and wish I could tell you this in person. I'm getting married in March of next year. Levi Yoder has asked me to be his wife, and I simply don't know how to make this easy for you. I have prayed, considered refusing him for your sake, but I love him as much as he loves me. He confessed his past transgression, said it was born out of frustrated love for me, while dating you. I hope you can find it in your heart to accept this, and I am so looking forward to your return, when we can meet face to face and discuss it in a mature fashion.

I love you, Susan. You've always been my supporter, my loyal confidante, and you will be again.

Rose, Liz, and my parents are all against my choice, which is very hard for me to accept. I see so much good in Levi. He's so good with the children and will make a wonderful father to them.

The children are well and send their love.

Our wedding date is March 29, 2021, and it will be at Dave and Liz's place. I'm wearing navy blue, so when you arrive home, I have the fabric for you.

Please write and tell me your feelings. I'm prepared to hear your objections, and I apologize for hurting you, but Levi is everything to me—so talented, such a good business man, so kind, and to think he picked me. I'm not worthy of a man like this. I adore him as he adores me.

Please come home soon. I miss you.

Love,

Kate

Enclosed is a letter from Emily and Nathan.

FOR A LONG time, Susan merely sat, as if frozen in time, staring at nothing. Her thoughts were like bubbles, appearing and disappearing in a second. Nothing seemed to make sense.

What did he see in Kate that she, herself, was lacking? Her size? Her dark hair? Her sweet personality? Would it really be able to accept Marie, Kate's Down's Syndrome child, as his own? She knew Levi as one who had to have the "best" of everything, name-brand sports equipment, the best horse and buggy. Would he see Marie for the amazing girl she was or would he feel like she was somehow "less than" other children.

Slowly, as she remembered the times they'd spent together at Kate's house, the way he had played with Marie, the way he had looked at Kate, she decided he really did love Kate and each of her children.

She sat up, shook her head to clear the infusion of hurt and jealousy and the oncoming rage. One thing was certain. She could never go home. She would not enter Lancaster County as the laughingstock of the family, the reject. Poor Susan. The poor thing. Well, you know how it is, some girls just don't have what it takes. Men just aren't attracted to them. And then they would quickly add that they were "leftover blessings" in the community.

Which they were, but the phrase still stung. Who wanted to be a leftover?

She considered a life in which she stayed single, started some enormously lucrative business, and became rich. She could run a bakery or deli, sell fresh cut flowers, become an interior designer. She was smart and driven. She could do it. She'd spend the rest of her life proving to everyone that she was absolutely fine. Instead of pitying her, they'd talk about her success and secretly wish they themselves could have her life for a day rather than being burdened by snotty-nosed kids, endless diapers, the struggles of marriage. Levi would wish he had married her, the strong, smart, and successful sister.

But her tears were liquid compliance to a better way, the way of the cross. Her Christian upbringing was put into place and she gave herself up to the will of God. In the space of time it took for Isaac and the children to do chores, she had run the gauntlet of her inner turmoil and submitted herself to the one and only God she served. She bowed before the throne of Grace, allowing Jesus to wash away the outrage, the pain, and the caustic wish for revenge.

And light dawned.

Like pieces of a puzzle, everything was found, everything fit, from her unexpected trip to Wyoming to teach school, her return, Dan's death and Kate coming home to be Amish, even Titus's wandering had been the hand of God. Isaac's proposal, her reluctance, her stupid, foolish self.

She probably didn't love Isaac the way he should be loved, but if God obviously meant one person to be a life companion to another, then who was she to argue?

It was the opening of the door to the laundry room that brought her out of her reverie. She grabbed a dishtowel and wiped her eyes, straightened her apron, and threw the letter quickly into the trash can. She was wiping countertops when they came in, faces red from the cold, Titus charged like a full battery, able to walk and run on his own two feet since the cast had come off.

"Hey! Daddy says we're going to have our Christmas presents tomorrow night after he gets home from work!"

"Really? I still have baking and wrapping to do."

"You can do that tomorrow."

Isaac hid his face, said nothing.

"Did you say that?" Susan asked Isaac.

"I did. Sorry."

"We'll see. If I can get everything done, it might be okay."

"They're calling for a blizzard on Christmas Eve. I met Bud Dawson from across the creek and he says we could get up to three feet of snow and ice. Cow-killing weather. So I'm going to take off work and help him round up a bunch of his cows. I love doing that. You want to go?"

"Me? Are you kidding? I can't stay on a horse."

"Your back's healed. You need to practice."

"I will. Come spring."

"Spring? You hear that, Dad? She's gonna be here in the spring. Yay! Dippy eggs and bacon before I go to school. Help with my arithmetic." Titus followed with a somersault across the kitchen floor.

Isaac searched her face. She turned away and said nothing. They played a game of Uno, then another, before Susan told them to take their baths and tell her when they were done. Isaac was bone weary and folded his large form into his recliner and fell asleep in a few minutes. When the children were in their pajamas, she went up the stairs with them, knelt side by side with both of them to recite the German prayer at the end of their day, the same prayer she had been raised on, then tucked Sharon in, kissing the soft, warm cheek, telling her she loved her.

"Love you, Titus," she said from the doorway, knowing a kiss was off limits for this one.

"Love you, too," from the depths of the covers.

With Isaac asleep on the recliner, she turned off the lamp and went back upstairs to a hot bath and a long night of retrospection.

She retraced her steps, her thoughts cohesive now, blending and molding her life to a perfectly decipherable entity. Here was her place, here in this great house in the vast plains of Wyoming. Here with this man Isaac, whom she wasn't even sure she liked. He came with age, a fractured face, two children, a love of logging, the most dangerous job on earth, she was quite sure.

She marveled at her own groping blindness. How ill-suited she had been to muddle around back in Lancaster, thinking she could find happiness, hanging on to the unstable thread of her relationship with Levi, obscuring the true light of God's will.

Her future would not be a bed of roses, but life wasn't that way. God didn't promise a life free of sorrow, of bitter disappointment, hurdles that were hard, really hard. But He was always there, always ready to make even the highest hurdle possible to get over.

She slept well after deciding one thing. She would attend Kate's wedding as a married woman, resplendent in her western dress.

True to Isaac's word, the children's gifts were given two evenings before Christmas Eve. Titus was hyper with excitement, ejecting himself off the couch, up the stairs, sliding down the railing in a split second, holding his lower back and hopping around in pain after he hit the top of the post. Sharon giggled and ran in circles, her skirts flaring as she whirled until she became dizzy and fell to the floor.

Susan had decorated the house with fragrant pine roping, candles, a small fir tree in the corner with popcorn and cranberries strung on a thread. There were brightly colored packages with ribbons attached, the scent of cinnamon and cloves bubbling from the hot cider on the stove.

She watched Isaac as he handed out gifts, noticed the pleasure on his face, his eyes lighting up at the squeals and shrieks of delight. A new doll, of course, for Sharon, a faux stainless steel cooking set that resembled the ones in Isaac's kitchen. (*My kitchen?* Susan thought.) There was a new pink bridle for the pony and bags of little brushes and combs to groom him. For Titus, there was a new pair of real leather boots, the handcrafted ones costing a large sum of money for footwear, a new aluminum baseball bat, a pair of binoculars, and a crossbow.

Titus was speechless for once in his life, never imagining these gifts, or not all of them at once.

There were games, snacks, and drinks, laughing and talking till the clock struck eleven and Isaac hustled them off to bed.

Susan was washing dishes when she heard his footsteps behind her.

"Need help?"

"You can dry."

So he did, putting the dishes away while she wiped countertops. When she was finished, she turned to him and said very soft and low, "Isaac."

He caught his breath, unsure of this tone of voice.

"Yes?"

"Do you still want to marry me?"

"Of course I do."

She walked over to the crumpled, half straightened out letter she had retrieved from the trash can, and handed it to him. He looked at her, a question in his eyes, but she motioned for him to sit down.

"Read it."

His eyes scanned the pages, his breathing so light Susan could barely hear or see he was alive. Like a stone, he sat there reading, then slowly put it down. He would not meet her eyes, but got up, walked to the kitchen window and stood, staring out into the dark night.

When he turned, his face was twisted with pain.

"So you're marrying me now only because you've been hit with a double dose of humiliation this time."

He pointed to the letter.

Susan gripped the back of a chair, her face gone white with shock, the reality of what she had been assuming almost more than she could bear.

"I'm sorry. Yes, it does seem like that. But since this letter arrived, I've done a lot of soul searching. I can't go on, resisting God's will for my life, blindsided by my own, which I can see now, was my way of serving my old nature, wanting what I can't have. How many of us are like that? Our eyes filled with stars, chasing the elusive fairy tale called romance, when in real life, relationships are hard. Marriage is hard."

She stopped, spread her hands.

"Here I am. I am willing to be your wife if you'll have me. Nothing about our marriage will be perfect, but I think we have a rock solid foundation, which is honesty and truth."

"But do you love me enough?" he asked, his voice hoarse with emotion.

"Probably not as much as I should, but I'll grow into it."

"Is that enough for you?"

"It is enough. I'm only being brutally honest here. I think I may be the type who never loves as deeply as some, always remaining a bit independent, but I have a sneaking suspicion you're much the same."

He smiled, then he slowly closed the gap between them. When he reached her, she stepped out from behind the chair, her eyes on his, taking in the question in his, answering with a question of her own.

"But will it work?" he whispered.

She nodded, then went into his arms, felt them close around her, and she enjoyed, again, the feel of his wide chest, the strength in those arms.

Their lips met in mutual consent. Susan gave herself to him in spirit, conveyed by her willingness to accept him, and in spite of the imperfections of her past, all the realities of her life in the West, she would take him to be her husband.

He looked down at her, she looked up at him, let her eyes tell him of the awakening of a sleeping love, one that was new and tender, not very steady, but was there.

"Susan, you know I love you, but not enough for both of us. I don't want to force you into something you'll regret."

"I'll probably regret it a few times. That's marriage. We're in this together, and we'll manage. We might even thrive."

"You know, you're probably right. No marriage is perfect."

"Absolutely not," she answered.

Far into the night, they talked, made plans. They would be married in February, but she would not return to Lancaster County to be with her family. She wanted a very small wedding, her family, a few close friends. They'd have to travel out here, and the wedding would be held here, in this big lovely house.

"The weather in February can be unpredictable for travel," Isaac said.

"It'll work out."

They told Titus and Sharon on Christmas Day, both their reactions something Susan would never forget. Titus was speechless, then cleared his throat, stood very straight and said, "I'll try and be a good boy for you, Susan," then looked as if he could easily burst into tears. Sharon, in typical fashion, hopped on both feet, clapped her hands, then threw herself into Susan's arms and stayed there for the longest time, while Isaac blinked back tears of happiness.

WHEN SUSAN'S FAMILY received her voicemail, her mother called back, her voice in the usual high-pitched frenzy when things spiraled out of control. Her reaction was what Susan expected, saying, "You can't, you can't do this."

"But I want to, Mam. Do you have any idea how terribly low I would have to go to attend Levi and Kate's wedding alone? Levi and Kate! Who would ever have thought? You know the old saying, 'truth is stranger than fiction'? Well, it is. No, you can travel out here, I don't care how, and if Doddy and Mommy Stoltzfus aren't fit to travel, we'll come for a visit another time. Mam, try to understand. This is Titus and Sharon, too. I feel at home here in the community. Everyone will be thrilled. I don't know what it is, Mam, but I want to be married here, in this house."

"But in winter?" her mother shrieked, close to hysteria. "What if something happens and we don't make it back to Kate's wedding?"

"Stop, Mam."

"Well, I mean it. Susan, I'm about to start crying. Liz and Rose are having a fit."

"Well, good for them. It won't hurt them to get out of their comfort zone for once in their lives."

"But they're sewing for Kate's wedding, and now they'll have to sew for yours. They won't get it all done."

"Tell them they can wear whatever they want. Nobody out here will know the difference."

SHE WAS MARRIED to Isaac on a calm winter day, the roads plowed from the previous week's snowfall, the passengers on the bus able to enjoy the two-day trip without the anxiety of inclement weather. The whole community had rallied around them, women cleaning and cooking for weeks, the love and happiness like an infusion, scents of pure joy.

And when the wedding day turned out to be perfect, Roy Edna whispered to Sam Barb that she didn't care what anyone said, God had put a special blessing on this day—it wasn't just any old wedding.

Sam Barb frowned and told her every wedding had a special blessing, that she held Isaac and Susan too high, they were only people like everyone else. Roy Edna clamped her mouth shut and thought a buzzing retort, which never materialized, knowing full well she could never get the best of her anyhow.

She thought Susan was plain down astonishing in her new style of dress. Tall and slim, her dresses fit like a dream, the full pleated skirt, the tight sleeves and neckline, her hair combed loosely up over her forehead, thick, wavy and that color between red and brown. Her bowl-shaped covering was so neat, so perfect.

Ach, she hoped Isaac would appreciate her beauty. His first wife had been so completely opposite.

They had all chipped in to help Susan find the right navy blue dress, had sewed for her, helped fit her coverings, showed her how to comb her hair, all so new and so different, but a requirement to be a member of the western church.

Isaac and Titus needed new suits and white shirts, and Sharon would wear a pale blue dress and pinafore-style apron.

So by the time the bus rolled up to the ranch, there was nothing left undone, everything fully prepared, the house emptied of furniture, benches set, food prepared.

Susan was unprepared for the emotion she felt, seeing her parents alight, looking around, bewildered, feeling like strangers. Isaac and Susan hurried across the porch and down to the bus, their faces showing their eagerness.

Strange, indeed, this unusual introduction. None of her family had ever met Isaac, and with the polite reserve of the easterners, he likely felt underappreciated, but did not show any disappointment.

Her father beamed, shook hands, dwarfed by this giant man, but approving of him. Her mother seemed to have swallowed a lemon, her face strained and set, but she managed a smile, a handshake.

Liz, Rose, their husbands, the children, dear Beth and Mark, a bored looking Elmer, and last, Kate and Levi. Grandparents, a few uncles and aunts. Another vehicle arrived with close friends and cousins.

Hugs, so much exclaiming and admiring, a dizzying whirl of family, excitement running high.

And in the middle, Isaac, tall, wide, relaxed, in his element, exuding confidence, talking, laughing, his wide smile flashing easily.

Susan found herself watching Liz and Rose, wondering what they thought, especially Rose. Sure enough, she was downright coquettish, slapping Isaac's arm, laughing too loud, giving him a second lingering look.

They fell on Susan, squealed, hugged, plucked at her dress, touched her covering, fussed and laughed and told her she was crazy.

Susan leaned back, arched one eyebrow, asked them to explain.

"This!" Rose waved a hand. "This place is amazing!"

Susan smiled, "I know."

"You are marrying him so you can live in this house, I guarantee it," Rose hissed.

"I'd take him with the house," Liz laughed. "He's not bad."

Kate came over, hesitant, her eyes begging forgiveness, so small and scared, followed by Levi, his eyes darting, like a firefly, never focusing on one thing. In a jolt, Susan realized Kate had done it again, a wave of pity followed by exasperation.

"Hello, Kate."

"H . . . hi, Susan."

A handshake was enough. Levi, then, sidling up to Kate, an arm around her waist.

Those light eyes, that perfect mouth, the straight nose with only the merest bump, the flawless complexion, wavy brown hair cut and combed to perfection. Oh, Levi. His eyes slid away from her accusing ones. He mumbled some form of greeting and stepped away, so ill at ease he turned his back completely.

"Good to see you, Kate," Susan said, smiling genuinely, holding nothing against her, knowing by some womanly intuition that Kate had truly done it again, fallen head over heels, tumbled down the slippery slope of star-dusted romance, blinded by his good looks and stealthy way of winning her hand by his words. He had cheated on Susan, was redeeming his sense of guilt and shame by marrying the poor widow, Kate. He would be highly esteemed by those around him, reaping honor and admiration, would lead songs in church, a benevolent father to his stepchildren, enjoying the spotlight, until he became bored, his new found status as a hero sliding into everyday life, and he'd be tempted again.

Or would he?

God only knew. Her thoughts might be only a form of revenge. But when Kate left her side and went to Levi, a hand on his back, her face lifted to his, her large brown eyes beseeching, Susan had to look away.

Kate, Kate. So dear and sweet. She hoped with all her heart it would be different this time.

SHE WAS PROUD to sit beside Isaac, proud of the house, the wondrous patio, the large horse barn, the place she had come to love. She knew the family was duly impressed and felt redeemed from the pain and humiliation of her past. The minister from Illinois, his family, all of it so new and complex, yet she felt no confusion, only a rare sense of belonging.

And when they stood in front of the bishop from Indiana, her hand clasped firmly in his oversized, calloused one, she felt safe and secure.

The words of the bishop were meaningful, and when she answered with a quiet *ya* (yes) after each question, she felt no regret, only a sense of quiet assurance. When the congregation stooped to pray with the bishop, she was deeply grateful for her faith, the only thing she could always depend on when the going got rough.

As the last hymn of the wedding service was sung, Isaac found Susan's eyes, his own filled with tears of love and happiness, and she was deeply touched, and conveyed her own fledgling love back to him with a discreet smile.

They ate a wonderful wedding meal, with Titus and Sharon by their sides, served by the young girls of the community. There was no traditional Lancaster roast and creamed celery, but instead the western-style wedding dinner of fried chicken and all the trimmings, complete with a resplendent wedding cake and an abundance of rich desserts.

There was the opening of gifts, the house rocking with the volume of wedding songs as everyone pitched in, praising God for the loving union of these two people. Susan sat with her mother and sisters afterward, shared her thoughts and feelings, said they'd be there for Kate's wedding, and Kate appeared elated.

And when the last buggy wended its way home, Isaac took Susan into his big arms and told her he was the happiest man alive. Titus took this all in, rolled his eyes as he unwrapped another Reese's peanut butter cup, and thought this was what he had to put up with now. Sharon clasped her hands in her lap and laughed out loud.

"My mom!" she said. "I have a mom!"

They all turned to look at her, so small and proud, announcing this fact with joy. Titus grinned up at his parents, nodded his head up and down.

"Yep," he said proudly.

Isaac's mouth trembled as his arm around her waist kept her close to his side.

"Aren't we the luckiest people in Wyoming?" he asked.

Sharon nodded happily, and Titus reached for more candy, grinning.

"I'd say we're pretty lucky."

CHAPTER 13

As if on cue, the weather turned nasty, low black clouds showing up on the horizon the next forenoon, the wind whipping bare aspen branches, sending loose snow whirling off into the distance, fir trees bent to the south by the force of the powerful, frigid gale. Loose garage doors slammed against the barn, anything unanchored rolled off the porch and down the stone walkway to become embedded in a snowbank.

Isaac looked out the window and frowned at the darkening sky, the force of the wind. Susan put away the dust rag and came to stand beside him, a hand on his back. She felt an ownership, a newfound sense of belonging, as if she had been teetering along on loose stepping stones, and suddenly, there was a cement bridge, well-engineered, a place easily navigated, an easy access to a new love.

God was so good to her, had been faithful to allow her an introduction to womanhood with a kind and wonderful man.

He looked down at her, his eyes liquid with love. He put his arm around her, drew her close and sighed.

"I'm so happy," he said gruffly, the tears on the surface.

She said nothing, the peace and quiet enough for her now.

"You're everyone a man could ever want, Susan. I love you."

"I love you, too, Isaac. I really do. It's mysterious, this thing called love. I don't know if anyone will ever understand it fully, but for me, now, being your wife, I know it is enough."

"I'm . . . I'm not a disappointment to you?"

"Not yet," she teased.

When the clouds turned threatening, Isaac worried about the children coming home from school, saying the bus driver, a man in his seventies, lived here all his life, didn't take these winter storms seriously.

"I'll go with you," she said quickly.

"Alright. I'll get the horse ready. You bundle up real good."

She put on her heaviest sweatshirt, a coat on top, a woolen scarf and two pairs of stockings, insulated boots. The air was cold and getting colder; they had no time to waste. The driving horse, Roger, was eager to go, so gravel and frozen snow spit out from under the wheels as they rattled along at a fast trot. They passed a few ranch houses, dilapidated trailers, men in fluorescent hunting caps nailing plywood over loose windows, dogs braying like coonhounds at the ends of long driveways. A few pickup trucks careened by, glittering eyes beneath heavy brows and lowered Stetsons, gloved hands held up in greeting.

Loose branches whirled through the air, pine cones skittered across the road. The horse's mane was whipped to a frenzy as the force of the wind slammed into them. Isaac watched the clouds ahead of them, said he didn't like this one bit.

"I hope your folks drove out of this okay," he commented.

She nodded. That had been the only hard part of her wedding day, the family returning immediately after the wedding, saying they couldn't take more time off with Kate's day coming up. They'd be back, they said.

Rose said her husband didn't know it yet, but he was coming out here with her for two weeks. Maybe more.

"Seriously, Sue. I had no idea anyone in Wyoming had a home like this. It's three times as nice as you ever let on. And Isaac is actually good looking, in a patched-up, rugged sort of way. He's attractive, like, *manly* attractive."

Susan laughed, told her she'd noticed Rose thought so, trying to get his attention whenever possible. A good feeling, though, Susan aware of her sisters' approval. And yes, Isaac was attractive in a very different way than Levi was. He was a man, had worked hard in all kinds of weather, been assaulted by a falling tree, lost his first wife to cancer, been scarred and weathered by life and its circumstances.

As they approached the school, more buggies were waiting for school to be dismissed, the parents uncomfortable with the force of the wind.

"Hey there! The newlyweds!" Abe Mast called out.

"Hi, Abe! Yep, it's us."

"Better get our kids home. Looks like a humdinger."

"Sure does!"

And Susan grinned widely, waved, called out to well-wishers, her chest puffed out with a true sense of belonging. She was Isaac's wife, a mother to Titus and Sharon, proud to welcome them into the buggy as they came running through the breathtaking force of the wind.

After a few miles, Roger was tiring, taking it slower as the first bits of ice pinged against the windshield. Susan glanced at Isaac, whose face registered nothing.

"Daddy, is Roger tired?" Sharon asked.

"We're headed into the wind, so the buggy is harder to pull, sweetie."

"It's snowing hard," Titus said suddenly.

And it was. It was unbelievable how the snow came down in thick squalls, driven by the relentless gale. Visibility was cut in half, Isaac's mouth set as he opened the window, shook out the reins, and called to the horse.

"Better get home," he muttered.

Roger sensed the urgency, leaned into the collar, and did his best.

Susan realized he was an extraordinary horse, the kind who had reserves of strength when the going got rough. By the time they reached the ranch, the whole landscape was a sea of whirling whiteness, a roaring wind bending bare branches, slapping loose doors, shivering and moaning around eaves and cracks in the logs.

Susan grasped Sharon's mittened hand as they headed to the house, faces lowered to the biting wind. She fumbled her way to the front door and gratefully inside to a blessed quiet warmth.

The venison roast was delicious, the leftover mashed potatoes made into potato cakes with onion, leftover peas, and brown gravy, wedding cake and tapioca pudding. Snow scraped against the window panes, but inside, fire leaped in the great stone fireplace, the couch was warm and cozy, nothing could frighten or worry any of them.

Titus brought out the Sorry game, and Susan reluctantly pried herself off the couch, putting aside the weight of a warm throw. Isaac smiled at her, whispered she didn't have to, but she said she wanted to, of course.

She was a mother now, albeit a stepmother, and she had a role to play. She would do it with all her heart, achieve the admiration and respect that too often fell by the wayside, innocent young women unaware of all that would be required of them. Susan felt it would be different for her, having been the children's teacher, knowing beforehand that troubled Titus would need special care. He'd been at his best behavior over the wedding, so perhaps her load would be lighter than she'd planned on.

The game of Sorry did not turn out well, however, with Titus becoming more and more agitated as he drew unlucky cards, was bumped off the board and sent home repeatedly. Susan sensed the brewing anger, but Isaac seemed oblivious, laughing out loud when he drew on eight and couldn't move into the home line.

"That's not funny!" he shouted.

"Here. Simmer down, Titus," he said.

"You just want me to lose, so you look smart in front of Susan," he yelled, his agitation increasing.

"Titus."

A warning this time.

Susan breathed easier when Titus looked at his father with a serious expression, quieted down, and lost the game to Susan. She felt bad for him, wished there was some way she could have let him win, since he always had a hard time losing.

"You want to play again?" she asked hopefully.

"No."

And he stomped off into the living room, rolled himself into the throw Susan had been using, turned his face to the back of the couch, and that was it.

Isaac looked at Susan, his eyes sympathetic.

"Sorry," he said softly.

She shook her head, mouthed, "It's okay."

But the perfection of the evening had been ruined, reality raising its dark head, a foreboding of things to come.

That night when Susan awoke to the sound of the wind and the scouring snow, her husband breathing steadily beside her, she felt the wonder of total security, this solid log house, the good heat from the massive cast iron stove in the basement, everything she could possibly wish for where material things were concerned. Isaac was a hard worker, a good provider, the future before her, a smooth path free of anxiety about Levi, about running around with the youth, the years of *rumschpringa* behind her now, and good riddance.

Would the happiness and gratefulness be a lasting thing? She wondered, before drifting off into a dreamless sleep.

THEY BOARDED THE Amtrak two days before Kate's wedding on March 29. The children were so excited they could barely keep track of them, running from window to window, Titus gesticulating, half yelling to Sharon, his blond hair literally standing on end with electricity when he removed his stocking cap, only to smash it back down on his head with excitement when he spotted a herd of mule deer.

They were going east, two thousand miles away, and he was wound up like a musical toy. Sharon caught his enthusiasm, bouncing up and down in her seat like a puppet.

Isaac was in good humor, settling back in the comfortable seat, relaxed, at ease, ready to enjoy a mini vacation with his family.

He was so in love with his new wife, he sometimes felt as if he was walking on air. She'd had a hard time getting her hair done the way she liked that morning, prodding and combing, spraying and clipping berets, then taking it all down and starting over. She had the most beautiful hair he'd ever seen, and found it hard to keep his hands off it, watching her.

She snorted, put down the comb, and said she could do this much better if he'd get out of the bathroom. He gave in helplessly, caught the luxuriant hair in both hands and buried his face in it, then put his arms around her and distracted her completely.

He realized God had spoiled him, like an overindulged child, given him this beautiful woman to be his wife, in spite of not even coming close to deserving her. He'd fallen away from his faith, pitied himself, blamed God, and here he was, blessed beyond reason, his faith blooming to life again. His head swam with the wonder of her. He looked over to find her frustrated, repeatedly putting her head back against the seat, then leaning forward, her eyebrows drawn.

She had perfect eyebrows.

"How do you relax with these bowl-shaped coverings?" she asked.

"I have no idea. I never wore one."

"That supposed to be funny?"

"I think it is."

His eyes narrowed, watching Titus.

"Hey, Titus. Titus! Sit down, buddy."

Pairs of eyes from the passengers followed as Isaac made his way toward the children, who obviously hadn't heard.

When he reached them, he spoke quietly, then brought them both back to be seated across the aisle, Titus's eyes sparking with anger.

The train ride was long, the nights uncomfortable, but the children seemed to think the whole trip was a great adventure, filled with all kinds of strange sights and sounds.

Titus didn't miss a single thing, found a boy about his age who was going to Johns Hopkins University to be treated for a rare disease of the liver, which was explained to him in detail. He talked to an elderly gentleman about raising corn in Iowa, cutting wheat with the great combines, watched a middle-aged lady of considerable girth applying her makeup, and wondered out loud to Sharon why you'd bother with all that gunk on your face if you were old and fat.

Susan held a warning finger to her lips, drew down her eyebrows, then glanced at Isaac for help and found him sleeping soundly. She crooked a finger in Titus's direction and mouthed, "Shh. Come here."

"Titus, please be quieter. The lady might hear you."

That worked for a while, but only until he forgot himself, picked a fight with Sharon, and everything started all over again.

She was glad to see the city of Lancaster, glad to finally embark on home territory, the air sharp with the tang of approaching spring.

There was no one to meet them, but she knew her way around quite easily.

A taxi driver, threading their way in and out of solid lines of traffic on the interstate, bare brown fields being torn up by a steel knife-edged plow, six brown horses plodding in unison, a ribbon of gleaming brown soil behind, the air thick with wheeling gulls following the plow for the fat, protein packed earthworms the plow left behind.

There were school children on colorful scooters, wire baskets containing bright lunch boxes, horses and carriages stopping obediently at traffic lights, women wearing black shawls and bonnets standing beside fancy teenage girls dressed in red and orange, gray hoodies with the PINK insignia across the back. Black-hatted old men with flowing white beards pedaling scooters, driving spring wagons, hats pulled low against March winds.

And they were home, though home was different now that it was emptied of her and Mark. The upstairs seemed hollow. Only Elmer's room remained lived in, the remainder of the rooms for guests. *Gute schtuppa* (good rooms).

Mam was in a tizzy, clean tired out, she said. Much easier to make a wedding yourself than letting any of the girls get involved, especially Liz. She was so terribly determined to have her own way. This was Kate's second wedding, so why would Liz have all these flowers and candles in the gift area? And those fancy signs?

"Seriously, Susan." She said she was plumb embarrassed but Liz wouldn't listen to reason, so if the preachers came to see them then she was the one who would have to answer to them, and not her. She'd warned her.

Susan smiled, loved to hear her mother's fuss, placed a hand on her shoulder and said everything would be fine. Times changed, and it had been a long time since Rose had been married.

Dat and Isaac hit it off immediately, Isaac in full logging mode, regaling him with stories of logger's adventures, the history of Wyoming, the price of lumber here and overseas, both men avid conversationalists, drinking coffee and staying up well past midnight.

Susan received more than her share of attention at the wedding, friends and acquaintances fussing over her western dress, her husband, asking if she could make herself feel at home out there, as if "out there" referred to Mars.

She greeted Kate and Levi with an air of reserve, knew she looked good and hoped he'd notice. When they shook hands, his felt small and a bit too smooth. In her mind she compared them to Isaac's hands and was glad to know she loved Isaac's better. Levi grinned up at her from his place beside Kate, seated on a bench in the proper manner, greeting guests.

She glared down at him, gave him the benefit of her disdain, and walked away with her head held high. She felt powerful and proud to be the wife of Isaac Miller.

Kate was lovely in her wine-colored dress with the neat black cape and apron, the status of a married woman, although her face was beginning to show the ravages of time. Small lines appeared around her mouth, her eyes sliding downward, showing the shape of sadness, of terrible disappointment and grief. Susan loved her so much, although a part of her still felt like shaking some sense into her.

How could she trust Levi? And she realized her own sense of throwing caution to the wind, chasing after him like a nectar-soaked butterfly, drunk on infatuation, weaving crazily along as blind as a bat.

Looking at Kate, she knew she would talk to Levi, bold as it was. He was going to hear a few words from her.

The service was conducted in the traditional manner, a beautiful service, complete with an old bishop, an uncle of Levi's, giving them together in matrimony. Kate seemed so small, so shy, her whispered "ya" barely audible, Levi's ringing answer firm, assured, and masculine.

Little Marie was not present, being kept by a neighbor girl, and Susan wondered if this was Kate's doing or Levi's. Susan did her duty, waiting tables with Isaac, helping relatives set the dishes on new table-cloths, serve food, wash dishes, and set the table the second time. Isaac pitched in, helping to serve coffee, always smiling, stopping to talk to perfect strangers.

To see Levi and Kate seated side by side, enjoying their wedding dinner, the pure adoration in her eyes for him, was harder for Susan than she'd imagined. She knew Levi too well, recognized the body language, the boredom, the lazy way his eyelids drooped, the wandering eyes beneath, noticing the pretty girls, eyeing buxom young women.

She cornered him when the wedding was over, out in the yard, where the wash house was built out from the main house, creating a secluded area.

"Levi. Stop," she called.

"What? Oh, it's you, Susan," he said, smooth as silk.

"It's me. Yes. I just want to remind you of the fact you are a married man now, tied to your wife with bonds of honor from God. You are the husband of my sister Kate, who has seen far more than her share of grief and pain, so I don't want to hear that you have ever mistreated her in any way."

He drew in a sharp breath.

"Now what makes you say that? My goodness. It is the farthest thing from my mind."

"I bet. Men take advantage of her. She's too selfless, too much a servant. How long before you'll want another nurse? Or decide you need another adventure in the wilds of the Yukon?"

"Susan!" he gasped. "The very idea!"

"Oh, stop acting like some sissified gentleman from the 1800s. You know exactly what I mean. And I want you to know you're no more to me than a . . . a skunk."

"Susan, you alarm me."

"Do I? Good. It's about time you woke up and saw yourself. I mean what I said. If you mistreat Kate or those children in any way, you'll have me to deal with. Kate and I are very close, so think about it."

"Well, I consider myself blessed to have picked Kate over you," he hissed.

"Oh, you're not rid of me, Levi. I'll be watching."

And with that, she turned and disappeared, melting away into the dark night, joining the throng of wedding guests as they prepared to take their leave. Her heart pounded in her chest, but it was a good, solid sound, the sound of courageously standing up for herself, facing him, giving him a dire warning about the way he treated Kate. After vacations and new business ventures lost their appeal, he'd be looking for other sources of amusement.

She found Isaac, seated in the middle of the wedding area, a group of men huddled around him, drinking coffee and listening to his hilarious accounts of logging in the West. Isaac was waving his arms, shouting almost, laughing uproariously, his appreciative audience captivated. She stopped, went to help Rose and Liz clean the worst of the mess in the cooking area, her face pale, nostrils distended.

Rose took a good long look and asked what got her goat now, so Susan told her.

"You didn't."

"I did."

Liz stopped, set down a stack of plates, eyed Susan with keen observation.

"Susan, you're just miffed about Kate."

"No. Absolutely not. You weren't for this, either, and you know it. What makes you think he'll change?"

"Oh well, we have to forgive. He's so sorry. You can't hold his past against him if he's sorry. That's wrong. Even the Lord's prayer teaches us that, Susan."

"I do forgive him. Have forgiven him. But that doesn't mean I trust him or like him."

"Oh, just get over yourself. Here, sit down. Let's finish off this lemon pie," Rose said, grabbing a fork and digging in.

"Ew, that's gross," Liz said. "I'd rather finish the blueberry doughnut holes."

"Coffee, coffee," Susan sang out.

"Where's Isaac?" Rose asked.

"Out there. A whole bunch of guys listening to him. He loves telling logging stories."

"Are you happy you married him, then?"

"Yes. I'm very happy."

"The West? You'll be okay? Not too much homesickness?"

"Probably I will be homesick sometimes, yes. But I think with all the circumstances in my life, God was clearly getting me ready to be a wife to Isaac and a mother to his children."

"That little Sharon is such a doll," Rose said, scraping out the bottom of an aluminum pie plate.

"You'll soon be in the family way," Liz quipped, popping a doughnut hole in her mouth.

Susan slapped her arm, the conversation turned to subjects only sisters share, and when Isaac came to find her, they were laughing and talking so fast he found himself thinking about how far away he would be taking her, away from this tight familial bond.

He sat down in the middle of them and told them exactly what he'd been thinking.

Rose said, "Aw, aren't you one in a million? Well, you can always live here in Lancaster. Move back."

"I could probably survive here."

"No . . . Isaac, that wouldn't be right. We belong in Wyoming. You'd be miserable and you know it."

Rose and Liz talked about the look she gave Isaac for weeks, said they guaranteed if God's will was carried out, there was a special blessing no matter what. They nodded their heads and felt quite proud of their own wisdom.

Mam cried when they left, clung to Susan, and told her to call more often. She was lonely and often bored, now that everyone was gone except Elmer. Susan felt an overwhelming love for her mother, regretted having to say goodbye so soon, but looked forward to her spring in Wyoming.

Here in Lancaster, daffodils were blooming profusely on well-manicured flower beds, forsythia like sunshine on a branch, fertilized lawns already greening in low places. Women were housecleaning, wheel lines laden with curtains and rugs and bedsheets, colorful quilts punctuating the whites, grays, and pale beiges. Calves and baby lambs were sprightly on young legs, kennels filling with litters of puppies, sold to eager city dwellers for exorbitant fees.

All this was the world Susan knew, the world of trade and business, hundreds of lucrative enterprises making up the commerce, the hub of Lancaster County. Plain folks everywhere, taking on well-established shops and markets, skills honed from one generation to the next, living shoulder to shoulder with men of the world.

This life had no hold on her, however.

Perhaps it was God's way of preparing her to live in Wyoming, to actually enjoy the solitude and immensity of the rural West. And she took her seat in the train and turned her face to the west, ready for whatever it was that God expected of her.

She told Isaac what she'd told Levi, which made him open his eyes wide and say he'd really better hope he stayed on her good side. She laughed, cuddled Sharon on her lap, smiled at Titus across the aisle, and told him so far, so good.

But how were they to know the days that would arrive in quick succession, bringing challenges and droughts of the spirit, frustrations and loss of control? For we set our face to the future without any idea of the twists and turns to come along the road of life.

CHAPTER 14

WHEN TITUS WAS THIRTEEN YEARS OLD, AFTER BABY KAYLA WAS born, Isaac caught him in the haymow, smoking cigarettes, one right after another, according to the litter of brown butts surrounding him. It was in spring, when the haymaking crew had just put a huge mound of well-stacked bales on the north side.

They came to the house, where Susan was asleep on the recliner, Kayla in her white crib in the new white nursery, Sharon patiently waiting till they both woke up.

"Mom asleep?" Isaac whispered.

"No. I'm awake now."

Susan pulled the lever on the recliner, her feet hitting the floor. For a moment, she felt lightheaded, disoriented, before regaining her bearings.

She saw Isaac, tight-lipped and stern, Titus sullen, flopping into the glider rocker, his face pale.

Her eyes went to Isaac's, questioning.

"Tell Mom what you were doing," Isaac prodded.

"Smoking."

Susan felt the sickening jolt, the sudden proof that Titus was rebelling, a distant thought she'd pushed away for too long. He had continued to get in trouble at school, was often getting into arguments with the teacher or with Isaac at home. Suddenly, the hope she had clung to that he might change was dashed to the ground by his sneering announcement.

She looked at Titus, but his eyes dropped away.

"Do you want to talk about it?" she asked, kindly.

"Course not."

"Titus, you need to realize how hard that is on your health. Your lungs will be damaged. It's dangerous. A bad, bad habit."

"Ron does it. He's old. Works hard."

"Who's Ron?"

Isaac said he was the owner of the Bar T, a few miles north.

"Oh, that Ron. You helped him unload hay," Susan said.

They talked of taking away privileges, gave him a clear picture of what happens when a person begins the journey to becoming addicted to nicotine, and in the end, grounded him for a week, taking away his privilege of hunting with Wolf or riding horses.

He was a great rider, fearless in his attempts to tame even the most determined horse, and he had a keen interest in the stables. He still went exploring with Wolf, his steps taking him into the back country where the land gave way to rocks and cliffs, scrubby forest, and acres of wild and untamed territory. But he was older now, and Susan didn't worry so much about his getting lost or hurt.

Susan was regaining her strength after the birth of an adorable baby girl they both loved at first sight, a wonderful, unforgettable experience, their very own newborn baby. Susan was introduced to mothering a newborn, the wailing at night, diapers, breastfeeding, weak and tired and in pain, but could fully understand why families wanted children of their own.

And she certainly wanted more.

But here she was, confronted again with another of Titus's escapades, this time a serious disobedience, rife with devastating consequences.

The first cigarette at thirteen years old seemed a harbinger of much more to come, the dark cloud of portent a very real emotion, now more than ever.

What did Titus need? This one who had been in trouble countless times, a hyperactive, outspoken, adventurous child who was definitely tainted by the loss of his mother, the years his father had often been absent, left to his own devices. She thought of his wandering, the time he'd been lost for three days, the event turning her life in the direction of Isaac and all that had occurred between them.

She was steadily becoming a fixture in the community, attended social gatherings, quiltings, school programs, parent and teacher meetings, church, and often having coffee with Roy Edna, her substitute mother. Isaac's days were spent logging, from five in the morning till six or seven in the evening, leaving Susan to find something to do till the children came home from school.

But now there was Kayla, the impossibly sweet daughter of her own, with a mop of brown hair, wide eyes, and a perfect elfin face.

She spent so much time bathing her, choosing cute outfits, combing her hair into a perfect wave in the center, then laughing aloud to herself how absurdly cute she really was. She could hardly wait for the arrival of relatives sometime in July.

For now, though, there was Titus to think about, to pray for, which Susan did as she flung the burp cloth over her shoulder and gently patted the small, sleepy infant. Titus was rebellious all week, never admitting he'd done anything wrong or showing remorse, merely sitting around stone-faced, bristling with anger. Susan thought Isaac should try a bit harder to coax him out of his foul mood, a self-inflicted trench where every sound above him was an imagined gunshot.

Weary to the bone from lack of sleep, her patience thin, she clung to the back of a kitchen chair for support, asked Isaac if he couldn't take him along on his day's logging, anything to occupy his mind and energy.

"I tried that before. He hates anything having to do with my business."

"Have you tried recently?"

"No."

Isaac was spreading a generous amount of peanut butter on a graham cracker, ready to put another cracker on top before dunking it in milk. His bedtime snacks were legend, entire sleeves of Ritz crackers with almost a pound of cheese, hot pepper relish, and hot mint tea, or slices of deer bologna rolled around a dill pickle and more cheese. He inhaled chocolate chip cookies, ate six at one sitting, and if Roy Edna brought one of her famous berry pies, he easily ate more than half. Titus would sit and watch his father, with admiration when he was little, but now, as he showed signs of adolescence, Susan caught the insolence in his eyes, the turning away.

Titus was tall enough for a thirteen-year-old, but thin, his skinny arms and legs like matchsticks. He ate when he was hungry but had no real interest in food. His preference was to be out and away from everyone, by himself, or with Wolf.

When Isaac didn't ask him to go logging, Susan brought up the subject herself on a day when an unexpected cloudburst had ruined her plans of working in the garden, finally feeling as if some of her old strength were returning.

He responded by shaking his head from side to side before she completed her sentence.

"No. Nope. I ain't going."

"Titus, why not? You can't sit around all summer."

"I can't stand Dad when he's with his crew. He's a giant, total control freak. He acts as if he owns the world, and I'm some . . . some slimy little worm."

Susan said nothing, merely watched his face go from a relaxed stance to one stony with remembered bitterness. She thought of her own brothers, the times they'd have run-ins with her father, but could never remember a hardened bitter expression on a face as young as this.

"I'm sure your dad doesn't look at you like that."

"I'm sure you don't know. You weren't there."

"No, I wasn't."

"Well then, there's stuff you can't fix, you know."

"What stuff?"

"Just stuff."

He got up, walked outside, and didn't return till late that evening when Isaac called him to supper. He shoveled his food in his mouth and then sat unblinking and unmoving until everyone else was finished. He didn't answer his father's questions before going upstairs to bed.

Isaac disagreed with Susan about what could be done, saying he'd get over it, he was pouting because he was mad. It was that simple. Susan lost her temper at his utter lack of understanding. What kind of father wouldn't see his child for what he was? How was she supposed to deal with this with Isaac on one side and Titus on the other? The lack of sleep coupled with his stubborn refusal riled her to the point of yelling at him, raising her voice and hurling accusations, causing him to get up, slap his hat on his head, and walk out. She was left sputtering with righteous indignation.

So that was how men dealt with matters they could not control? Blame the opposition and get off scot-free. He hadn't done anything wrong. He was the father, his son was disobedient, punishment had been carried out, and now it was up to Titus to get over it. Well, far be it from her to change his mind, being only the stepmother in this situation, but he had a big surprise coming in the morning. It was time he sat up and took notice of what she had to say.

To make her life more complicated, there had been a succession of rosy letters from Kate, saying how undeserving she was of a perfect husband in every way, how blessed, how happy. And Susan still harbored a wound, picking at it with each announcement of marital bliss.

So hers wasn't pure bliss, not with Isaac and Titus, for sure. She wasn't about to lower herself far enough to allow Kate a glimpse of life here in Wyoming, so she painted a colorful description of the newborn Kayla, and the well-behaved Sharon. She said that Titus had gone to work with his father, which wasn't a lie—he had gone a few times.

She remained frosty all the next morning, Isaac watching her as she packed his lunch and made his egg and cheese sandwich, her back turned.

"Kayla sleep well?"

No answer.

"Susan, I'm talking to you. Why are you angry?"

Still no answer.

He sighed, took his lunchbox and Thermos jug, said "Bye" without attempting the usual goodbye kiss, and thought now there were two, Titus and his wife. Hoo boy. But being Isaac, he swung his lunch and Thermos in the back of the truck, heaved himself into the seat, and began a lively conversation, putting his wife and Titus on the back burner till he returned, when hopefully they'd both be in a better state of mind.

So THIS WAS marriage, Susan thought, as she took up her crying infant. Unwashed dishes in the sink and on the countertop, bread rising ready to be kneaded, and what was she to do with this poor Kayla? She'd been crying most of the morning, with Susan dashing from packing lunches to combing Sharon's hair. She yelled at Titus, regretted it, and felt like the worst mother ever. She wasn't cut out for this, had no experience dealing with a thirteen-year-old, especially a thirteen-year-old with a chip on his shoulder.

Why did this poor baby keep crying?

She rocked, she tried feeding, burping, walking the floor, and finally laid her in her crib to allow a space of time to knead the bread dough and put it in pans to rise again. She wept a bit, wiped the back of her hand across her cheeks, and felt like a child.

As Kayla's wails turned into shrieks of hysteria, she dropped the last mound of bread dough into the greased pan and ran for the white crib in the nursery.

"Sweetie, poor, poor Kayla. Aw, come on," she crooned. She felt a failure as a mother to all her children, from the newborn to the angry son, and Sharon in between. Even their father, who went off to work all day, took for granted the fact his wife would handily take care of everything, seamlessly managing housework, laundry, the garden, school-aged children, and a wailing newborn.

Plus, her parents and sisters were a million miles away.

When had he told her he loved her? When had he noticed her enough to tell her she was beautiful? Was she still beautiful to him? She was puffy-eyed, scraggly-haired, still had an extra twenty pounds from being pregnant and had a ravenous appetite because of breastfeeding. How was she expected to lose any of that weight?

Self-pity washed over her like a noxious wind, and for a few hours nothing seemed right, including the fact she'd consented to marry Isaac, whose life remained basically unchanged while she struggled every day to accept the huge transition from a young, privileged girl from Pennsylvania to a mother of three in this empty, dusty West.

Sometimes she thoroughly disliked this country.

There was never enough water. They had to drag the hoses around, setting up sprinklers, lugging watering cans. And the wind never stopped blowing, drying up in a few hours what she had worked to accomplish. Isaac told her it was all part of life here in Wyoming, she might as well get used to it.

Susan sighed, feeling lonely, isolated, fat, and tired. She sat by the front windows, the views she had so often enjoyed now turned into a gray landscape complete with dirty windows, windows that spoke of her inability to manage everything properly.

She looked through half open eyes, sat upright at the sight of a horse drawn surrey moving down the sloped, curved driveway, and on up to the house. If she wasn't mistaken, it was Roy Edna.

Her heart swelled at the sight.

Just what she needed, a good visit with the closest person to her out here, the nearest thing to her own mother. She would know what to do about Kayla, could listen about Titus.

The two women greeted each other warmly, a genuine affection creating a bond. The coffee pot was set on the stove and Edna produced an insulated bag containing the latest recipe she'd clipped from her favorite cooking magazine and a steaming hot bacon, cheese, and broccoli quiche. It smelled delicious and Edna was not humble at all, when all was said and done, nodding her head, eyes shining at Susan's quick words of praise.

Kayla had a stomachache, Edna said. You could tell by the way she drew up her knees and scrunched her little fists. She was so kind and understanding, Susan felt the lump in her throat long before she was ready to admit she wanted to release a bucket of frustration, homesickness, despair, and most of all, disappointment in marriage, love, romance, the whole nine yards, in the form of big tears. When Edna saw Susan's chin begin to wobble, she gave her a piercing look, told her if she had the blues, she might as well let them out.

And Susan's face crumpled. She wept a bit, quietly, before releasing a stream of real, honest tears.

"I'm just not happy, Edna. And I was so sure my marriage would be so much different than my sister's. I thought Kate was stupid marrying Dan, and here she is, married to the one I really wanted, and he's a perfect husband."

She lifted steaming sheep's eyes at Edna, a Kleenex pressed to her swollen, purple nose.

Edna clucked, rolled her eyes, and asked if she was sure about that.

"Of course. She writes to me every week."

"Well, good for her. I'm assuming Isaac doesn't fall under the Prince Charming category right now."

Susan shook her head, a bit of disbelief on her face.

"No, not really. I feel so guilty, so worthless."

"Which is perfectly normal. You just had a baby, which is one of the most strenuous jobs you will ever have. You're not going to be okay in a day, a week, a month. It takes a while to get into a schedule that works for everyone. And if I'm not mistaken, Isaac is gone too much of the time."

Susan nodded.

"And there's this thing with Titus. The boy still wanders these fields and wild places like some tramp, works for a rancher and has now, at the grand age of thirteen, taken up smoking. What does Isaac do, but takes away privileges, grounds him, leaving him mad as a hornet and does absolutely nothing to ease his anger. Just shrugs his shoulders and says he'll get over it. I could pound him."

Edna laughed.

"Well, I must say, it sounds very much like marriage. Sounds exactly like Roy and me. It's real life, and as long as we're here on earth, the fairy tales we imagine aren't going to come true. We are human beings, two different people who try to blend opinions and lifestyles. Especially you and Isaac. Our culture is different. You're from Lancaster, you're not like us."

"No, we're not."

"But you can learn. It's not as if you have a choice."

No response from Susan.

"That's the thing. We're in this for life. Our faith doesn't allow divorce. We can never walk away with a free conscience."

"We can if it's bad enough," Susan corrected her.

"Well, yeah. But we have to stay alone from there on out."

"Don't tempt me," Susan said sourly.

Edna choked on a swallow of coffee, spluttered and gasped for breath, laughed and slapped her knee, wiped her eyes, then took a deep breath.

"I gather the honeymoon's over."

"You gathered right."

Edna laughed again, cut herself another generous slice of quiche, shook her head as she sliced neatly through the tip with the side of her fork.

"You know you have a double portion, being a stepmother."

"Tell me about it."

"Titus was thrilled to have you marry his father."

"Till he began to resent me for bossing him around."

Edna nodded. "Can you try to win him?"

For a long moment, there was silence as Susan wrestled with her answer.

"I don't know if I will ever be able to. He's so angry, rebellion literally sizzles out of him."

"It's too bad. Although I sincerely hope you realize he has been this way since his mother passed, not just since you're in the picture."

"But I make it worse."

"Stop, Susan. You need a good night's sleep, some good nutrition, and Isaac needs a talking to."

After Edna left, leaving Susan in a better frame of mind, things didn't seem quite as terrifying. Perhaps it was normal to have this in a family where the real mother was cruelly taken away, leaving hurting children, a new person to call Mom. Was it true that stepmothers were never truly accepted, never even coming close to taking the deceased mother's place?

Susan took a deep breath and imagined wings of prayer on their way to Heaven, begging for strength and wisdom to begin again, fresh and new. To rid herself of her own will, her own determination, allow Isaac to lead, to love in the way he deserved to be loved.

To try again with Titus.

Kayla slept most of the afternoon, and Susan decided to forego the longed-for afternoon nap and instead washed windows, cleaned floors, folded laundry, and made a stuffed meatloaf for supper, complete with brown gravy and mashed potatoes. She welcomed the children home from school, asked about their day, told Titus there was fresh bread and grape jelly.

Titus appeared interested, then sat at the kitchen table, one knee bent, his heel propped on the chair seat, eating one slice after another, grape jelly over his shirt front, his knee, the table.

"I hate school. That teacher is a buffalo."

"Whoa," Sharon said quietly.

"Titus, really? Surely not."

"She looks like one. That thick neck and bulging eyes."

Darlene Borntrager was heavy, an older single girl who was the long sought-after teacher everyone had been thrilled to hire.

She had her own house, her own sturdy mountain bike, a keen interest in the school and its pupils, as well as the surrounding community.

"She doesn't like me," Titus said, licking grape jelly from between his fingers.

"Maybe you just don't like her. You didn't like me, remember?"

"Well, at least you were better looking."

"You really think so?"

Embarrassed, Titus didn't answer, got to his feet, and said he was going to start chores. Susan opened her mouth, wanting to ask him to weed the string beans, then decided against it. At least she had a few words out of him, even if they were describing his teacher in a rude manner.

"Mom, you know what he did today?" Sharon asked, nervously tearing a browned crust from her slice of bread.

"I'm always afraid to know," Susan said.

"He brought two earthworms and placed them on the teacher's chair. She sat on them and couldn't tell. Titus laughed so hard on the playground I thought he would choke. A few of the upper grade boys laughed with him, but I think some of the girls didn't think it was funny."

"Does Darlene know?"

"No. They were smooshed on her skirt the rest of the day, until they dried up and fell off."

Sharon spoke in her sweet lisping voice, her large brown eyes serious, clearly appalled at her brother's behavior.

Susan smiled at Sharon, said not to worry, if there would be trouble, the school board would talk to them. Titus would simply have to learn to behave himself.

Isaac's work truck came up to the drive and stopped in a swirl of dust. He swung out, slammed the door, and bent over the side to retrieve his lunchbox. Susan stood by the front window, watching the way he walked, this big, unshaven, unkempt man, his hat smashed on his head, his denim pants black with oil and logs, his steel-toed logger's shoes a solid size thirteen. Likely, he'd spent all day hoisting that enormous chain saw, and still he came jauntily up to the porch. He remembered to go around to the flagstone patio and into the laundry room to wash up, leaving his hat and shoes.

When he came into the kitchen, swung his lunchbox on the counter with a bang, turned to her with that crinkly way his eyes flattened when he smiled, his white teeth flashing in his tanned face, she went into those strong arms and remembered the love between them, a haven of purely having been found and appreciated. When he kissed her, his breath smelled of black licorice, that disgusting candy he loved so much. There was always a bag opened in the glove compartment of the truck.

"How was your day, Susan?" he asked, his big hands on her shoulders.

She looked at him and said it was okay after Roy Edna's visit and after Kayla had stopped crying.

"Good. Roy Edna was here. You needed that."

And because he was so kind, and because he knew she'd been struggling, she went back into his arms and loved the solid feel of him the way she had that very first time.

"Thank you for knowing I was having a hard time," she said.

He smiled down at her.

"I was married before, you know. I think most women need a bit of special care after a baby is born. And I'm not always very good at that."

"That's about right, Isaac. You aren't here when I need you."

"I know, and I'm sorry."

"But every husband has a business to attend to, or a job, whatever. I will survive."

Their supper was almost perfect, with Titus snapping out of his mood, Isaac praising the meal, especially the meatloaf, and baby Kayla sitting on her little bouncy seat watching them all with her bright eyes, like a deermouse, Titus said. Isaac laughed at his description of her, Sharon giggled and squirmed happily in her seat, and Susan thought this was the reason you fell in love, this soul satisfying feeling of providing a safe haven for children, enriching the life of the man you chose to travel the path of life with.

CHAPTER 15

DARLENE BORNTRAGER WAS A VERY CAPABLE PERSON. AT THE AGE of forty-two, she was well aware of who she was and what she was about, which included a love of school teaching and making hand-thrown pottery.

Raised in Ohio, moving to Wyoming after she agreed to teach school, she set her face to the future and clomped through her days with her black Nikes and woolen gray socks below the sea of pleated fabric covering her more than two-hundred-pound frame. She put her whole heart into the betterment of this northeastern Wyoming settlement.

She lived in an old abandoned house that had barely been salvageable, but Darlene waded through hip-high brome grass, stepped up on the porch, and watched calmly as thin, scruffy rats squealed their sniveling way out from underneath. The front room was filled with spider webs, dried mouse carcasses, and skeletons of other rodents. She kicked at them and asked Vrie Yoder why all the little varmints came inside to die. She stomped on floors, put a hammer fist to walls, sniffed at moldy remains of food in the rusty tin cupboard by the pewter sink, and said she'd take it for forty thousand and no more.

She paid cash to Orvis Scuttle, a grizzled old man so thin he appeared to be little more than a flesh-covered skeleton. Orvis peered at her through rheumy eyes sunk into folds of leathery skin, graced her with yellow teeth protruding from stretched facial muscles, and said, "Much obliged, ma'am." Then he turned away and got into his '68 Dodge pickup and backed out onto the dirt road.

Darlene told the school board men that there would be a frolic for the community on Saturday. The women could bring food. It was an order, not a request, which they all obeyed.

The frolic was directed by Darlene herself. Building supply trucks rolled in on time and construction was underway by nine.

A few months later, she resided in a neat little home with gray siding, new windows, a solid steel roof complete with snow catchers, and a lovely porch. The grass was bushwhacked and mowed, the perimeter of the house dug up with shovels, and greenery planted. By the time school started, she was ready to go, happier than she'd ever been, living along out on Beebe Road, the cranky Orvis Scuttle as a drive-by neighbor who was curious but would never stop in or even give a friendly wave.

Darlene had been brought up in the heart of Holmes County, one of the largest Amish settlements in Ohio. She was the oldest of ten, her mother's health often failing her, which meant Darlene had to step in and take hold, basically raising her siblings with strong arms and a loud voice, two dependable attributes. She scared away any possible suitor, deciding she didn't need a man. Look what they put you through, bringing ten babies into the world whether you wanted them all or not.

No sir, that was not her cup of tea, going around with your dress front soaked with milk and your back hurting for the rest of your life.

She planned to keep her health intact.

She developed an avid interest in pottery after watching a potter at the Old Towne festival in Mount Hope. She acquired books on the subject and established her own side business making and selling mugs and bowls.

She loved mashed potatoes, yellow gravy, and dressing and ate fried chicken and macaroni and cheese often. She loved children and food, not necessarily in that order. She knew she was a top-notch school teacher, had no humble bone in her body, spoke in loud, affirmative tones, and could wield a hammer alongside the men.

Her first week of teaching in Wyoming was not fun, not even close to enjoyable, with that scraggly little Titus Miller acting like someone with no common sense in his head. She couldn't figure that one out, and she thought she'd seen it all. He was tall enough for an eighth grader, but skinny as a rail. She honestly couldn't see how he'd kept his feet on the ground in this stiff breeze that swooped down between the high peaks of the Bighorn Mountains.

After that first week, she decided the word "devious" fit him perfectly. He whispered behind her back, threw bits of eraser at the girls, then put on a serious face complete with limpid brown eyes swimming with innocence when he was caught. Smart enough to realize he wanted attention, negative or not, she chose to ignore him until he cut off Marlena Troyers's covering strings with his scissors and she began sniffling and then finally crying outright.

The poor thing, meek and gentle, always ashamed of herself.

Darlene's righteous anger began like a slow cauldron boiling, simmering gently, and she pinned Titus with her bold hazel eyes, but said nothing.

When he raised his eyebrows and taunted her with mockery on his thin face, she drew herself to her full height, which was a good five ten, and took a very deep breath.

"Titus Miller."

The voice was volcanic in its power. Titus blinked, sat up straight.

"What did you do to Marlena?"

"Nothing."

She marched back through the aisle, her black Nikes coming down on the wooden floor like the hooves of a moose, her heavy arms swinging, multiple pleats swaying. Her face turned to a deep, thunderous purple.

"You did something, Titus. Look at her."

Every word was dripping portent.

Marlena's head was on her desk, her arms covering her face, the pitiful sniffling amplified by the wooden desktop.

"It looks to me as if you cut off her covering strings. This is rude, disobedient, and just plain mean. Tell her you're sorry."

The classroom was completely silent. A dropped pin would have been like a gunshot. No one had ever heard Titus Miller apologize to anyone, no matter how he treated his classmates.

"I ain't doin' that."

Oh, so now he was intimidating her with his cowboy slang. She didn't hesitate, but reached out and grabbed him by the collar, hauled him up to Marlena's desk, and repeated, "Tell her."

And Titus told her he was sorry. He was hauled back to his desk, dropped into it like a sack of potatoes, and that was the end of that.

For months afterward, he plotted his revenge, carrying it out in every conceivable manner until she asked the school board to intervene. They pointed out it was nearly the end of the year and he was about to graduate, so hopefully she could stick it out just a little longer.

Titus never tried to contain his glee of being free of her, the four walls of the classroom, all his classmates, and school in general in just a few short weeks. But as luck would have it, he was never completely rid of Darlene.

The last weeks of school were filled with stupid tests, planning games for the picnic, having to write a composition on plans for the summer, which he thought was the dumbest thing. He refused to comply and had to be inside with her after lunch, when Wesley was organizing a game of baseball without him, driving him to distraction.

Darlene was eating an apple and disposed of the core neatly, bending over the side of her desk to make sure she hit the waste can.

"So tell me, Titus, what do you have against telling me what you'll be doing this summer?"

"Ain't none of your business."

"Really? That's not why you're writing it. It's to exercise your skills."

"Yeah, well, I don't have any."

She acted bored, lined up her ruler on a piece of art paper and drew a line.

"So what are you going to do?"

"Work on a ranch."

"Are you? That's interesting. I'd love to watch someone rope and brand calves. Can you do that?"

"Not yet. But I'm going to learn."

"That's good. You know, I wonder if I could get a job on a ranch."

"You?"

"Not roping and riding. Driving a tractor, making hay, fixing fences."

"They don't hire women."

"How do you know?"

By the time summer was upon them, he was working for Ron Busker on the Bar T, wearing a battered Stetson, aged cowboy boots, slouching his shoulders, swinging his hips, and keeping a pack of cigarettes in his shirt pocket. He felt tough, strong, in control of his life, for the first time ever, smoking and swaggering, riding horses with the best cow hands, driving a tractor and an old sagging pickup they used to run the fence line. It was hot, the wind as dry as desert wind; he was thirsty and hungry and in his element. The longer he stayed away from his father and Susan, the better off he'd be. He couldn't bring himself to call her "Mom," or think of them as his parents, because his real mother shouldn't have died. He'd loved Susan, wanted her as a parent, until she really was, and now that he was older, she didn't seem right. She shouldn't be there.

He looked up from pounding a nail into a fence post to find none other than Darlene Borntrager getting out of an outdated old pickup truck, flouncing toward him in the usual mess of navy blue pleats.

Who in the world was with her?

He straightened his back, pushed his Stetson up to wipe his face.

"Hey there, Titus."

Titus didn't say anything.

"Whatcha doin'?"

Oh come on. Now she was acting like a cowboy. That was disgusting.

"We need a young boy to help us out this afternoon. We got a cow stuck in the fence."

"We? Who's we?"

"Me and Orvis."

Titus wasn't convinced she wasn't out to get him, to teach him a lesson, get back at him for all the ways he'd made life hard for her, so he stood beside the post and squinted up at her. She was as wide as a barn, still resembled a buffalo in his opinion, and he didn't trust her one bit.

"Who's Orvis?"

"Orvis Scuttle. My neighbor. Guy I bought my house from."

She gave him the willies, trying to talk like a westerner. It turned him off so bad he could barely stand to look at her. Why she didn't go back to Ohio and fry chicken he didn't know.

"I'm busy."

"Come on, Titus. She's seriously stuck. She'll die in this heat. We need someone to rope her from a horse. She's vicious."

He blinked, gave her what he hoped was a cool stare that would turn her away, but instead she crooked a finger and said, "Come on."

He followed the vast acreage of navy blue pleats out of the fenced-in pasture and into the truck held together by a few rusty welds and good luck.

"This is Orvis. Orvis, Titus."

He heard a grunt from somewhere underneath the vicinity of the hat brim. Titus looked down at the bony claw grasping the clutch and slid an inch or two closer to the soft mound that was Darlene.

Rattling away, Titus felt a decided sense of unease, the old rancher beside him like a stick man. The only sign of life was the engorged purple veins running across the backs of his hands, like mountains or rivers on a map.

Darlene hooked an arm out of the truck window, leaned back, and squinted into the midday sun, for all the world like one of the many seasoned old ranchers in trucks all over the countryside.

They rode across a few gravel roads, stopped at a macadam road and made a left, before moving in behind a cattle trailer, the gate held shut by a stout rope, cattle bawling and milling thirstily.

"Russ Wedge," Orvis said, in a voice like cracking glass.

"Who's he?" Darlene asked.

A bony thumb was jerked over his shoulder.

"South a here."

Darlene glanced at Titus, saw the bulge in his shirt pocket, drew her eyebrows down and glared out the window. She'd figured it out. This child would push all the boundaries, try everything just to see if he could get away with it, thinking only of himself and never worrying about his parents.

That poor Susan was already showing the stress of being a step-mother. Not that she hadn't felt the ravages of mothering herself, raising those youngsters at home, barely thinking of them as her brothers and sisters.

This one, though, was going to plow his own way through, no doubt about it, and she wasn't sure that Isaac was up to the task. For one thing, he was gone all day. For another, he allowed him to do anything he wanted. Folks still talked about him wandering off and getting hurt like that with his dog, surely teaching his father a lesson. But no, he was still doing the same thing. Someone had seen him clear down by Clean Springs.

In due time, they rolled to a near stop, turned into a dirt lane, passed under gray poles with one notched across the top, a wooden sign hanging by one side, the rusted chain on the other side long gone.

Titus could not decipher the words on the weathered sign, so he asked Orvis, his curiosity greater than his fear.

"Ranch named the C.W. Stands for Crazy Woman."

He looked up at Darlene, who raised her eyebrows and held a finger to her lips. Titus looked away, wished he hadn't asked.

They rolled to a stop in front of a barn with unpainted boards, a corral in dire need of repair, and fifty-gallon oil drums, tires, remains of a few trucks, and wagons with missing wheels all resting in a bed of weeds.

But Titus could tell the longhorn cattle roaming the dry pasture-land were sleek and fat, well cared for. They found the trapped cow, her hind leg caught in a twisted barb wire, her eyes wild with pain, blood flowing freely from a hind leg. The sun was beating down hard. Darlene mopped the beads of sweat from her forehead.

"Kin you get a rope on 'er?" Orvis asked.

Titus eyed the belligerent creature, thought those horns could easily pass the whole way through him, but swallowed and nodded his head. Here was his chance to show Darlene what he was made of.

The horse was fat and lazy, the tack cracked and dusty, but the lariat was in passable shape. A few swings and he hooked a horn, drew it tight, and sat, one hand resting on his thigh, elbow out, the way he'd seen men at the rodeo. He had never imagined his time to shine would be this soon, and especially in front of Darlene.

"Keep the rope tight, boy," squawked Orvis.

He snuck in with the wire cutters while the cow was preoccupied with loosening the rope from her oversized horns. It was smart, quick, and efficient, but when the cow felt her foot being freed, she lunged at Titus on his horse with a mad bawl, the rope slipping off the smooth horn like warm butter. The horse was used to herding the longhorns, so he cut to the left when the cow came to the right, sending Titus flying off into the dusty, sparsely grassed cow pasture, landing on one shoulder. He was up in an instant, wild eyed, watching over his shoulder as the cow stopped, turned, shook her head, and ran off to join the rest of the herd, leaving Titus gingerly rubbing his shoulder. Orvis lifted his head to the sky, hooting and howling at the sight of Titus lying in the dirt. Darlene's face was puffed up with the effort to keep from laughing, but she finally gave in, bending over and slapping her knee with the pure hilarity of the moment.

Titus, rigid with anger, stalked toward the truck and got in, glowered through the dirty windshield until the others joined him. The horse was grazing peacefully with the cows, and Orvis didn't seem to be bothered by this at all.

"You okay, Titus?" Darlene asked kindly, still smiling.

"Shut up."

And Darlene did, realizing they'd hurt his pride. She couldn't blame Orvis. This was the way of ranchers, young boys accustomed to rough and tumble lives.

Orvis spoke up as they got in the truck and pulled away. "Now boy, you don' need to get your britches on wrong 'bout thet. I took many a tumble afore I learnt. You done good. Thanks fer yer help."

He slid a glance sideways, but Titus stared straight ahead. The truck rattled on, Darlene's arm out the side, but her mind was churning. What could she do for this boy? This was his first summer out of eighth grade, out of school forever, and she could sense he was headed for trouble.

The world around him was large, a vast rural area made up of generational ranches, mostly seasoned old men and their tough women, offspring who worked the cattle, hauled livestock, lived the way their parents had lived before them, and on back to the rough and tough settlers who pioneered the country.

They were much like the Amish, except for the lack of religion for many of them. They had only a respect for the land, cattle, horses, and the concrete conviction a man needed to hang on to his acreage no matter what. Most had a deep mistrust of the government, every man for himself, not complaining about whatever life threw at them.

And if a man was in trouble, you helped him out.

They took Titus back to the Busker ranch, where Ron was loading a few yearlings from the corral onto a questionable cattle trailer, mostly the odd brown color of rust.

"Hey!" he yelled. "Where'd you find him?"

"Borrowed 'im for a bit," Orvis yelled back.

Darlene got out, watched as Titus slid across the seat, strode toward Ron, already a hand to his shirt pocket, extracting the box of cigarettes. He stopped to light one, right there with Darlene in full view.

She wavered between sadness and anger. She was about to give him a piece of her mind, but then turned back and climbed into the truck. She wasn't done with Titus yet.

Darlene was hired on by Orvis Scuttle that summer. The two unlikely neighbors had hit it off tremendously, meeting along the road one day when a sudden cloudburst left her stranded in a three-sided cow shelter at the adjoining property, and he drove up and offered her a ride home. The unspoken law of Wyoming was that you helped each other out. Didn't matter if she was a large Amish woman wearing one of those white bonnets.

She, in turn, invited him in to see what she'd done to the house, and he followed her in, amazed at the transformation, and in so short a time.

He accepted a cup of water and then said he guessed he'd better be on his way. Didn't want to interfere with prayer time. "You get down on the ground and pray to the East, right?" he asked, feeling some pride in his knowledge.

Darlene laughed so hard he thought she might split a seam, and said no, no, they weren't Muslim but Christian.

"Whatsa difference?" he asked.

And she, being a school teacher, well versed in history and origins of religion, sat him down and explained it to him. He said, yeah yeah, his mother was a Christian, always went to church somewhere between here and Clearmont, but he'd never taken to it much. Said his wife died of cancer o' the stomach, suffered terrible. He paused a moment and then said he needed a housekeeper if she'd oblige.

And she did oblige. She cleaned up the garbage in the kitchen, got the old wringer washing machine going, took a hatchet to a few scrawny chickens and made him chicken pot pie.

And so a strange but comfortable friendship was formed.

When they dropped Titus off at the Busker ranch and he began to smoke, showing a total lack of respect for her, she decided to go berry picking, bake a pie, and take it over when Isaac was home.

He was going to listen to what she had to say if she had to hog-tie him.

The pie turned out great, purple filling thick with berries, a heavy topping of oatmeal, nuts, and brown sugar. She set it on her bike cart, stopped at the gas station on Wild Horse Corner, and bought half a gallon of vanilla ice cream before pedaling wildly to the Miller homestead, well after six o'clock. The sun was slanting down toward the Bighorns and she knew she might arrive with melted ice cream.

Sweating profusely, out of breath, her legs aching, she came to a stop, kicked the prop on her bike, swooped up the offering, and made her way to the great side patio where the family was seated around a table, relaxing after the evening meal.

Darlene never worried much about her appearance, had no idea her hair was windblown, her covering crooked, or that her dress was much too tight and too short. Her old sneakers were cracked and dusty, but she walked right up and yelled, "Looks like I timed this just right."

She held up the pie, her eyes closed, her jaw tilted.

"Ta-da!"

Isaac grinned and Susan laughed, getting up from her chair to pull up an extra one for her. Sharon smiled shyly and little Kayla watched with her bright eyes. No Titus.

"I brought you a berry pie and ice cream," she exulted.

"Wow! Thank you, Darlene. This was thoughtful of you," Susan said, welcoming her warmly.

"How are you, Darlene? Haven't seen you since the picnic," Isaac offered.

"I'm good. Got a summer job. Well, he'll want me all year, but I hardly know how I can do both."

"Who are you working for?"

"Orvis Scuttle. Not far from me."

Isaac blinked, Susan caught her breath.

"But . . . is he . . . okay?" she asked.

"Of course. Ugly as a mud fence, but he can't help that. He's a nice old man."

Isaac looked at Susan, and she looked at him, when Darlene bent to cut the pie. Stranger things had happened, they supposed, but local gossip didn't do poor Orvis justice.

Isaac's eyes narrowed when she told them why she had come.

Susan caught her lower lip in her teeth, her eyes frightened.

"I need to talk to you about Titus. You know you have a problem, right?"

Isaac opened his mouth, closed it again, his dark eyes sparking black fire.

"So . . ."

Darlene held up a hand.

"If you'll stay quiet long enough for me to explain, I'll give you a heads-up on your son."

This was too much for Isaac.

"Seriously, how can you come in here and tell me about my own son? I guess I'm the one who knows him better than you do."

Susan took a deep breath. "Isaac, why don't we hear her out?"

Darlene was highly perceptive, could gauge a situation with laser accuracy. So, it was just as she'd always thought. Isaac was the too lenient father and Susan saw the situation for what it was, but who was she? The stepmother.

So Darlene told them about Titus's inability to lose with any kind of grace, the hatred toward authority, the smoking and how it was already leading him down the road to substance abuse, or worse. He blamed those around him for everything and was clearly bitter over his mother's death.

Unless they were willing to invest time, extra love, and attention, and take him to a good counselor, she could see only trouble and heartache for Titus down the road.

"Let me tell you, Isaac. Teachers see a lot more than you think. You're married to your logging job, always were. Your wife and children don't rank that high on your priority scale. So unless you change something here, you'll reap your reward of negligence down the road."

Isaac sat, lips compressed, eyebrows drawn.

"What I'd like to know is what gives you the right to tell me how to raise my child?"

"Because you're blind where Titus is concerned. And because I don't care what anyone thinks of me. It's just tough if you don't like me. I'm giving you a fair warning. The rest is up to you."

She finished her pie, invited Susan to come for coffee sometime, and took her leave, pedaling off into the dusk.

Chapter 16

That summer, Darlene approached Orvis about setting up a mini rodeo for the youth. She thought it might be a good idea to get Titus involved in something competitive, especially with horses.

Orvis Scuttle lived alone and had been alone for quite a few years, resigned to being a widower. He had turned into a recluse who saw less and less of his acquaintances, no longer went down to eat at the Wagon Wheel, and lost many of his contacts, sliding into an unhealthy abyss of depression and loneliness. He had his cattle and a few horses, so that was basically the reason he kept going. He'd lived on the ranch his whole life, was born there, fiercely proud of his five-hundred-acre spread, no matter if the buildings fell into a state of decay. He still had his land.

So when he caught sight of the large woman huddled beside the road in a downpour, he helped her out by stopping his truck and yelling at her to get in. Later, he saw it was the woman he'd sold the house to, the one he'd thought was a nun, then thought she might be that other religion. He wasn't much for any of that stuff, never had been, didn't plan on it now. He believed there was a God somewhere up there, but he didn't give Him much thought. He didn't have much patience for self-righteous Bible-toting Jesus people, either.

His language was laced heavily with curse words, which wasn't unusual for ranchers around there. He tried to keep this in check for the Amish woman, but it was a part of who he was, and most of his sentences were peppered with words Darlene would never say.

She'd remind him, "Language, Orvis. Watch your language."

Over time they got to know each other and it was a strange friendship indeed, but it was one that worked for them both. He took her to town for groceries, didn't give a hoot if folks stared and snickered. She kept his house clean, scolded and fussed about the lack of decent kitchen equipment. What was wrong with buying a decent refrigerator that worked? And why couldn't he have a normal stove instead of one from the stone age?

And so little by little, week by week, the house was saved from rack and ruin, with Darlene at the helm.

She cooked beef roasts with potatoes, onion, and carrots, made a German chocolate cake, and he thought he might be a lucky man after all.

So when she brought up the subject of the rodeo, he didn't say no, but struck a bargain, saying if she helped with repairs and getting rid of some stuff around the place, he'd think about it.

AT THE MILLER homestead, things seemed to be going well, with Isaac having an extremely good run of logs from an especially lucrative timber tract just off Route 14, along the Little Bighorn River. It was a month's work, sure to enlarge his bank account quite efficiently. He left the house between four and five every morning, jaunty, well-rested, and eager to go, carrying a huge plastic Coleman lunchbox with an ice pack, two ham sandwiches with cheese, lettuce, onion, and mayonnaise, chips, pretzels, dip, cheese, cookies, a pint of canned peaches, and a doughnut or TastyKake.

He often felt blessed, redeemed from a life of sorrow, Susan being a gift in every way. She was strong, healthy, kept everything in running order, and seemed to be happy, settling into the new culture so far away from her family without complaining.

Plus, he truly believed she loved him. He smiled to himself, thinking of her arms around him, her willingness to be a wife to him, the long talks they shared on the patio after the children were in bed, the night mellow and sweet around them, the stars so close they were like tiny windows into the heavens. The sounds of night insects, the occasional call of an owl, the scurrying of night creatures with the sighing of pine trees always made them both want to linger for another few minutes.

And Susan never complained about being tired, was up early with the duty of packing his lunch foremost on her mind, working efficiently to make sure he had everything he needed for the day. Kayla was only a few weeks old when Susan was back to her normal routine, and when he told her she should be careful, she pooh-poohed that idea and kept going.

At times, when she was overwhelmed with Kayla's crying or Titus's misbehaving, she longed for home and her former life of freedom, but Isaac didn't know this. And she always felt better after spending an evening with her husband on the patio, talking about everything and anything. Isaac had a great sense of humor, a knack for describing the antics of his driver, the ponderosa pine tar, the fir trees that held all kinds of scared critters, deer, mule deer, an occasional black bear or badger. He loved being in the wild, thrived on his dangerous occupation, the chainsaw roaring in his ears, driving the iron wedge expertly, laying the tree down in the exact spot he meant for it.

Always, he spoke of his hope for Titus to take an interest in logging. He'd be so proud to teach him the way of it, but so far, Titus wanted nothing to do with it. Instead, he hung out with that Ron Busker who was not a good example for him.

The subject of Titus seemed to always bring tension into their conversation. Susan simply refused to talk about him with Isaac anymore, disagreements cropping up like land mines, and she hated the futility of circling around one another, never seeing eye to eye. Susan felt he needed Isaac's attention, some one-on-one conversation, so they could develop a better relationship, but Isaac insisted this wasn't possible. How could you force a child to spend time with you if they didn't want to? Susan felt he needed to try harder, and Isaac would shrug his shoulders and say they'd already lost him to his own self-pity, anger, and outright rebellion. It was that simple.

But at thirteen? Susan thought. Wasn't he still pliable, still able to take instruction, respond to love, even if it meant counseling? And now here was this Darlene, stirring the whole uneasy swamp of disharmony with her threats.

Darlene simply annoyed Isaac. He said she needed to stick to school teaching and stop trying to run his life. He thought it was disgraceful, the way she rode around with that old Orvis Scuttle, she being an Amish woman of good standing, and Susan told him that it was totally her own business and no one else's if she wanted to make a lonely old man's life a bit easier.

But Isaac loved that about Susan. She was sure of her own mind, and not afraid to spar with him, freely giving her own opinion . . . except, now, when it came to Titus.

She knew when she'd met her match. She was not his biological mother, so it was up to Isaac. She figured they'd be in for a long, wild ride, and she'd just have to depend on God's strength to stay patient and loving.

THE LOCAL CHILDREN were all sent flyers from Darlene inviting them to the mini rodeo. It was for anyone who felt the need to ride better, or who was already very good but wanted to learn new tricks, or how to train a misbehaving animal. Darlene was too heavy and a bit old and creaky to be demonstrating anything on horseback, but she had been raised on a horse farm and thought herself quite the knowledgeable equestrienne, and so looked forward to a few weeks of competition before school started. If she admitted it even to herself, it was all for Titus, a way of keeping contact, of asserting herself into his life, hoping to make a difference somehow.

For hadn't she seen too much in her life? She could handpick the troublemakers in school, the ones who went on to live sad lives of rebellion, going out into the world, leeching onto questionable characters who exuded false confidence and who herded them down the slippery slope to alcohol addiction and worse. It remained a pang in her heart to think of the sweet first grade children who now lived lives of hardship, the shield of anger and rebellion their only protection in years to come.

And Titus was a problem if she ever saw one. It seemed unfair, God taking his mother at a tender age, but He made no mistakes. There had to be an underlying reason, one only He knew, and the poor humans here below could only muddle through the ensuing grief and heartache.

Which was exactly what that big bear of a man, that Isaac, was going to have to do yet again if he didn't listen to reason.

Susan, bless her heart, did the best she could. She was a brilliant person, really, recognizing her role as a stepmother, one who was at the bottom of the totem pole when it came down to it. Stepmothers were very rarely liked or appreciated by hurting children who were grieving for their first mother and had to watch the love story unfold between this woman and their father.

Darlene always gave her all to a community, caring deeply about the life of the church, the well-being of her school children. She knew most children were raised in loving two-parent homes where God was at the helm, but you never knew what went on behind closed doors, and it never failed to show up in the children.

So here in Wyoming, she went right on sticking her nose into other people's business, without ever second-guessing herself, fully confident in her own ability to fix things. She cared about Titus, could only see heartache for his parents in the future, and so she went about being who she was.

THE SUN ROSE in a glamorous display of red, orange, and yellow, a soft outline of lavender and blue framing the vibrant colors.

Darlene was on her way to the Scuttle ranch, her black Nikes solidly pushing the pedals with tremendous force, moving along at a good clip. The gravel road was dry and dusty, the air so clean and pure it felt unreal, as if all the man-made inventions ever created had never been, and the air was as glorious as the day God created the earth.

She'd been up early, greeting the day with her usual alacrity, rolling out of bed, brushing her teeth so furiously her gums bled, wincing as she drew the hairbrush through her thick, wavy tresses. One of these days, she was going to whack off this mess of hair, she didn't care if the old tradition of never cutting hair remained in place or not. She didn't have time for this.

After a bowl of oatmeal and a handful of raisins, there was a sweet taste in her mouth that called for a few slices of toast, liberally buttered. After that she felt satisfied, so she was off on her bike, savoring the wonders of a midsummer morning.

Everything was dry as powder. She could hardly see how these ranchers could feed their cows and make a profit. They could wander around all they wanted, but couldn't live off rocks and sagebrush.

It was kind of stupid, living out here, really. She thought of the verdant soil, the frequent rain and deep green of Ohio fields and forests, rolling hills thick with heavy cornstalks and alfalfa. Still, money wasn't everything. She supposed the West grew on you if you were here long enough, as she was beginning to see herself.

She greeted Orvis with her usual forthright manner, no greeting, just a brusque "I thought you were going to mow this grass."

Orvis spit a thin brown stream of tobacco juice, looked her in the eye, and told her if she wanted that grass mowed, she could do it herself.

And that's exactly where Titus found her when he rode in on a striking black gelding. Darlene was not in a good mood, having moved pallets and buckets, pieces of old lumber and concrete blocks to get to the derelict old riding mower, a total piece of junk, and she was no expert at lawn mowers.

She'd already worked up a good sweat removing all that stuff, wasn't thrilled to see half a dozen mice run from under the pallets, and had a notion to tell Orvis to forget about this endeavor. He brought her some gasoline, dumped it in, and tried the starter to no avail.

Darlene told him to back off, she'd do it. She had no experience with a riding lawn mower, but didn't imagine it would be that hard.

She got the mower roaring into life, backfiring like a cannon, and went bouncing across the potholed driveway and nearly into the fence. As she was backing up, she spied Titus. She stopped the mower too suddenly, jolting her so hard she half fell off.

"Hey there!" she called, trying hard to cover up the goofy maneuver.

He waved, stopped his horse, and threw the reins across the saddle horn. He leaned forward and crossed his arms on top, for all the world like a seasoned cowhand.

"Just trying to mow some grass here, before the children arrive," she offered sheepishly.

"You're not too good at it. Want me to finish?"

"You think you're better?"

But she caught herself. It was never a competition with the children. Move down a notch, lift them up by putting yourself last.

"You almost flew off," he observed dryly.

She was going to deny it, but found a bubble of laughter rising in her throat. She caught the twinkle in Titus's eye and burst out laughing, throwing her head back and howling to the sky. She wiped her eyes, saw the smirk on his face, and laughed some more. He actually joined her, giving a few yelps of laughter in spite of himself.

"Hoo boy," she said. "Yeah, I was definitely unseated, so maybe you better give it a whirl."

He almost liked her as he drove around the perimeter of the corral, mowing off the dusty brown grass, while Darlene cleaned up junk and ordered Orvis into some semblance of helping.

The children came in pony carts and on horseback. There were girls riding good fast horses, children riding ponies, some no older than six or seven. She knew them all, had taught them for nine months, and was more than pleased to see them arrive. Louise Mast and Marianna Stutzman came in the surrey to make sure the children reached their destination safely, then carried folding lawn chairs to the corral fence, spread a quilt for the little ones, and prepared to watch the show.

Darlene was in her element. She'd seen plenty of riding and knew the intricacies of the tricks she'd seen performed, so she stepped up on a box and was the ringmaster, calling out orders, pointing a riding crop. At first, Titus hung back, looking bored and disinterested, as if he had advanced far above this baby stuff. Darlene was working the eighth grade girls' horses, putting them through their paces. Hannah was a tall, slim, quiet girl with bad skin and tightly curled hair, obedient and conscientious, always getting good grades and being helpful to the lower grades.

Millie was in seventh, and Trisha was going into eighth. They were both dark-haired and dark-eyed, with skin the color of honey, good athletes and outstanding in everything they tried. Quick to display their talents, neither shy nor humble, they were soon leading everyone riding around the corral, their horses obeying every command.

That was the deciding factor for Titus. No way was he going to be outdone by two girls, so he turned his horse and left.

Darlene realized what had occurred and motioned to the girls to ride after him and persuade him to come back.

They were happy to oblige, allowing their horses free rein, and soon caught up to him.

"Hey, Titus!"

"Wait up."

Titus reined in his horse, glared at them.

"What?"

"Darlene says you're to come back."

"I'm not going back. That's silly. All that fancy riding isn't for me."

"Come on, be a sport. She'll be disappointed. It's actually fun."

"Nope."

"Seriously, Titus. Do it for her."

"Her? You mean Darlene? Why would I do that?"

"It's not all about you, Titus," Millie said, clearly exasperated.

"I don't want to do this baby stuff, and if I don't want to, nobody's going to make me."

The girls gave up and watched him ride away, a thin figure with defiance in the set of his shoulders, the way he wore his hat, but most of all, the finality of his words which seemed to be written in stone.

HE SLOUCHED INTO the house, slammed his hat on a hook, kicked his boots into a corner, and flopped on a kitchen chair. Susan was changing Kayla, but finished and wrapped her into a blanket before looking at Titus. Her heart sank, but she approached him cautiously.

"Hi."

No answer.

"How was the rodeo?"

"You don't need to know. It's none of your business."

"Okay."

Sharon looked up from the book she was reading, her large brown eyes filled with worry. She placed her book on the end table and came out to the kitchen, leaned her elbows on the tabletop, and gazed at her unhappy brother.

"You okay, Titus?" she lisped.

"Yeah." He smiled at her, but with the side of his mouth away from Susan.

"So, you weren't into Darlene's rodeo?" she asked.

"I told you. You don't need to know."

And suddenly Susan had had enough of the boy's attitude. She spoke firmly, letting him know in no uncertain terms that she did not expect to be treated unkindly, and that was no way for anyone to talk to a parent.

"You're not my mother."

Susan sighed. No, she was not his mother. She had merely married his father. Did that amount to anything at all?

"No, I'm not."

"And you never will be."

"Titus, please."

Susan was heartsick the remainder of the day. She went about her duties mechanically, tried to pray away the feelings of inadequacy, begging God to give her strength. She hadn't bargained for this the day she wed Isaac.

She never imagined the troubled little boy turning on her, a mutiny of sorts. She felt betrayed, closeted with nowhere to turn.

She managed to cook a good supper, but found herself chewing her fingernails with apprehension, knowing she must talk to Isaac, and was unprepared for the lack of courage. When the truck drove up to the house, the passenger door opening before it came to a full stop, she felt a quick instinct to hide, then berated herself.

Filthy dirty, sweat creating dark rivulets on his blackened face, his eyes alight with the challenge of the day, fresh holes in his shirt and trousers, he yelled his goodbye to the driver and clumped into the laundry room, catching Sharon as she ran to her dad for a hug. Susan managed a wan smile and got through the evening without being too obvious about her state of mind. She put the children to bed, showered, and joined her husband on the patio, grateful for the cool of the night.

"Something wrong, Susan?"

"A little bit."

"Titus?"

She nodded.

"Was he being mean?"

"Oh, I don't know, Isaac. He simply doesn't accept me as his mother."

"He did at first."

"So, you're insinuating it's me. I am the problem."

"No, not really. Just give him time and he'll come back around."

"You'd think a few years would be enough time."

"Susan."

"What?"

"It's not going well, is it?"

"It's Titus."

"Hasn't it always been Titus, every single upheaval in school or at home? You knew how he was when you married me."

"I did. But somehow, it's much harder than I thought. He doesn't respect me. Evidently, the rodeo did not go well, and he told me it was none of my business. Sassed me."

"Don't take it from him."

"I didn't. But, Isaac, please. I need you to step up to the plate and do your part. You are the one who needs to talk to him. He needs his father, and you're hardly ever around."

"What am I supposed to do? Stay home and babysit him and allow my business to go to pot?"

"No."

There was a long silence, a time of dashed hopes for Susan as she grappled with the heartless answer her husband had given her. Why couldn't he go to Titus, sit down, and have a father and son discussion? And how many times had she asked him to do that with no response?

Far away a coyote yipped and another answered, followed by a chorus of howls and high pitched calls as the pack ran together.

Isaac shook his head.

"Hope the calves and lame cows stay with the herd. Those unruly animals need to be shot."

"Isaac, is this as far as our conversation will go? Are you actually done with our discussion, leaving me dangling in midair?"

"I don't know what to tell Titus. Look, Susan, my dad never talked to me. He didn't know what to say. Our feelings were never discussed. If you did okay, he was nice. If you didn't, you got whooped. So what's the big deal? We turned out alright. Mam and Dat are gone, and we're all Amish, keeping the faith, so that's something. All this craziness of therapy and figuring out who you are and what happened years ago when you were a child is for the birds. It's stupid. Titus will grow out of this. He's just being a thirteen-year-old."

"So every thirteen-year-old smokes, swears, and talks back to his parents?" Susan asked, without trying to hide the sarcasm.

"A lot of 'em."

"Isaac, really?"

She lay awake far into the night, Isaac's large form beside her stone quiet except for the rising and falling of his big chest.

Oh, Isaac, she thought, as fresh tears sprang from her eyes, ran down the side of her face, and soaked her pillow. The night seemed fraught with anxiety, the yawning gorge of wretchedness taunting her.

He had been so kind, so loving, so attentive, giving her no reason to believe in anything except a great love that would carry them through the worst of times.

Was this real life then, marriage and romance and love put on a shelf, while you were expected to carry on by yourself, taking the hurdles as they were thrown in your path?

She decided to pray, rolled on to her side, closed her eyes and began, giving her thoughts new wings, carrying her overwhelmed concerns to Jesus. She imagined his kind face, his shining white clothes and nail-scarred hands, the great love God had given to fallen man, giving His only Son as a Redeemer. With her eyes on the spiritual part of life, she felt the cleansing tears begin, but this time, they brought healing peace.

This love was the only kind that would last forever, that would satisfy her soul, quell every thirst. Isaac was her husband here on earth, and as long as they were in the flesh, their bodies, minds, and hearts were imperfect, and nothing was always without fault.

As she prayed, she felt a renewing of her spirit, a fresh hope and courage for another day. With that came a love for Isaac, the kind that had eluded her in the past weeks. She felt a need to be close to him, to touch this man God had given her, so she snuggled close, put a hand on his huge chest, and felt comforted.

And two shall be one, she thought. So his father had not talked to him about his feelings, and he didn't think it was necessary for him to do that with his own son. Well, she was his wife, and she planned on carrying out a bit of common sense of her own. If Isaac was going to be this way, she had a strong feeling there was a God-given advocate in a navy blue dress and a large pair of black Nike sneakers.

CHAPTER 17

"Liz, if you want to come for a visit, the best time is before October. It can snow in September, so you better get this planned."

Susan sat in Isaac's office, the sun casting an honest light on the dust and dried mud, the filthy doormat, the windows peppered with fly dirt, cobwebs, and dead flies all over the windowsills, empty coffee cups, and trash.

Everything was planned. The two school-aged children would stay with her parents, which made Liz cry to think about it, but Dave couldn't leave the farm till September, after the corn was in the silo, and the children shouldn't miss that much school.

"So, if it snows, it snows, Suz. It won't snow that hard in September."

"I hope not. Oh, Liz. I am so excited. Okay, let me call Rose."

And a great flurry of words ensued, Rose steamed up like a fired boiler. They were traveling in an RV, a big one, not some piece of junk that would fall apart halfway. She told Susan she really had gotten some housework done and the garden cleaned out in preparation for coming.

"Don't tell Liz, but I threw a bucket of tomatoes across the fence. The horse ate a few. I can't see any sense in making all that pizza sauce if you can buy it in the store for what? A dollar? I hate my Victorio strainer. The dumb thing is so hard to put together and take apart I could just scream."

And Susan had a good deep-down belly laugh. She loved Rose so much it hurt. How badly she needed her sisters, she thought. And how she looked forward to their arrival.

SHE SPENT THE last weeks of August house cleaning, her feet encased in wings as she sped from room to room with Kayla swinging from side to side in her little swing. Sharon was her self-appointed babysitter, calling anxiously up the stairs if Kayla as much as stretched or grunted. And Susan ran down the stairs, laughing, saying the baby was alright, that's what babies did in their sleep.

It was a joy stretching fresh sheets across freshly washed mattress pads, plumping pillows, arranging quilts perfectly, running from room to room deciding which throw pillows looked best with which quilts, knowing Rose thought herself an expert on decorating. Susan smiled as she arranged pictures on the wall, old ones she'd bought at a yard sale in Gordonville, years ago.

How long ago was it? And how far away the area seemed. A wealthy land, teeming with the tourist trade, outstanding crops, and lucrative business establishments, the plain people thriving among it all.

She had heard her grandmother talk of the Swiss brethren, how prosperity caused them to adopt the ways of the world, hiring servants to do their housework, changing their lifestyle and their dress, with the love of money the root of all evil. Her grandmother was very sharp for a person in her eighties, her wisdom rolling off her tongue like water. She'd warn others about taking the *ordnung* (rules) ahead of a personal life with Jesus, being justified by the law instead of Him.

Our righteousness is not our own but Christ's, she would say, and Susan remembered struggling with that concept. Why adhere to a man-made rule if it meant nothing? Or was the *ordnung* inspired by the Holy Spirit, same as the Bible?

Grandmother assured Susan it served its purpose by keeping a group in unity, but if it wasn't practiced out of love, it wasn't worth much. "We love the brethren. Therefore, we keep the peace in our churches."

But the boundaries of the *ordnung* kept stretching, being elongated by restlessness, discontent, the way of humans.

Susan missed her grandparents, wished they could have come for the wedding, but they'd both declined, saying they had their limits. Traveling was not for them.

She picked up a woven rug, tossed it out the window, hung on to one end before slamming the window down to hold it in place, then picked up a corner of her apron to wipe her streaming face.

My, it was hot. But nothing deterred her from preparing for her two sisters' arrival.

TITUS APPEARED TO be reasonably happy, riding his bicycle to the Busker ranch five days a week, where he was taught how to herd cows and how to repair fences, paint buildings, and fix leaking stock tanks.

Wolf was no longer in his prime, his muzzle turning gray, and his hips achy as he rose from his bed of hay each morning. But in the evening, when Titus was ready to scout the surrounding areas, his binoculars hanging from a strap on his neck, Wolf would take off running and circle back, hysterically yelping, eager to see what could be found. They watched coyotes, an occasional badger flattening himself in the tall grass, mule deer in rocky valleys, and nervous whitetails stepping from a stand of fir trees. The most exciting thing of all was the rare sighting of a bison or black bear, or watching golden eagles in clefts of red rock along creek bottoms. The world was endless, the intricacies of nature a continuous source of entertainment.

He loved the dry season, when the land was dusty and yellow, when creatures shared few watering holes and overcame their fear of people because of their thirst. The danger of fire was very real, then, so he knew enough to be careful of his cigarettes, the isolation a good opportunity to enjoy the habit already firmly entrenched by the power of nicotine.

The only uneasy thing in this smoking deal was that Darlene. She kept sending him that annoying literature about the dangers of smoking, and he could no longer enjoy the cigarettes the way he used to. For the hundredth time he wished he'd never met her. She was worse than a conscience, that uneasy feeling he was getting good at ignoring.

He was not really okay with his job at the Busker ranch, being told what to do every single minute of the day, but then, he didn't want to allow himself to get involved in his dad's logging business, either. To be out of school before you were fifteen was like being caught on a ledge. There was nowhere to go. He wasn't always comfortable around Susan, nursing that Kayla, the wary look in her eye as if she was afraid he'd come around, and when he did, she'd tug the blanket up over her shoulder and look away. Kayla was cute enough, and he did like her, but all that nursing . . .

His dad was never around, and when he was, it was either chore time or supper. It seemed as if they never had anything to talk about anymore, nothing in common, because his entire brain was taken up by Susan and logging, or logging and Susan, or just logging.

He hated the world, couldn't stand to think of his furious chainsaw murdering the beautiful fir trees, the whole backbone of the wildlife habitat in this area. If he dared mention it, he was made fun of, with a sarcastic remark about being a tree hugger or a hippie. These comments were accompanied by a giant hand on his head, ruffling his hair to make it look like a joke, but the mockery snagged like a fishhook.

He'd liked his dad well enough before Susan, and he'd liked Susan by herself, but those two together were like the wild honey he sometimes found in tree notches. Way too sticky and sweet.

He couldn't watch his dad put his arm around Susan. It seemed all wrong. He remembered his short, plump mother, blond-haired and blue-eyed, so weak and gentle and tender. He'd never done that to her.

So why was he all over this tall, skinny Susan who wasn't nearly as sweet and soft and lovable as his own mother?

He couldn't take it, so he roamed the fields and forests, stayed out of everyone's way, and hoped he could move out soon enough.

WHEN THE LONG-AWAITED visitors arrived, Titus watched from the bird's-eye view in the haymow, the door wide open toward the house.

It was a lovely day in September, one of the rare warm, languid ones, where grasshoppers whirred in the dusty grass. The aspens were turning yellow, the wild creatures were still enjoying the warmth before winter, and the rains were on their way.

Isaac had asked Titus to stay home from the Busker ranch to be present when his aunts and uncles arrived, but he decided they were not his relatives and he wasn't planning on making an appearance.

He was surprised his dad quit making money long enough to welcome anyone, taking a day off from his destructive logging.

The RV was amazing, though. Wow. But that fat woman in a red dress was a bit overboard.

As he kept watch, Susan reached for Liz, gathered her into a warm hug, then Rose, who squealed and yelled and hugged Isaac, her sister going for a formal handshake. Children circled warily around Sharon, Amos, and Dave with wide smiles of pleasure, Isaac pumping hands, as gregarious and outgoing as ever. Susan wiped tears of joy, laughing and crying simultaneously.

Isaac put a protective arm around her, and she cried more. Rose thought it was so sweet her face crumpled, and she cried, too.

What a fuss about Kayla sitting in her little stroller, just as cute as a button with her delicate pink dress. Liz said she looked like Susan did when she was a baby, and Rose said how could she know, she couldn't possibly remember and Mam didn't have baby pictures.

But no matter, Kayla was scooped up, cuddled and kissed, examined from head to toe, and pronounced the cutest baby they'd ever seen.

Liz, always the thoughtful one, hugged Sharon and said she was growing into a little lady and she bet she was a big help to her mother. Sharon was won over immediately and latched on to Liz for the remainder of their stay. Isaac was in his glory. He loved visitors, anyone to sit on the patio or around a campfire at night, anyone to swap stories with, to eat and drink and enjoy life.

He took the men to his logging site the following day in the RV. Titus could not turn down a chance to ride in the massive vehicle, so he appeared at the last minute and went along.

The women drank cups of coffee around the table and caught up on every aspect of their lives. Susan had prepared a western-style egg casserole, which Rose couldn't get enough of. She rolled her eyes and moaned, "Seriously, what is in this stuff?"

And Susan laughed, said butter, half-and-half, and loads of cheese.

Rose shrugged her shoulders and said it was delicious. Susan sized up the heavy arms and substantial waist, smiled, and loved her just the way she was. Liz, however, picked at her food, ate mostly baked oatmeal with raisins and cranberries, her dress loose on her thin frame.

They discussed Susan's life in the West, the adjustments she had had to make, the loneliness and the dry weather, her husband gone so much of the time.

Susan's face fell.

"Yeah, well, does anyone know what to expect when they get married? I didn't date for so long because I didn't want to deal with the struggles that come with marriage. None of this Kate and Dan stuff, or you, Rose, with your picky in-laws."

"So being married to Isaac isn't as perfect as it seems?"

"Oh my, no. I do not have a perfect marriage at all. That's not what it's about, believe me. You love your husband in spite of his imperfections. My two biggest hurdles are his logging and Titus, both sometimes so hard."

"I believe that. I surely do. Stepchildren wouldn't be my thing. Sometimes I don't love my own the way I should. How would it be if they weren't your own?"

"I try, but since Kayla, there is a difference. Your own flesh and blood, carrying them for nine months, the joy of birth, it's just so different. The bond so complete. Then I feel guilty if I don't feel quite the same about Sharon and Titus. And to be truthful, Isaac is an absent father, never that close to any of them."

"Seriously?" Liz asked.

"That was my biggest issue with him when I taught school. I made the mistake we all make, thought I could change him. Huh. I can't."

She went on to fill them in on Titus, mentioning Darlene and her endeavor to form a summer rodeo, his refusal to participate, the battle to fight the sense of failure in himself.

Susan sighed. "But, you know. If I would have married Levi, I would have had another set of problems."

Rose raised her eyebrows. "Something doesn't sit right with me there."

"What do you mean?"

"It just doesn't. Levi is weird. Kate is always fluttering around trying to make everything appear perfect, but I don't understand him. I personally think he's too *schmächlich* (smooth)."

Liz lifted a forefinger. "The only way to describe him."

"Why didn't they come, too?"

"I have no clue. Kate thought they were going to. Made plans with us and everything. Last week she called to say Levi thought it best to stay home. Marie gets sick easily and he was afraid the change in climate might trigger something."

"Really?"

"Oh, and all she did was go on and on about how caring he was about Marie, what a wonderful father to her children and how blessed she was to have him."

"She was naive enough to marry Dan, and she probably got duped into another winner. I personally can't stand him," Rose said, without mincing her words.

"Well, you're too hard on people," Liz said quietly.

"Not on him, I'm not. Did you ever notice how he shows off in church? It's like he needs everyone to know he's the best father in the world. All it makes me think is that he's hiding something."

Susan watched Rose quietly, knowing she always said what others might only think, and most would berate themselves for having thought it in the first place. She was open and honest, as truthful and unvarnished as the day was long, but tended to come across as harsh and judgmental.

"The thing that irks me the most is, how could she be so dumb? Marrying one loser, grieving for him, and on to the next."

"Rose! Stop." Liz said, conscientious upbringing coming swiftly to the rescue. She was appalled. "You simply don't talk in those terms."

"You know it's true."

And there was nothing to say to that.

Susan pondered Rose's words, thinking how all of this could only be evil surmising.

Oh dear.

She sighed. "Well, everything appears okay on the surface, so we'll take that and be happy for Kate. She seems to thrive on serving her man and her children, which is what God expects of us."

Rose choked on a swallow of coffee.

"You have got to be kidding me, Suz. What in the world has crawled over you? Must be the loneliness got to your head. You can't be serious. If you think that's what marriage is all about, then you just go right ahead bowing and scraping, 'cause I'm not. I'm not doormat material."

"I didn't mean it that way."

A bit miffed, Susan got up to wash pans, keeping her back turned till Rose called out, "Now you're mad."

"I'm not. You're just . . ."

"Different? Modern? *Ungehorsam* (disobedient)?"

They all laughed.

"I bet Amos is as happy as any man, and I guarantee he doesn't get away with not helping me. They're his children, too, and I'm not doing it all by myself."

The visit came and went alarmingly fast, the time so precious, Susan trying to be present in the moment, remember every conversation. She cooked and served, checking to see they were all comfortable in the evening, going sightseeing with the affable driver of the huge RV, his wife as friendly and personable as anyone Susan had ever met.

They had been born among the Amish, were all acquainted with their ways and peculiarities, made a good living being paid drivers. On this trip, they thoroughly enjoyed themselves, especially Rose and her outspoken ways, her devoted husband in tow. Which added plenty of humor to the time they all spent together.

Susan was so proud of her husband. The perfect host, he was always seeking ways to make their stay enjoyable, taking time off from his logging job, which in itself was amazing. An extrovert, for sure, he thrived on entertaining company, the level of which Susan had never seen. Talking, laughing, showing off Kayla, always looking out for others, except Titus, who disappeared, or sat on the outskirts of every gathering, every conversation, never contributing except when Rose would sit beside him and ask questions about his job, his friends, his life in general. He did give her a scant outline of being lost, the broken leg, grinned wryly about Susan's return to their home, but offered no further information.

Rose told Susan he was hurting, and they better look into getting him some counseling, the sooner the better. Susan's eyes opened wide, showing the surprise she felt. She was reminded of Darlene's words the night she brought over the pie. She shook her head no, no, it wasn't that bad.

"But it is, Susan. You and Isaac don't see it." She made an impatient sound.

"This Isaac thing. Every Isaac in Lancaster County is called Ike. Why not him?"

"Oh well, that shouldn't bother you."

"It does. I'm going to call him Ike. It's much easier than Isaac. For some reason, I think of that somber story in the Bible, about Abraham offering up his son Isaac as a sacrifice, and it gives me the blues."

"Oh, but that one has a happy ending. God's voice stopped Abraham, a ram was provided, all symbolic of Christ's sacrifice for us," Liz said airily, clearly thinking herself superior to Rose.

"Yeah, Liz. I know you're an avid reader of the Bible. Better than me. I hardly ever read my Bible, it's just so boring. Sometimes I don't feel right, you know. Kind of like I did something wrong, or God is just some figment of my imagination, not really close, and I open my Bible and read just to get closer to God, but I'd much rather read my current book or one of my magazines."

"That's your whole problem," Liz said, sniffing.

And this was what Susan missed most. The way sisters could be open and brutally honest, hashing and rehashing opinions and observances, getting each other's jokes, sharing the same sense of humor.

Nothing was humorous about Titus, though, which was where the conversation turned, seated around the campfire in the backyard on an unusually mild September evening. It was the last evening before they would leave, a bittersweet time for Susan.

Titus had retired to his bed earlier than usual, allowing a space of time for Rose to open the discussion.

"Ike," she said loudly.

Isaac was unused to hearing the shortened version of his name, and did not answer immediately.

"Ike," Rose repeated, louder.

"What? Oh, hey Rose."

"I think you need to take Titus for counseling. He's hurting."

A long moment of silence. The fire leaped and crackled, the stones around it holding in the heat. The sound of children playing hide and seek in the dark recesses of the yard was the only other noise on the isolated homestead.

"I don't know what he'd be hurting for," Isaac said gruffly.

"His mother died. He has a stepmother."

"So? It's happened before and will happen again. That in itself doesn't necessarily mess a kid up."

"Really? How do you know? Did it happen to you?" Rose's voice rose an octave.

It was only Isaac's good manners that made the best of a situation that could have turned uncomfortable. He told Rose it hadn't happened to him till he was in his twenties, and perhaps it was harder for a child of eight, which left Rose nodding her head righteously, exulting in the upper hand.

"But this thing of taking children to counseling over every little thing didn't used to be. I don't have much patience for it. We all have our path to follow, and the sooner we grow up and accept what life throws at us, the better. Titus is a rebel. He's always rebelled against everything he doesn't want to do. Take my job. He won't go along, refuses to show an ounce of interest, got himself a job for some no account rancher, who is a negative influence, take my word for it. So what is a parent to do? Beat it out of him? That's the old way. He would be logging alongside me or get a good whooping. Children were expected to buckle down and obey their parents, do what they were asked."

"They still are," Amos cut in.

"Are they? How many Amish kids nowadays are working a job they don't like, but doing it because their parents want them to?" Isaac asked.

He got up and put more wood on the fire.

Rose, always the outspoken one, answered in a huffy tone of voice. "Why should they? It's not right."

"I'm just saying. Children used to obey without question where now they're given a choice. Titus doesn't like logging, so he doesn't go, which is my fault. And I feel if he'd give it a whirl, he'd learn to enjoy it, take an interest in it. But I can't force him, just have to wait till the time is right."

"It might never be right," Liz said softly.

"You're right, Liz. And if it isn't, then we'll go from there, right?"

After that, a more harmonious atmosphere prevailed, sparks shooting into the night sky, like millions of twinkling lights, the stars blinking off and on like tiny diamonds. The silhouette of black fir trees were like the teeth of a giant comb poking into the beauty of the starlit sky, the air so crisp, so pure and clean, Liz said she wished she could bottle some up and take it home.

"I love my home in Lancaster, but the congestion of cars and trucks, the cities and towns always growing . . . I bet if we knew the disgusting quality of our air, we'd have a fit."

"You can always move out here," Isaac offered.

"And wear that covering? No way. I'd look like the moon. Completely round," Rose said, laughing.

Susan would remember that night for a long time, the thought of Rose and Liz moving here to Wyoming raising uncomfortable questions. Was it fair to live the remainder of her life so far away from family, missing out on numerous family get-togethers? But she decided she had chosen Titus, had chosen his father when he was lost, and had surely been guided by the hand of God.

Here she was, married to a man she had never imagined she would be even slightly attracted to, but he was her man, and sometimes she loved him more than she thought possible. Sometimes she didn't, when he made her so angry she couldn't see straight, and she yelled at him like some simple fishwife, which was so satisfying she didn't regret it at all. But in his strong arms, his lips on hers, there was a haven of peace and trust, a gratitude and contentment only found in the blessing of a union called marriage.

CHAPTER 18

DARLENE WAS FURIOUS AT TITUS. HERE SHE WAS, WORKING SO hard in the heat of summer to organize a rodeo for his sake, hoping he'd reach out to his classmates and make some friends, and what had he done but gone home because he was a poor sport.

She rode her bike the five and a half miles to the Ron Busker ranch, red-faced, dripping perspiration, in no mood to tiptoe around Titus or anyone else. This boy needed to be told his behavior was unacceptable, and that was her mission.

The place looked much like every other ranch in Wyoming, unpainted outbuilding, or weathered white paint turned a sickly shade of gray, gray weeds, rusted wagon wheels, flat tires. The house was a long, low rancher made of cement blocks and vinyl siding, with no porch, giving it the appearance of a doctor's office, or a dentist. They could have added a porch and some shrubbery to give the place some character, but that didn't seem to be very high on the list for most of these people. Land or oil or both, that was what divided the haves from the have-nots, here in the West, so you kind of had to go with it.

She kicked the stand on her bike into place, looked around, and decided the place was deserted. She heard a woof and a mangy German shepherd dragged himself out from beneath a hollow by some shed, his coat in lamentable shape. Darlene eyed him with distrust and thought this might well be the end of her if this oversized dog decided to have her for dinner.

A deep-throated growl, followed by a series of barks.

"Good dog," she called out.

The door on the front of the house opened and a middle-aged woman in jeans and a loose T-shirt called to the dog, stopping him in his tracks. Darlene resumed breathing and felt a tremendous sense of relief.

"Come on in. Don't worry about Buff. He won't hurt you."

They all said that, these dog owners. Snarling Rottweilers, mean German shepherds the size of a pony, Dobermans like vipers, supposedly kittens to their owners. She mopped at her face with the hem of her apron as she made her way to the front door, the supposedly affable Buff sniffing her backside, lending speed to her sturdily clad feet.

The woman stepped aside.

"Come on in. I know who you are. Orvis talks about you. I been wanting to meet you."

Her face was lined, her deep-set eyes a dark brown, her graying hair cut short, but there was a warm friendliness about her that Darlene trusted instantly. She stepped inside, found a living room with threadbare furniture, pillows, and hand-crocheted ripple afghans hiding the worst spots, a large fireplace, bookcases and a scattering of cheap pictures and knick-knacks. Everything was fairly clean. Two enormous cats were stretched out on the back of the couch, blinking their large yellow eyes in her general direction.

"And don't worry about Shem and Ham. They're too lazy to give you the time a day," she said, laughing good-naturedly.

Darlene chuckled about Shem and Ham, the sons of Noah. Were these people Christians?

She was seated at a kitchen table on which a pile of magazines, sales slips, bills, advertisements, empty quart jars, and many other items were piled, but the iced tea was served in tall, clean glasses, sweet and dark, just the way she liked it, the rest of the kitchen in some semblance of order, which made Darlene feel right at home.

"What brings you here, Darlene?" Winnie asked, giving her name as Wynona Busker, but saying she could call her Winnie, same as everyone else did.

"I wanted to talk to the boy who is working for you, Titus Miller."

"Oh, Ty. He's gone to town with Ron. They're putting in fence posts and ran outta fuel."

"Ty?"

"Yeah, he's Ty to us. We had a son named Tyler. Was gored by a mean longhorn mama with a calf. He lived for three and a half weeks after, but in the end, we couldn't save his life. It's a terrible thing to be put on life support, but even worse having to make that decision to pull the plug. You're never the same afterward. So when Ron met Titus out with that dog a his, they hit it off."

She was a true rural Wyoming rancher, the way she shortened the "of" to an "a" sound, something Darlene had almost picked up herself, listening to Orvis unspool his half-truthful recollections. In Winnie, it was completely endearing.

"I'm sorry. I had no idea."

"So yeah, it was tough. And Ty just fills an empty spot."

"Was he your only child?"

"No. Bonnie's in Arizona. Married some highfalutin real estate developer she met in Casper. They have money, their lifestyle so different from what she was raised. But what're you gonna do? Kids make choices, and nothin' you can do."

She paused, went to the refrigerator for more tea, then sat down.

"Rudy is in the East somewhere. She got mad when she was nineteen, got into a fight with Ron about going to college and lit out. She sends an email every once in a while, just to let us know she's still okay. Like I said, kids make choices."

Winnie tapped her nails on the tabletop, her eyes on the back of her hand. She seemed calm, but suddenly raised her eyes to Darlene's.

"Ron was hard on the kids. Could never get along with none of 'em. I tried to fill in, but seems every kid wants their dad's approval. His love. They never got much from him, but that was the way of it. Not much to do about it now."

"This is why I'm here," Darlene said. "Titus needs someone, and I plan on stepping in. His mother passed away after a long illness, his dad remarried, and he's not happy with the arrangement. Typical rebel. Doesn't have much of a cause, in my mind, living in the beautiful place, horses, his stepmother a real sweetheart. He makes life miserable for her."

"Aw, you think? Now how could he do that? He's one of the sweetest kids I ever come across."

Darlene said nothing, merely took a sip of her iced tea and wondered if these ranch women didn't serve a snack when they had visitors. It was almost lunchtime, and she'd skipped breakfast.

"Winnie, he's a problem to his parents. He was a real mess in school. I should know. I was his teacher in eighth grade."

"Well, now, that don't make sense."

Darlene gave her a sharp look.

"Well, it don't. Ron said he'd do anything for him. Just anything. Follows him around, learnin' things easy like. We just love Ty."

There wasn't much to say to that, so Darlene took her leave, feeling as if a strong foundation had been kicked right out from under her.

How could you figure that one out? Titus acting like a sheep to Ron and his wife, then being a burden to his parents? None of it made sense. She would live to be a hundred and never understand the intricacies of human nature, the strange foibles that made a person who he was.

She wasn't sure what to do. He obviously didn't like the idea of a rodeo, but she had to carry on with the rest of the children, seeing how much they seemed to enjoy it, plus she was terribly behind with preparations for school to begin.

In church on Sunday, she listened to an inspiring sermon about humility, felt she'd fallen short of that virtue on numerous occasions, and decided to approach Susan.

"How's Titus?"

Susan eyed Darlene with a sad expression in her beautiful green eyes.

"Just absent so much of the time. He comes home late, often not eating supper with us. It's hard."

"I can imagine."

Darlene smiled and placed a hand on Susan's arm.

"Well, at least he has a place where he's well thought of. I paid a visit to the Busker ranch, met Ron's wife Winnie, and she says he's the perfect hired hand. Obedient, learns easily. Now why do you think that is?"

Susan shook her head as Darlene continued to fill her in on everything Winnie had said about their lives and Titus's special place in it.

All around them, the congregation was setting up tables, spreading tablecloths, placing dishes, glasses of water, an assortment of bread and cheese, pies, pickled beets and cucumbers. Children threaded their way among the women and men lined up the walls of the large shop, their hands in their pockets as they conversed easily. It was much the same as the church services Susan had grown up with in Lancaster, only the women's dress and some of the men's clothes were different.

But now more than ever, it felt like home, being a mother, a part of the community, dressed in the bowl-shaped covering made of stiff fabric unlike the eastern heart-shaped ones she'd always worn.

Darlene was rambling on about Titus and her failed rodeo, how it had all taught her humility and how she had connected with the words of the minister today.

Wasn't it something how God taught us from time to time? Then she went on to tell Susan about her delicious meatball subs, and would they like to come for supper that evening? Titus, too.

Susan smiled, said she'd see if Isaac was up for it, her heart sinking to her shoes, knowing neither Titus or Isaac would want to go. She felt bad for Darlene, who led such a solitary life.

After lunch, when Isaac came to ask if she was ready to leave, she said yes, but mentioned the invitation to Darlene's house.

She saw the shadow pass over his face, was ready to accept the refusal, but much to her surprise, he consented. Susan was happy, having wanted to see Darlene's house all summer.

No amount of coaxing would get Titus to budge. He simply refused, stalked off and said he was walking home. Isaac shrugged his shoulders and said fine, be that way, and let him go, which did not sit well with Susan. As she watched happy families pile into waiting buggies, she thought again of the added weight on a stepmother's shoulders. You simply had to unspool the long and ragged thread as you moved through your days, hoping the way back could hold a few life's lessons.

For one thing, she'd learned to stay quiet in situations such as this one. If Titus kicked up a fuss, his father unable to persuade him, then she certainly wasn't capable of it, either. He disliked her too much.

To know a stepson couldn't stand you was sickening, like a kick in the stomach. She had grappled with this fact for a few years, tried to outmaneuver him with kindness, gifts, special food, going to his room at night to talk about his ill feelings, but nothing made an ounce of difference. She had to take care of her own emotional well-being, so she distanced herself to some extent, showed outward kindness and let well enough alone.

She mentioned his loyalty to Ron Busker, told him what Darlene had said.

She'd always remember the dusty road, the dying grass by the side of the road, the smell of drought and pine tar, the crunch of stone under steel wheels as Isaac's condemnation of Darlene tore through the air between them.

"That woman needs to start minding her own business. I'm raising my children the way we were raised and she needs to stay out of it."

He snapped the reins across the horse's back, startling him into a much faster gait.

"But Isaac, we can learn from this. What is at the ranch that changes him so? What do they have that we don't?

"What are you talking about?"

Isaac turned to face Susan, his eyes dark with disapproval.

"Just that it seems Ron and Winnie have an ingredient we're missing."

"Oh, so now it's Ron and Winnie."

"Darlene calls them that. I never met them."

"An English couple like that? Not even Christians. All they have for Titus is letting him do whatever he wants. Smoking? That's okay. Swearing? Okay, too. That's the only reason he's there, 'cause he can get away with everything, and he thinks he's cool doing it."

Susan was shocked into silence. His self-righteous attitude was appalling.

Susan mulled over what Darlene had told her and began to understand. With Ron and Winnie, Titus felt needed, respected, filling a place in their aching hearts, knowing he was someone. He was Ty, and they loved him for what he was—they didn't just put up with him for what he wasn't and never would be. A failure to his own father, a skinny child with no muscles and a deep fear of chainsaws and trees falling to the earth.

Should she tell Isaac? Drive the wedge between them even farther? She knew it was not the right time to try any correction, so she stayed quiet. Fortunately, Darlene's house came into view, the fluttering yellow aspen leaves a quaint backdrop for the small gray house, the shrubbery thriving, the grass brown but neatly cut.

Isaac stepped into his role as an invited guest and was talkative and entertaining as she served glasses of tea, corn chips, and salsa.

She mixed ground beef with spices, egg, and breadcrumbs, talking as she worked, asked about Titus and his whereabouts, clucked and fussed and repeated her lesson in humility, having failed at including Titus in the rodeo. Susan caught Isaac's eye and they both grinned, both still looking for the humility she had seemingly acquired.

The subs were delicious—so good, in fact, Isaac said he almost liked Darlene and would be happy for another invitation. He told Susan this on the way home, and they laughed together. They talked about how Darlene had shooed them out right after dinner, saying that Orvis would be swinging by any minute to pick her up for evening chores.

They smiled together, contemplating the odd arrangement between the two of them.

So perhaps marriage was hit or miss like this. Some days, even weeks, were very good; pick another day or week, and you were sorely tested. But she'd take it, Susan thought.

She still loved her husband, and planned on keeping it that way, in spite of his despicable attitude about Titus.

They wended their way home, pleasantly full, both becoming sleepy, lulled into relaxation by the drumming hooves, the clatter of wheels, their shoulders gently touching. Sharon and Kayla both fell asleep, so by the time they drove up to the house, Susan was almost asleep herself.

She gave the girls their bath, listened to Isaac clattering through the house, singing the remains of the "Lob-Lied," the song of praise everyone sang in unison at every single Amish service. Isaac loved to sing, often led the German songs in the *Ausbund* (song book), his voice a pleasing baritone, never faltering as he led the congregation. And Susan felt a certain pride, a sense of belonging, the wife of a prominent member of the church.

The singing stopped.

"Where's Titus? He in his room?"

His head appeared at the bathroom door where Susan was snuggling Kayla in a towel, Sharon wincing as she drew a brush through her wet hair.

"I don't know. I just imagined he would be."

A few steps across the living room and a thundering voice calling up the stairs, a pause, another call, before the heavy footsteps of her husband sounded through the house. In a terrible voice, he told Susan he wasn't in his room.

"Are you sure? Check the guest room. Sharon's room."

But her mouth was already dry, thinking of one skinny thirteen-year-old walking alone on country roads after dark. He often missed dinner, but he'd always before been home before dark.

He'd been spared before, oh surely, he'd be alright now.

Kayla was strapped into her swing, Sharon told to keep an eye on her, and Susan helped Isaac search the barn, the haymow, the outbuildings, everywhere they could think of, Wolf whining, searching with them.

Twilight had cast its chilling shadow across the homestead, the snow-covered peaks of the Bighorns in stark relief to the darkening sky. Scrub jays called their night song, the final bird call before the sounds of owls, night hawks, and coyotes began.

Susan felt a mushrooming sense of panic, fought it back with the sword of God's word.

"I am your refuge and strength, a very present help in times of trouble." *Yes, Lord. Help us, help us.*

Walking home from church at Ray Yutzy's was a distance of perhaps four miles, perhaps closer to five. Her mind traveled along the road, the houses, the few scattered ones, the endless vista of grassland, tumbleweed, scrubby pines, none of it a safe haven if a man inclined to taking a lone young boy would set his evil snare.

Had they taught him anything about strangers in cars? Susan couldn't remember warning him, but perhaps Isaac had.

Oh, dear God, please help us find him.

Isaac appeared in the half light, his ruddy face pale and drawn.

"I don't know where else we can look."

"Should we call the police?"

"I don't know. We'll be taken as negligent parents."

"So many things could have happened. The West is so . . . so wild."

"Yeah, but most of these scrubby old ranchers and their sons are pretty decent down deep. If . . . if someone would have taken him, he wouldn't be local."

"What should we do?"

"I don't know. Let's wait a while. Maybe he found some wildlife and got carried away again. That's what happened the last time."

Susan took a deep steadying breath. With Isaac beside her, she felt calmer, or at least rational.

"You don't suppose he's at the Busker place, do you? Maybe he just dropped in for a visit and forgot the time."

"I'll call."

He turned and left. When he returned, shaking his head, Susan's spirits dropped, and the panic took root again.

"Isaac, it's getting late. We have to do something."

"You're right. I guess the only thing to do is call the sheriff, and I'm ashamed to do that. Unless they forgot the incident before."

"Go, Isaac. I'd feel better if we had professional help."

He turned on his heel to use the telephone again, when the sound of a truck slowing, turning in the drive, and making its way down the winding lane to the house froze both of them in place, their hearts beating like drums in their chests. Susan couldn't breathe, couldn't think except to plead over and over.

Let it be. Let it be.

"It's old Orvis," Isaac said.

The truck ground to a stop, the engine was cut, and the passenger door flung open. Darlene stepped out, and Susan could see a thin young person, Titus, slide across the seat and down, flinging the door shut.

Both of them were by his side immediately, Susan reaching for him, an arm across his shoulder. He shrugged her off, stepped away, and asked what was going on.

"Titus, we couldn't find you! That's what's going on," she said, doing her best to keep from crying with relief.

Darlene opened her mouth, but Titus broke in.

"Hey! You guys will never guess what happened."

He looked around expectantly, waiting till Orvis hobbled around the truck and joined them.

"I decided to do a little hiking on my way home and sort of lost track of time. When I saw the sun getting low, I turned back to the road and was walking along, minding my own business. You know where the bed in the road out of the plateau is, where it dips down past those rocks? On Hog Road, on out past that yellow trailer with the rusty roof?"

"Go on," Isaac said gruffly.

"I saw a yellowish-brown flash, and right in front of me, a big cat leaped across the road. A mountain lion. I saw him."

"Oh, come on."

Isaac, a disbeliever, taking the wind out of the boy's sails.

"Yeah, it was! I saw him!" Titus yelled.

"Okay, go on."

"Well, then come along these two."

Titus jerked a thumb in Darlene's direction, Orvis shifting his wad of chewing tobacco.

"And Orvis said we could follow him, see where he went. Darlene's a pretty good tracker."

"You can't track a mountain lion," Isaac snorted.

"We did. A few broken twigs, some leaves. The scattered dust. Hey, she knew what she was doing."

"Hope we didn't scare you," said Darlene, though she sounded more excited than apologetic. "We weren't tracking it for that long, but the sun sinks fast when you're caught up in something exciting."

From the house came an anxious call from Sharon, so Susan hurried away to tend to Kayla, her heart and mind filled with gratitude.

Little Kayla was crying, hungry and tired, Sharon's large dark eyes filled with worry.

"You're such a good babysitter, sweetheart. Thank you for watching her for me. Titus is back with Orvis and Darlene. Thank God."

"I'm going to say my prayers really good tonight."

"You do that, sweetie. God is so good to us."

"Titus should be more careful of us."

The door opened, and they all piled into the kitchen, Isaac putting on the coffeepot as the chairs scraped across the floor, everyone talking at once. Susan stayed in the living room, feeding Kayla, listening with renewed appreciation of Darlene. It seemed as if God kept throwing her in Titus's path, and she wondered whether it was meant to be, these two unlikely people. With Orvis Scuttle in his rattling old pickup as the means of bringing them together.

That night, Titus talked more than he had in weeks. His excitement carried him along, forgetting all his ill feelings toward his father or Darlene. He kept up a constant chatter, even led the conversation at times. Susan rocked Kayla to sleep, her body relaxing from the tension of a few hours ago, the thankful feeling almost overwhelming.

She stiffened as she heard Titus ask his father to take off work tomorrow to see if the mountain lion could be found. Isaac hesitated before telling Titus he couldn't do it. There was a schedule to be met before the snow came. Darlene said it was too bad she had to teach school, which she definitely had to do.

"How did you learn to track like that?" Titus asked her.

"Oh, when I was a teenager, my dad was a big hunter. We went to Illinois, Iowa, Texas."

"You're kidding me."

Absolute awe in his voice, Titus began another volley of questions. Isaac's laugh rang out, Orvis's chuckle like gravel from a tin pail.

Darlene recognized an audience when she saw one and was quick to take the stand. She kept up a string of lively stories of wild boar hunting, huge whitetails, following her father and brother on too many excursions to count. That was partly why she was here in Wyoming— she had always loved the wilderness, and teaching school.

"Will you teach me?" Titus asked.

"I will. Although I'm older now, and heavier, so you may not be too thrilled with the outcome. You have your license?"

"No. Dat didn't take me yet."

"I will. I will," Isaac said quickly.

"You better. If the boy has an interest in these things, ain't no good to keep pushin' it off," Orvis said, unafraid of anyone at his age. He'd had a boy of his own, knew the importance of giving them your time, and the way this place looked, he'd given plenty of his time making a pile of money.

CHAPTER 19

THE FOLLOWING SATURDAY THE SKY WAS LOW, GRAY, AND THREAT-ening, the dark clouds piled up like roiling puffs of smoke, the dry air dense with promise of a cold rain, snow, or both.

Before it was fully daylight, Orvis drove his old truck up to the house, his passenger dressed in a camouflage coat, a bright orange bill cap, and the navy pleated skirt beneath. She carried a rifle, an incongruous sight, indeed. But Titus had been up for an hour, banging around upstairs, his excitement running so high he almost fell down the stairs. Susan handed him a breakfast sandwich made of bacon, egg and cheese, plus one for Darlene and one for Orvis, waved from the front door, and stood watching as Titus climbed into the truck.

And where was his father, she thought? Logging on a Saturday to meet the deadline, leaving Susan caught in the crippling net of resentment.

There were two sides to this. One, she should be appreciative of his work ethic, the beautiful house and barn that was now her home, never wanting for anything.

But the price for Titus was high, having to do without a present figure in his life when he needed him most. She was happy he and Darlene had found a way to connect, especially after the rodeo idea failed.

Yes, God worked in wondrous ways for sure.

But to show love and approval, to win over the disapproval, was, in fact, one of the toughest jobs she'd ever undertaken. How often had she viewed her sisters' marriages from her self-designed pedestal, looking down from the lofty heights of singleness. She had never imagined in her wildest dreams she would marry a widower who was too single-minded to accept the needs of his only son, too bullheaded to take advice.

To talk about it was to invite calamity, so she stayed quiet, which meant more and more frequently she was visited by her friend and prickly companion called resentment.

She resented the one she was supposed to love. But how did one go about getting rid of it? By agreeing with his view when your whole being rebelled against it? Oh, it was hard.

To be a quiet, submissive wife, to truly throw your own opinion out the door and allow your husband's to enter in, took discipline, prayer, and constant soul-searching. There had to be a better way.

She needed a friend to confide in. A sister. Someone who knew the ropes so much better than she did. But her sisters were almost two thousand miles away, and she couldn't simply hitch up the horse and impose on anyone, either. Most families did things together on a Saturday, except for her and Isaac. He was always logging.

As she turned back to the kitchen, she felt the first wave of self-pity. Here she was, her house cleaned, washing and ironing done, a long Saturday ahead of her with nothing much to do. She poured another cup of coffee, then decided to call one of her sisters to see if they were available to talk for a while. She should call her mother, but she had such an old-fashioned view of marriage. She supposed years ago it was all very simple, cut and dried. The husband was the head of the house, the wife willing to submit to whatever he decided, even if that meant logging on Saturday and pooh-poohing the idea that Titus needed a caring father. Submit, submit, Give in.

If children misbehaved there were consequences, not much thought given to emotional needs. Everybody just shaped up, grew a backbone, and went on with their life.

She sighed, looked at the clock. She couldn't go out to the telephone in Isaac's office till Sharon woke up, so she got out a few cookbooks, paged through them half-heartedly, wondering if she should try a new pie recipe. Or whoopie pies, maybe.

Or perhaps call a driver and go the long way to town, where she'd spend far too much money and become flustered when Kayla got cranky, which she did, every single time.

Oh, here was a good recipe indeed. Chocolate chip whoopie pies. Hm. She bet Titus would love them.

Not so much Isaac, though. Well, he could just deal.

See, that was the resentment talking right there. Before, it was all about Isaac. She loved to cook and bake for him, loved to watch him inhale the mounds of buttery mashed potatoes and chicken gravy, the golden fried chicken he loved so much.

She'd have to work at this.

She heard light footsteps on the stairway and Sharon came out to the kitchen, her long flannel nightgown with the flounce around the button like an angel, rubbing her eyes sleepily, a smile on her pretty face. Waking up cheerful was one of the most endearing things about Sharon.

"Well, good morning, honey pot," Susan sang out.

Sharon giggled. "I'm not a honey pot."

Susan laughed, thinking how children could so easily take the edge off clouds of worry or discontentment and transform selfish thoughts into more worthwhile ones. Sharon was the easy one, the guileless child who had no memory of her biological mother, who accepted Susan as her own without question. Susan was still aware that her connection with Sharon was different than her connection with Kayla, but at least their relationship was easy and enjoyable.

"Sharon, would you please listen for Kayla while I talk to my sister on the phone? Here, why don't you snuggle into the blanket for a while?"

Yawning, Sharon nodded, and Susan covered her up on the couch and bent to kiss her warm cheek.

"You know where I am."

Rose and Liz did not answer, and Susan was not in the mood to leave a message, so she dialed Kate's number. Three rings and Levi's deep voice answered.

She swallowed, had to clear her throat.

"Hello?"

"Susan! How are you?"

"How did you know it was me?"

"Oh well now, Susan. You know we talked on the phone a lot."

"Yeah, guess we did. Can I talk to Kate?"

"Of course. I'll go get her. So how's Wyoming?"

"Good."

"I'll get Kate."

There he went acting all nice and smooth, almost flirty, as if he had never betrayed her and broken her heart. She'd been so in love, so reluctant to fall hard for him, but after she'd allowed her heart to lead . . .

"Hello?"

"Kate?"

"Susan! Oh, it's good to hear your voice. How are you?"

"Doing good. Really good, except for one huge problem I thought you might be able to help me with."

Kate was instantly all concern and caring, so Susan told her about Isaac's work schedule, his lack of time spent with Titus, explained about Darlene being a helpful presence in his life.

"I mean, think about it, Kate. There he is, the poor boy, tramping around with his fat old teacher instead of his own father. Darlene is a piece of work, you know. She was so unbelievable this morning in her camo and orange bill cap. Kate, it's so bizarre."

Kate let out a sweet peal of laughter, then said she'd love to meet Darlene, she so enjoyed unusual characters.

"But, Susan, I can see where you're coming from. I really can. The secret to a good marriage, though, is learning to understand your husband's view. Perhaps he knows what is best for Titus, even if you can't see it now."

"You can't be serious."

"Oh, I am. Our husbands are smarter than we are. Men are."

"And Dan was, too?"

"Susan, he died. May he rest in peace. I will never talk about him in a negative way. He had his struggles, but he was a Christian, and I know his sins are washed clean. I hope to join him someday, in his heavenly home."

"Well, Kate, no wonder Levi picked you. You're a much better person. I have a real struggle with Isaac and Titus."

"I know you do, and I keep praying for you. You were always more outspoken, more sure of yourself than I am, so it only stands to reason. Just keep trying to understand Isaac."

"But . . . he's wrong. Flat-out wrong. How can you justify not spending time with your children? He eats, sleeps, and breathes logging. He makes money like crazy, and believe me, it's his . . ."

Kate interrupted her. "Susan, don't ever talk bad about your husband. It's not a virtue. We love our husbands and support them no matter what. We are the weaker vessel."

"Oh, for Pete's sake, Kate. Dan dragged you all over creation, beat you, and . . . and ruined your life and you know it. It wasn't right. That's not a marriage. It's a dictatorship. You weren't even allowed to think for yourself. Sorry, Kate, but I disagree."

"I'm sorry, too, Susan. Your life would be so much easier if you could learn to give yourself up."

"But it's Titus," Susan wailed, her voice raising an octave.

"If you give yourself up, Titus will be blessed by a strong union between man and wife."

"Whatever."

"Mom!"

"Oh, Sharon's calling. Kayla's awake. I have to go. Goodbye, Kate."

"Goodbye, Susan."

Susan dressed Kayla, fed and cuddled her, and got breakfast for Sharon, but her thoughts were in a freefall of bewilderment. There was no way she would ever be reduced to Kate's flimsy outlook. Kate had been honest for the first few years, when Dan struggled with depression, telling her he wasn't sure she loved him anymore, but eventually she was worn down by his control of her until she had no backbone, no will, no nothing. And Levi saw his chance at the perfect life, doing whatever he wanted without any resistance from his wife. It wasn't right.

Susan's day seemed to be the length of two as the afternoon dragged on and neither Titus nor Isaac made an appearance. Finally, at five-thirty, Darlene's boots thumped on the porch, followed by Titus, exhausted, filthy dirty, and exhilarated. Susan opened the door to welcome them in, a wide smile on her face, so glad to see another adult with whom she could share her day.

"Hey, how'd that go?" she asked.

Darlene was seated on a porch chair, grunting as she unlaced her boots, her face hidden beneath the bill of her cap. She said they had a grand day, kicked off her boots, and leaned back, shoving her legs out and sighing.

Titus did the same thing, and Susan wondered if it was a hunter's ritual.

"We saw him, Mom!"

"The mountain lion?"

He nodded, his face alight with an inner exhilaration.

Susan thrilled to hear him call her "Mom," but she kept it hidden. He hardly looked like the same sullen, pale, withdrawn young boy, but was alive in a way Susan had never seen. Darlene was clearly beyond exhausted, sitting and staring into space, a smile on her face.

"Yup. He was this long."

Titus jumped up, pointed to the front porch post, stepped back a few paces and pointed.

"A magnificent creature."

Darlene nodded.

"And Mom, we saw so many elk and deer, so many wolf tracks, a rattlesnake ready to strike. I can't tell you. Darlene knows everything about everything in nature."

Darlene nodded, said weakly, "I'm awful hungry."

And Susan forgot about Isaac being late, forgot her conversation with Kate, and opened her home and her heart to Darlene, the angel of mercy in a camouflage coat and a fluorescent orange bill cap.

FROM THAT DAY on, there was a decided change in Titus. He lived all week to spend Saturday with Darlene. Susan asked her if she was okay with this, and she was, doing her schoolwork and house cleaning late in the evening. She had a new goal, and that was helping Titus.

The snow came early but melted away during the unusually warm November, the creeks running high from the runoff, their edges laced with delicate shards of ice, the ground slippery with moisture, the sky a huge dome of blue with a scattering of clouds like clean wool.

Susan sang as she hung laundry on the line in her backyard, appreciating the view of the mountain that never failed to lift her spirits.

Kayla was down for her morning nap, Sharon off to school, and Titus at the ranch, the job he still seemed to enjoy. Isaac didn't like this, said the pay was pathetic and the kid wasn't learning anything worthwhile, but did nothing to change the situation, either. Titus never spoke of his work at the ranch, so Susan thought perhaps Isaac was right, hoped he'd want to go logging with his father when he was older, which would please Isaac, repair the breach in their relationship.

Today there was a quilting at Roy Edna's, and Susan was eager to go, longing for adult conversation, community news. Or was it gossip?

Susan smiled to herself, thinking of the fine line between the two. She loved to quilt, loved the food and general camaraderie of these western women. The cooking was so diverse, the dishes they tried and served so delicious that Susan never lost quite all of the weight she'd gained from having Kayla.

The quilt was set up in the spacious living room, the rows of windows looking out over the open area dotted with grazing cattle and horses. There were four women already seated around the appliqued quilt, a gorgeous spray of flowers caught in a ribbon in the center, with a smattering of butterflies appliqued on adjacent squares.

The women looked up as Susan entered, greeted her warmly, then fussed about Kayla, admiring her dark hair, her sweet dress, and asking about Sharon.

Susan put her thimble on her third finger, threaded a needle, and began to quilt, one hand underneath to feel the tip of the needle, another plying it up and down in tiny stitches, quilting the top and the filling to the bottom fabric, creating a lightweight bed covering in a beautiful design.

For hundreds of years, plain women had been creating objects of beauty, designing and hand-sewing works of art. Susan had been taught by her mother and grandmother, who both quilted "by the yard," or were paid seventy-five cents for every yard of thread that went into a quilt. The owners of the many quilt and fabric shops scattered throughout Lancaster County had women piecing quilts and quilting them, hanging them on great racks for the eager tourists, making a profit on each one. So really, it was quite commercialized, but the quilts were truthfully handmade by Amish women.

Susan remembered winter evenings when her mother sat at her quilt by the window, the DeWalt battery lamp above her, humming as she plied the needle. And Susan would pull up a folding chair and join her. Her stitches were large and slightly crooked at first, her back ached, and she wondered aloud why anyone would do this to make money, bringing a burst of laughter from her mother.

"It grows on you," she said.

And sure enough, that was exactly what happened. She began to enjoy the feel of the thimble, the satisfying emergence of a finished square, an appliqued flower come to life by being raised above the flat surface by the row of tiny stitches around it. Slowly, her stitches became smaller, evened out, her speed improved, and she won her mother's approval.

On winter evenings, after work, Susan enjoyed a quiet closeness with her mother. Sometimes they spoke at length about everyday occurrences, other times they were silent, each one lost in her own thoughts. She could still picture her mother with the flat wooden yardstick, measuring quilt thread, counting softly under her breath, then writing another fifty yards in the small tattered tablet with gray kittens on the cover. And when she received a check in the mail, she would always take it to her small writing desk and double-check the amount before carefully signing her name on the back and putting it in the small middle drawer with a small, satisfied smile. She was an active contributor to the household expenses, and this made her feel very important.

Susan thought about her own life, married to Isaac, with no need of being a contributor. He was generous with the amount he gave her each month, allowing plenty of room for living well. Susan felt a sense of guilt at first, but he liked good food, name brand chambray shirts, and good socks, so before she realized it, the amount going through her checkbook was shocking. He laughed when she told him that.

The quilt was filling up with women of the community, the clean white bowl-shaped coverings with the loose hair combed up over the head, which Susan found to be more attractive now, having changed from the eastern smaller, heart-shaped coverings, with the hair parted in the middle, combed wet, drawn sleekly to the head with rolls of hair on either side, a style she could barely picture for herself now.

A few years in the Wyoming community, and she did not feel a stranger. The women were friendly, outgoing, warm, and refreshingly honest and relaxed. They smiled, laughed out loud, and loved freely, the eastern reserve never present. Susan had been raised to present a proper portrait of goodness.

In Lancaster, everything was "good." If someone fell ill, it was all good, they were getting better. If a person was depressed, or was in financial trouble, or struggled with any other issue, it was still good, they were getting things sorted. Everything had to appear neat and tidy so that the high standard of the community's expectation could be met. Everything was good.

Here, there were more sighs, complaints, honest tears. And similarly, happiness was more robust. There was a loud expulsion of congratulations if a baby was born, if a weight loss goal had been met, if a woman struggled to make a pair of trousers and finally reached her goal. Even her first year of teaching, she had noticed the lack of inhibition at Christmas programs, laughing heartily and applauding wildly, something she appreciated.

And so, with each woman's remote setting in the vast country, get-togethers were frequent, well-attended, and extremely noisy, everyone talking at once and no one really listening.

Darlene was in attendance today, having hired Marlene Troyer to substitute that day, so as usual, she was delighting everyone with tales of her friend Orvis Scuttle.

"What a name," Ida Mae burst out.

"Orvis? It's like that fly-fishing catalog with all the clothes and stuff. You know, they have some nice-looking mittens in there."

"Well, I won't send for anything there. The prices are outrageous."

Murmurs of assent rippled along the quilt.

Susan didn't say this was where she bought all of Isaac's winter shirts, at twice the price she had ever paid for any shirt. But they were durable, soft, and warm, so it was worth the price.

Why did she think of Levi now, in his lemon yellow polo shirt with the Ralph Lauren insignia on the pocket? The sleek pressed black trousers, his perfect manners. It all seemed so lame. So ridiculous. She realized she wanted her huge logger with diesel fuel plastered to his trousers, the front of his shirts worn and stained from hefting heavy branches.

She felt a wave of love, realized love was still possible in spite of faults. Titus was a jolt of reality, but so be it.

"So when I got there the first day, you cannot imagine the mess in that man's house. I don't think his wife was much of a housekeeper, but let me tell you, it was all downhill after she passed away."

"I think a lot of these ranch women spend most of their time outdoors."

"They don't care that much about their house."

"No, but this was gross. The man didn't own a garbage bag, so I started throwing stuff in cardboard boxes. He got mad, but I stood my ground and told him if he wants me to cook for him, this goes with it."

"Doesn't he ever, like, want you?"

"What do you mean? Of course not, he's way past that."

"Are you sure?"

"Ach, Frieda, who would want me? As big as a house and a face like a burnt pancake."

Oh my, how they laughed, followed by many reassurances. Of course she wasn't fat or homely looking. She was a presentable middle-aged woman who was blessed with quite a few worthy talents indeed.

Susan spoke up.

"She hunts, too. Was raised on out of state excursions with her father. Now she takes Titus on Saturdays, and he lives for those days."

Titus. The one prickly subject no one wanted to talk about.

Except Darlene, who regaled them with plenty of action-packed scenes of the past Saturday, laughing uproariously about coming home, falling into the recliner with every bone and muscle in her body on fire.

"But I do it for him. He needs someone."

Susan nodded. All eyes were on her.

Instantly, she resorted to the reserve she was accustomed to from back East. No one needed to know. Their home was a haven of perfection. She kept her face to the quilt, her fingers flying, a wall erected by the bonds of her upbringing.

"Susan, I don't want to talk about this if it hurts your feelings," Darlene said, always forthright, straight to the point.

"No no, it's okay."

But was it, really? This was new, unaccustomed, the trouble aired and explored. Is that what was expected of her?

She mumbled her assent uncomfortably.

"We don't need to talk about Titus if you'd rather not," Darlene said.

Susan felt the beginning of a lump in her throat.

"Well, we could probably use all the help we can get."

Sympathetic murmurs all around, a ripple of kindness. A hand on her arm, a brace of caring.

Susan said very quietly, "It's just tough being a stepmother at times. He wanted me to marry his father. It's just after we were married that he turned against me."

Her voice was choked, but she went on, shakily. She wasn't used to sharing anything pertaining to her shattered dreams, or even displaying the slightest crack in the glossy sheen of perfection.

And she was brilliantly surprised by the chorus of voices starting up, the telling of experiences pertaining to stepmotherhood. An aunt, a sister, a friend. Someone who had walked nonchalantly into a marriage with children. The heartache and anxiety, doing their level best to win the children over, to replace the mother who had their hearts forever. How many women had been sent to plain facilities named "Haven of Rest," or "Green Pastures," or "Woodland Retreat"? They were crushed by an unbearable burden, slowly watching the husband turn to the children, protecting, supporting them out of pity, the mother dead, buried in the cold graveyard, the sound of the sod hitting the top of the wooden coffin creating a deep, infected scar they could never quite heal. There were exceptions, of course, when everyone appreciated everyone else, but that was rare.

Darlene listened, her lips pursed, thought herself fortunate to have the smarts to stay single. Selfish perhaps, but smart. And here God had given her this strange boy, laid those large brown eyes on her conscience, and there wasn't much to do for it but be led by the Holy Spirit. At least as long as she could decipher the difference between the Spirit and her own will, because she dearly loved to go hunting with him.

"Well," Abe's wife Louise went on, "Alma simply had a nervous breakdown, yelled and screamed and cried till they took her to a doctor and he prescribed a sedative. From there she went to Woodland Rest, and I'm telling you, she got help, once that husband of hers got it through his thick skull that he needs to support his wife and help discipline those kids."

"But you can't blame him. My word."

This from Barb Troyer, a loyal wife to Harvey. No one had ever heard her speak a disparaging word against him, no matter how loud or how conceited he became.

"Imagine how he must pity those precious children, like little orphans without their mother."

Heads nodded, a general agreement all around.

"But can you imagine loving someone else's children the way we love our own?"

"Oh, absolutely not a task for everyone."

Susan gave a small laugh.

"You definitely walk in completely unaware. Titus turned to resentment so fast it's shocking. He literally can't stand me or his father."

"But he was troubled long before this, Susan."

"I know. I'm aware of it, being his teacher."

"So don't be too hard on yourself."

"He's a child who needs a goal," said Darlene. "He needs to be guided to a goal that will hold his interest. I tried organizing that rodeo and didn't get anywhere at all. Then, and mind you, God placed that mountain lion straight in our path, and I saw exactly what his passion was. It's wildlife, the wilderness, hunting. I'm just curious how he'll react to fishing in the spring."

She gave a wry laugh. "At least fishing isn't as hard on these old bones. Honest, the first day hunting was very tiring, shall we say?"

"Oh, but Darlene. What a sacrifice. You'll be blessed in return."

Someone dared ask about Isaac.

Susan said he was logging six days a week, more than twelve hours a day, tried to explain the distance, the need for speed with winter coming on. When she was met with silence, she looked around, frightened.

"No job should take the place of a child's welfare."

"But I can't tell him that. He says they weren't raised that way. No one needs coddling. He said that. Says Titus needs to grow up and accept life for what it is."

She could not believe she was saying these things. It was fraught with social mistakes, the laying bare of a truth she should have hidden away.

"He's partly right," Abe Louise said, pressing down on the quilt top to create an incline for the thread to roll toward her.

"Not entirely," Darlene disagreed. "Any child who has lost their mother needs a father's love in double portion. Not all fathers are capable of that, so to me, it seems as if Isaac didn't experience that in his own life, so doesn't know how to reach out."

"Or doesn't want to."

Susan winced.

She didn't want anyone demeaning her husband. She loved him.

"Isaac is a driven man. He's extremely ambitious, loves his job and lives to go to the woods in all kinds of weather. He's tough as nails, thrives on danger and adventure."

"Why doesn't he take Titus with him?"

"Titus has no interest in logging."

"My word. Well, in my day and age, it didn't matter if you had an interest of not, you did what your parents told you to do."

"Amen."

"Absolutely."

And so the day passed, with good food, good companionship, the melding of different views, spiced with generosity of spirit, empathy, and caring.

Susan came away feeling the warmth of a great support system, a sense of genuine belonging two thousand miles away from her family.

CHAPTER 20

THE COLD SPREAD ITS FROSTY HANDS OVER EVERY PLAIN, ROCK, ravine, and cliff and turned the air into freezing gusts of snow-laden gales, the pale sun between weak clouds as ineffectual as a faraway lantern.

Susan shivered on her way to the barn, scuttled in from the clothesline shaking circulation back into her hands, and bundled Sharon into layers of sweaters and coats, woolen scarves, and mittens before sending her off to school. The wind tore at her skirts as she stood by the mailbox waiting for the school van, but Sharon hopped and bounced, staying warm with sheer excitement about another day at school.

Susan viewed the cold landscape, the beauty of gray and brown and yellow, dead weeds like uncombed, thinning hair around the perimeter of the board fence. Ice hung on the north side of rocks like fine lace, the lodgepole pines quivered and creaked in the cold, the distant Bighorns rising over the plains like a sentinel on guard, but unable to stop the ever-increasing power of northern blasts of frigid air.

She ran into the house, slammed the door behind her, and shivered. She shook the scarf off her head and shrugged out of her coat before noticing Titus hunched over a bowl of Cinnamon Life cereal, his favorite.

"Don't you want eggs and bacon, Titus?"

"No."

"So what are your plans for the day?"

"I dunno. Ron doesn't need me. Too cold."

"I see."

Susan felt ill at ease, so she busied herself immediately, afraid of saying or doing the wrong thing. She'd been scorned so many times, left to wonder if she would ever be able to understand how to get him to even mildly approve of her. It was a constant tiptoeing, figuring out how to navigate the complicated maze of his feelings, often leaving her drained and weary. She wished he'd notice Kayla, wished he'd lean to hold her, play with her the way Sharon did.

Titus lifted his cereal bowl, drank the milk, then poured himself a glass of grape juice. When his back was turned, Susan noticed how tall he was, how his thin shoulders were widening, his sleeves becoming snug. A form of pride tugged at her heart, thinking what a good looking boy he might turn out to be with that blond hair and brown eyes. If only he could find it in his heart to be rid of his anger.

Without warning, he said, "Darlene said we can go out on Saturday if it doesn't snow. She said wildlife will be moving, the elk are in rut. Can you imagine?"

For a brief second, he met her eyes. His danced, then slid away.

"Did your father get you your license?"

"We're going tonight."

"Oh, that's good. What about Darlene?"

"She's going along."

He blinked, then stared at her. Finally, he blurted out, "You want to come?"

"Where are you going?"

"That gun shop on Crazy Woman Creek."

"I'll pass. I don't want to take Kayla out in the cold."

"Mm."

He donned his coat and hat and was out the door. Susan stood by the window above the sink and watched him go, feeling proud to have had a decent conversation. He'd asked her to go, and that was something. Tiny steps, but in the right direction. She stood a while longer and prayed for her stepson with a vague hopefulness she hadn't felt in ages.

ISAAC CAME HOME earlier than usual, grumpy with the cold, his nose and cheeks wind-burned and sore, his eyes swollen, stretching his cold fingers to restore flexibility. He took a long hot shower and was still cold when he came out. He drank a mug of hot tea and glowered.

Susan finished preparing supper, then served up the pot roast and vegetables, a dish of coleslaw, and one of pickled red beet eggs.

The food seemed to brighten his outlook, and he praised her cooking, said it was wonderful to come home to a beautiful wife. Susan became flustered and shy and could not think of a witty comeback or a suitable answer. He said his day had been miserable, the cold creating one problem after another until he was ready to scream.

"Chainsaws aren't at their best in ten degrees. Nothing is, including me. I get so frustrated when nothing goes right."

Titus snorted, a loud derisive sound of total disrespect.

"Yeah, no doubt," he sneered.

Susan stiffened, waited for the battle to begin. Much to her surprise, Isaac spoke kindly and apologized for being a man with a quick temper.

He ruffled Titus's hair. Titus ducked, grimaced, looked as disgusted as possible, but Susan hoped that deep down he appreciated the affection.

"Why don't you go up with me one of these days, see what it's like?" Isaac asked, as he plied a dinner roll around his plate, sopping up gravy before popping the whole thing in his mouth. Susan looked away, thinking how some things weren't able to be fixed, and his table manners were one of them. It wasn't for lack of trying, but after a while, when she realized he ate with the same frenzy he did everything else, it was hopeless. The amount of food, the size of his bites, were phenomenal, that was all there was to it. Two hundred eighty pounds of muscle, although she sometimes noticed his stomach becoming more rounded as time went on.

"I'm not going out in this weather."

"You can sit in the loader. Operate it. It's enclosed, heated."

"I know that."

"Then why don't you?"

"Lay off, Dad. I have a job."

"So that's what you want to do with your life? Be a rancher who makes peanuts with a bunch of dried-up cows?"

Oh come on, Susan thought.

"Some people don't think of their lives in terms of money," Titus shot back.

Isaac lifted both hands, palms out.

"Okay, okay. Just saying."

Susan sighed with relief, mentioned the fact that the wood box needed replenishing.

Isaac looked at her, his eyes half closed.

"Nap first, okay?"

"Titus and Sharon can work at it," Susan agreed.

"Sure. I'll start a fire in the fireplace later. S'mores?"

Even Titus grinned, nodded, told Sharon he'd beat her to the woodshed, with Sharon scrambling off her chair and racing for the back door.

It was rare moments like this when everyone seemed so normal, the family ties so genuine, that Susan was happy with the decision she'd made, looked forward to the future with hope. Perhaps being a stepmother was doable if you merely took a day at a time, did your best, and didn't knock yourself over the head when things went wrong, which they would, inevitably. She sang as she washed dishes, shivered when the door was left open, took Kayla from her highchair into the living room on a blanket, away from the rush of cold air.

Pieces of wood banged into the wood box and Sharon squealed as she raced Titus to the door. Susan stopped at the recliner and planted a kiss on Isaac's nose, which didn't wake him at all. What did wake him was an itch behind his knee, and he lifted one leg and grabbed the fabric of his trousers, grimacing. He thumped the footrest of the recliner down, leaned forward, and scratched for all he was worth.

He sighed, leaned back, belched comfortably.

"I still have to do chores," he groaned.

"You keep Kayla, I'll go," Susan said. "I need to get out of the house."

So out into the frosted night she went, walking the distance to the barn, the battery lantern casting weird shadows on the dark lawn and driveway. The stars were so close.

She loved that about Wyoming. There were no lights, no constant movement of traffic, just the plains, the silhouette of the towering Bighorns, and the enormous sky with millions of cold little stars winking down on one lone human, as small and insignificant as the head of a pin.

Susan lifted her face, watched the stars winking, sparkling diamonds on a velvet cloth. What absolute beauty. How magnificent the night sky, the crescent moon as crystal clear as glass. So perfect.

She could smell the acrid odor of horse manure, the sweet scent of horse feed, the dried grass of the haymow as she pushed the door open, swung the lantern on the shelf. She was welcomed by soft nickering, the stamping of impatient hooves as she made her way to the feed bin.

One scoop for Rex, another for Goldie, and on down the aisle till she came to good old dependable Roger, the Standardbred driving horse.

She jumped when the door was flung open and Titus burst through, then turned his back to wait on Sharon. Laughing, she tumbled inside, and Titus said, "Beat you!"

"You're bigger!"

They helped feed hay, checked the cow's water level, then Titus grabbed the broom and began to sweep.

"Good job!" Sharon sang out. Susan grinned.

"Okay guys, race you to the house," she shouted.

"One, two, three, go!"

And they were off. Susan was careful to allow Sharon a small lead. Titus was off like a rabbit and arrived at the laundry room door long before they did, but Sharon was pleased to be ahead of her mother.

"Wow, but you are a fast runner, Sharon," she panted.

"I know. Remember? I won the race for first grade at the school picnic."

"You did. That was a wonderful race, wasn't it?"

Isaac was on the recliner, Kayla in the crook of his arm, both relaxed and peaceful. Susan started a fire in the fireplace with a few crumpled newspapers and some good kindling, the small flames leaping to catch the dry pine, crackling cozily.

Titus brought the marshmallows and the long tined forks while Susan spread a thick layer of peanut butter on Ritz crackers. Sharon happily broke sections of chocolate off a Hershey's chocolate bar, laying them carefully on top of the peanut butter before carrying a plateful to Titus.

"I want mine burnt, Titus," Isaac said sleepily.

"Make your own," he said, without turning his back.

"Come on, Titus. Your old Dad's tired."

"Not my fault."

Susan caught Isaac's eye. Isaac gave her a wink, pointed a finger at Titus.

Could it be, she thought, she was creating a mountain out of a molehill? Blowing this Titus thing completely out of proportion?

Perhaps Isaac had a certain amount of wisdom about adolescent boys she did not. Maybe just going with it, they'd grow out of it. Or was Darlene really making a difference? The fact that he had every Saturday to look forward to might be making the difference. Either way, she'd enjoy it while it lasted.

Titus handed his father a blackened marshmallow, which was met with a questioning look.

"Now how am I supposed to make a decent s'more with this baby Kayla in my lap?" he asked.

"I'll make you one," Sharon lisped, her voice as light and sweet as a little fairy.

Isaac thanked her so kindly, she promptly made another, and Susan quit counting after seven of them.

"Dad, you can't have any more," she said seriously. "I'm tired of making them."

"I had enough right now," Isaac said.

"Well, good."

And Susan cuddled into the soft throw, felt the heat of the fireplace, smelled the burnt marshmallow, chocolate, and peanut butter, and was contented, thankful for her family especially.

LIFE WENT ON, the winter spent keeping the house warm, watching the snow, going to church every two weeks, having friends over for coffee, and learning to grasp the intricacies of marriage and being a mother to Isaac's children. She had good days and days she could hardly believe she had been so dumb marrying Isaac, who came with two children.

Titus had taken to staying in his room, lifting weights. He was obsessed with his lack of muscles, watched his father's physique before putting a hand to his own skinny arm. And by the time his fifteenth birthday came around, his shirts were snug across the shoulders, his voice took on a gravelly tone, and a whisper of facial hair marched across his upper lip.

He still hunted with Darlene, a fast friendship opening like a flower, but something he never talked about. It was embarrassing going to the foothills and mountain ranges with her, but she surely knew what she was talking about. She owned a pair of binoculars she'd paid so much money for she wouldn't tell him the amount.

Orvis Scuttle was their driver, taking them all over Wyoming, and sometimes into bordering states, setting up camp and arranging everything to his liking—camp stove, bedding, everything.

When they stayed for a few days, he slept in the truck, wearing his hat and boots, saying it wasn't proper to sleep in the tent with a lady. The lady in question snorted and asked why not, she sure wasn't going to be trying anything inappropriate.

And Orvis laughed, said no, after his wife passed, he had no longing for another one. He wanted to keep her alive in his heart, and if there was a Heaven, he hoped to get there somehow.

As for Titus, Darlene became something of a mother figure, even more than Susan was. He didn't have to see his father all googly-eyed and mushy with Darlene, the thing that rankled most.

Darlene knew just about everything there was to know about wildlife. She hired a substitute so frequently, the school board had to pay her a visit, asking her to refrain from all the hunting. But Darlene told them she was on a mission, saving Titus from who knows what all, and showing Orvis Scuttle the way to heaven. She didn't even think she might not be capable, that the end result might not be what she planned, just disregarded the school board's admonition and went on doing what she had been. Besides, Abe Mast's Trisha was perfectly capable, a school teacher if she ever saw one.

When Kayla was two and a half years old, another baby was born on a windy November night. They named him Thayer James. He was the ugliest baby Titus had ever seen, so red it was alarming, and not a hair on his head. His eyes were swollen shut, his nose smashed flat against his face, and he was the size of a colt. They said he weighed ten pounds plus some ounces.

The whole deal turned him off so badly he couldn't even look at Susan, so pale and exhausted. She looked as if she could easily burst into tears, which she probably would after all the fuss died away. Titus decided Thayer would probably grow up to look like his father, be a logger, and Titus would always be the family's disappointment, still working for Ron Busker on his unkempt ranch. So he kept to himself, didn't have much to do with anyone, and wished his father would never have married Susan if they were going to fill up this house with a new baby every two years.

Darlene came to visit, said he was a real woodchopper if she ever saw one, cuddled him and burped him, acted as if he was the cutest baby she'd ever seen. Said he looked like Isaac.

His father was nothing to look at, but this baby sure wasn't either, Titus thought, wishing Darlene wouldn't sit there with her ridiculous cooing. She never had a baby of her own, he supposed, so she had to hold the available ones.

So now he was fifteen years old, with three siblings, not much of a relationship with his father, an okay one with his stepmother, a friend named Darlene, and one named Orvis. He really liked Ron and Winnie Busker, enjoyed his job, but as he grew past the gangly stage, all thin arms and legs, hands and feet too big for the rest of him, he felt hemmed in, like there must be more to life than what he'd experienced so far. He knew how to ride, how to rope, could drive a tractor and a skidloader, repair barns and fences, but there was something missing, some ingredient he couldn't name.

ISAAC SAT AT the supper table, going on in detail about his day, how they slid logs around in the snow, the angle of the slopes, the danger with the skidder, the crack of frozen logs, and Titus found himself drawn in, listening in spite of himself.

"I'm telling you, it's a rush."

Susan laid a hand on his arm.

"Isaac, I still need my husband. I hope you think of us before you do something too dangerous."

"Hey, somebody has to do it. Our reputation is on the line. We go places with a skidder where no one else will. That's why I get paid double what some of the others do. It's crazy."

Titus scooped more cream gravy on his mashed potatoes, kept his eyes on the plate.

"And I'll tell you another thing, these poor elk are in for a hard time. They're predicting the worst weather in years. The winter will be brutal. So I gotta keep going as long as I can."

"Isaac, we don't need the money. Why don't you simply stay home for a few months."

"I can't do that."

Thayer began screaming from the living room. Sharon slid off her chair and raced to insert his pacifier. Kayla thumped her spoon on the tray of her highchair, flinging noodles into the air.

"Kayla, no," Susan said softly.

Titus went to his room, thought how peaceful everything had been before Thayer was born. He was a grouch. Yelled all the time about nothing. And that Kayla got away with everything.

Before he knew it, he'd be sixteen years old, expected to go to the youth's gatherings, the circle of young men and women he would have to hang out with. Born and raised Amish, it was expected of him, a thought he did not relish. He just wasn't into silly, stupid games, sitting along a table singing German hymns, hitching up your horse and driving home in the dark. He'd much rather go hunting with Darlene. Now there was an interesting person. He couldn't believe the amount of things she'd taught him about stalking wildlife, about getting those binoculars on deer. "Glassing them," she called it. She was downright cool. You just had to get past the size of her, and that loud voice.

And now there was the program at school coming up, and he'd promised her he'd go. He didn't look forward to being in the schoolhouse, the place packed like a can of sardines. That place didn't hold very many good memories for him. The other students had been mean to him, the teachers were always tattling about him to the school board. The other boys made fun of him all the time.

But he'd do it for Darlene. She was the only true person who was always the same. Loud, cheerful, wise, ready to go on any adventure you could imagine. She was the only one who could get through to him about the dangers of smoking, and he had quit the cigarettes. She was strong, capable of tracking an animal for miles without tiring, and he was always huffing and puffing behind her, stopping for a smoke when he began to cough. That was ridiculous, she'd told him, and never quit berating him, giving him frightening literature, even going so far as taking him to Orvis Scuttle's house to watch a video of some gross old woman who lost her throat and part of her mouth to cancer from cigarettes.

He was glad for Darlene's friendship. So he guessed he better go to the stupid program. It would please his father and Susan, so he might crawl into their good graces for a while as well.

CHAPTER 21

THE SNOW BEGAN IN EARNEST A FEW HOURS BEFORE IT WAS TIME TO leave. Titus was upstairs, buttoning the red shirt Susan asked him to wear, glowering at his image in the mirror. He finished the buttons, then pulled on his trousers, ran a hand through his hair. He was as tall as Susan, maybe taller. His shoulders were wider, his arms no longer tan sticks.

The thing was, he always felt like an outsider. He never made friends in school, never connected with any of the other kids. There was Kevin, but he stuck with Fremont, the two tighter than burrs. They had always been friendly, but they never allowed him into their inner circle.

He allowed it all to run off his back and focused on causing mischief, which he found amusing.

But now he was approaching his sixteenth year and had no friends to speak of. Well yeah, Ron and Winnie, Darlene and Orvis, but they weren't going to help him through *rumschpringa*. He was expected to attend all the required places, show up and be a decent young man, do his parents proud. Frankly, it sounded miserable and a little scary.

All this was on his mind as he stood by the window, drew back the curtain, and watched the beauty of the driven snow. He loved the outdoors, the vast stretch of grassland, pine forests, and hovering mountains, knew every ravine and rock glade for miles around. If he was left to his own devices he would never, ever show up to any social function. People drove him crazy with their endless displays of interest and good humor, shaking hands and grinning like hyenas, slapping each other's backs in a burst of emotion. Surely, they weren't that glad to see each other.

At the school, kids would be running underfoot, babies yelling. He didn't know how his parents expected Thayer to endure the program given that he never shut up at home.

He watched the snow a while longer, then turned and went down the stairs, just as Susan was pulling on her black bonnet.

"Are you riding with us?"

She looked flushed, excited to be taking Thayer out. He said he'd ride his horse, the buggy was full enough. She nodded, hurried out the door to the waiting horse and carriage.

It was cold. The horse was eager to go, but the snow was like a thousand pinpricks to his face. He yanked his stocking cap even farther over his forehead and pulled back on the reins steadily, in spite of his horse prancing and lifting his head to loosen the pressure on the bit. By the time he reached the schoolhouse, he was chilled to the core, his gloved hands like icicles.

A row of carriages were lined up along the fence, the horses blanketed against the snow, their heads lowered, resting in a state of drowsiness after a run in the cold. A few bicycles leaned against the fence.

A group of boys were huddled on the steps, hands in their pockets. When they heard hoofbeats, they turned, acknowledged his presence with a knowing look, before resuming the conversation.

He tied his horse on the lee side of the schoolhouse, adjusted his stocking cap, and walked to the entrance to find the steps empty. Hm. They could have waited till he was ready to go in, but no, they didn't care. Nothing new. He opened the door and went in by himself, stood close to the group, nodded when he met their curious gaze.

Darlene, flushed and large in her burgundy dress, caught sight of him, raised her eyebrows and smiled widely, threw up a hand.

He gave her the briefest smile possible.

Everywhere, the classroom was a riot of color. Candy canes and green holly tied with a red ribbon on the windows, Christmas trees with brilliant red, green, and silver ornaments attached on the wall, cutouts of angels and wreaths. Many of the women wore green or a dark shade of red, the little girls in pink or mint green. Presents were piled on a table along the wall with urns of coffee, trays of cookies, cupcakes, homemade candy, and other snacks.

Darlene tapped a bell and all the pupils moved behind the curtain. She drew herself up to her full height as the classroom quieted. She faced the audience and welcomed everyone to the Christmas program, saying the children had worked very hard and she hoped they would all appreciate their effort, then thanked them for the ongoing love and support. She extended an arm toward the young girl seated by the wall.

"My thanks to Trisha Mast. Without her this program could not be possible."

Titus knew who she was, had gone to school with her, but thought she didn't look much like the girl he knew. She was blushing, a small smile on her face, clearly uncomfortable being noticed. Her face was round and smooth in the lamplight, and he remembered her large, dark eyes. She must have done a lot for Darlene, being acknowledged like that.

He was surprised to hear a rousing chorus of "Joy to the World" from behind the curtain before it was drawn aside to reveal the stage being filled with children of all shapes and sizes, from ages thirteen to six, dressed in Christmas colors, their faces alive with pleasure, finally able to recite the secrets they'd kept from their parents since Thanksgiving.

Titus found himself drawn into an entertaining repertoire of songs, stories, poetry, and plays the likes of which he had never seen. The children sang in harmony, spoke in clear, slow tones so the audience had no trouble grasping every word. Plays were done with such precision, lines spoken with the correct expression, humorous, and finally, simply so funny even Titus was won over.

They had never seen a finer program and the applause loud and long, everyone filled to the brim with the Christmas spirit.

They'd laughed, they'd wept, and best of all, they'd been conveyed by the children to a place where Christmas held the real meaning of Christ's wonderful birth, but also the humor of human folly. Darlene basked in the praise, her charming lack of humility refreshing.

Trisha stood, came to the back of the classroom to talk to her girl-friends, and Titus couldn't breathe. He honestly thought he had an obstruction in his windpipe, or a mild case of heart palpitation. He had gotten a tooth filled last week; perhaps the Novocain had done something to his breathing apparatus.

She walked with an easy grace, the way he imagined a ballerina would. Now where had that word come from? He felt his face go fiery red with that silly word confronting him. The insanity of it. She looked at him. She said, "Excuse me," and pushed past. He had a whiff of wild-flowers on a sunlit slope on the foothills of the Bighorn Mountains. His knees went weak. He didn't think he would ever get his breath back.

He filled a paper plate with food, talked to Kevin and Fremont and Harry, but didn't know what he said or how they answered. He had to keep track of where Trish was and what she was saying and whether she was looking his way.

She never was.

He couldn't leave without saying something to her. He couldn't think of anything he would say, but he had to say goodbye. Or hello. Or thank you for being here. No, he'd thank her for the good program.

Isaac came to tell him they were leaving, with the snow coming down so thick he might want to tie his horse to the buggy and ride along home. Titus shook his head. He couldn't leave now. He might miss an opportunity to speak with her.

"I'll be home," he said.

Isaac told Susan he felt good about Titus being with friends from school, that he'd learn to fit in if they gave him time.

Susan smiled, said yes, she'd noticed, and was so overcome with the Christmas joy that she squeezed his arm and smiled up at him. When they sat together in a buggy, there was barely room for her, and now, holding Thayer, she felt pinched, flattened. But the snow was so beautiful, the scenery so breathtaking, she thought it was a small price to pay, being able to enjoy this wonderland.

She began to hum. Isaac caught the tune, belted out the words, and Sharon giggled from the back seat, Kayla singing out of tune but joining in.

"Darlene puts on quite a show," she said after a while.

"That's her. She loves it."

"But I think Trisha Mast had a lot to do with it."

"She's really pretty."

"Really."

And so they drove home, happily unaware of poor Titus being pummeled by the onslaught of infatuation. Darlene noticed him lingering on the porch, opened the door, and asked if he'd help take down the curtains. He said he had to go on home, bolted, and rode his horse in a dead gallop on slippery roads, then arrived at the barn and had to restrain himself from turning around and going straight back to help. The last image was her reaching up to pull out the straight pins, her pose like a model. She looked like one.

He sighed as he slung the saddle on a rack and brought the curry comb down over the horse's flanks. Well, if he never saw her again, he'd probably be better off. She had nearly killed him just by being so beautiful. Besides, he wasn't nearly good enough for her. Not even close.

And so began the exquisite misery of being immensely attracted to a young girl, creating a whole new level of chaos in the household. For one, there was no work at the ranch after two feet of snow swept down off the mountains, putting a stop to the logging, the ranch work, all moving traffic except four-wheelers and snowmobiles, of which they had none. They cleaned the barn, washed windows, installed a heater in the tack room, drove each other straight up the wall, one or both clomping to the house airing a whole list of atrocities one had committed against the other, till Susan was ready to tear her hair out. And she was cooped up in the house with the colicky Thayer, all fourteen pounds of him.

She sat beside the three large windows, her recliner steadily rocking, gazing unseeing across the expanse of drifted snow. The wind clawed at the house and chewed at the eaves and downspouts with vicious fangs, hurled frozen snow across the level, treeless area in great white billows. The corners of the house were cold and chills raced up and down her spine as she went about her day's work, and now, she'd wrapped the irritable Thayer in a fleece blanket, covered herself in a heavy throw, and was finally warm through and through. She'd put a few heavy chunks of wood on the fire, adjusted the grate, and was feeling drowsy after a few minutes of back and forth motion . . .

Oh, for a good night's rest. Kayla had developed a cough, which was worrisome enough, without having to deal with Thayer's outraged yells from the crib. She felt drained, assaulted by the unbelievable force of the wind, the constant rigors of her household chores, and the demands of two little ones. Sharon, bless her heart, skipped home from school in a ray of sunshine, her bright face and sunny disposition a genuine spirit lifter. She always took Thayer, rocked and fussed and cuddled him like a second mother, called him *Boolly* (little boy).

Kayla toddled into the living room, talking to her dolls, just as Susan entered a blissful cloud of sleep.

"Mom!"

"Yes, Kayla?"

"Don't sleep, okay. Patty needs a cookie."

"You can get her one. In the pantry on the bottom shelf."

That was the reason cookies were kept on the bottom shelf, she thought. Toddler self-help.

"Mom!"

"What?"

"I can't get this."

Sighing, Sharon lifted the cozy throw, heaved herself and Thayer from the recliner, tiptoed across the living room floor to lay him carefully in the crib. He squirmed, made a face, then began his grimacing and squeaking in earnest.

Oh man, she thought, but hurried out to help Kayla remove the lid from the Tupperware container as the howls increased from the bedroom. Just then Isaac came through the laundry room door, already talking in his booming voice like a bullhorn, only gravelly, rough.

"I can't get that heater going. One more minute and I'm going to rip it out of the wall and throw it in the trash. Titus thinks he knows what it is, and he doesn't know a thing. Kayla, give Dat a cookie."

"See, Isaac? That's your whole problem with that boy. If you'd give him a chance instead of always thinking you know best. I'm about up to here with both of you."

"You go up and install it then."

Susan gave him no answer, but marched around the kitchen with an injured expression, hoping he would notice and feel awful for having said that.

"Why don't you get that baby?" Isaac demanded.

"That baby, whose name is Thayer, is your baby, too," she shot back.

One eyebrow went up, the rest of the cookie was stuffed into his mouth, and he walked stiff-legged into the bedroom.

Now he's mad, she thought, but she was too exhausted to care. She winced as a tree branch was hurled on the porch roof.

"What was that?" Isaac asked, holding Thayer clumsily, as if he was afraid of him.

"A branch."

"You sure?"

"Of course not. Go outside and see for yourself."

And so the wind blew, Thayer howled, the day dragged on, and no one was in the mood to see the arrival of Darlene on the largest of four-wheelers they had ever seen, holding on to a youth no older than twelve or thirteen years of age.

"Wheee!" she shouted as they tailspun to a stop.

Titus came from the barn, a wide grin on his face.

"Titus, this is Jared. Orvis Scuttle's grandson. Great grandson."

The wind tore most of her words away, but Titus got the meaning.

Susan stepped out on the porch, told them to come in and warm up.

The grandson was shy, spoke little, aware of the puddles beneath his boots, but Darlene was in fine spirits, slugging coffee, eating everything Susan set before her, saying Titus had to go for a spin.

"Exhilarating, is what it is," she yelled, thumping her coffee mug on the tabletop, her foot hitting it from beneath.

"It's not even Amish."

Isaac grinned, caught Susan's eye, and gave her a broad wink.

"What I can't understand is how you got through all the blowing snow, the drifts. They're almost six feet high."

"Oh, we hardly were able. Sometimes we had to stop and go around. It's the biggest thrill, though. Right, Jared?"

Jared nodded, grinning.

So the rest of the day was taken up with the four-wheeled entertainment. Thayer fell asleep, finally, and Susan reheated ham and bean soup for supper, too exhausted to cook anything new. Darlene headed home in a roar of engine exhaust and spitting snow, with the family watching from inside, the four-wheeler turning to a small black dot amid clouds of snow.

The laughter began as a chuckle from Isaac, a snort from Susan, then an all-out fit of loud laughing from Titus, an explosion of giggles from Sharon, until the whole family was slapping knees and wiping tears.

"Whoo," Isaac said, still chuckling to himself.

"She is one of a kind, believe me."

Titus could not keep from saying what a good sport she was, though, and how he admired that in her. Never too cold, too miserable, a hill too steep to climb, or anything like that.

"You two are unlikely friends," Isaac said.

"Just don't go around talking about it."

Isaac and Susan did talk about just that before retiring for the night, the small changes Titus was making with the family. He was no longer as sullen and didn't display the outbursts of anger at the slightest provocation.

"He's growing up. Deciding for himself what works and what doesn't."

"It could be. But I think Darlene gets some of the credit. She spent almost every Saturday with him for I don't know how long."

"And you're saying it should have been me."

"You said it. I didn't."

And because Susan was so exhausted, so dreadfully weary with the succession of near sleepless nights with Thayer, she knew the conversation would take on an argumentative tone, and she didn't have the heart for it. Either way, she'd end up yelling or crying, so she showered and fell asleep the minute her head hit the pillow.

UPSTAIRS, TITUS STILL lamented the fact he'd taken off like a scared rabbit, without helping Darlene at the school. Mercifully, she'd said nothing about it, and he deeply admired her for that. She was a regular trooper. A buddy. Who would have guessed? You never knew what was around the next curve.

He'd gone to school with Trisha Mast for years. She had never been anything special, never stood out from anyone else, so it was hard to figure out why she'd literally taken his breath away. Boy, it was embarrassing. He was lucky no one had seen it, and he certainly planned on keeping it that way. He was much too young to be thinking of girls.

But he put his hands around his head and thought of Trisha anyway. He wondered about that program, which parts she'd done and which were Darlene's. It had been very good, for a simple Amish school, the way the children had done their parts just right.

He wanted to tell Trisha, but he couldn't imagine facing her and actually getting the right words out.

IN JANUARY, WHEN the snow was packed down with a layer of freezing rain on top, Susan told Titus that Darryl Stutzman had left a message saying there was a sledding party at their house for the fourteen- and fifteen-year-olds. Titus tried to remain perfectly cool about it, and would have carried it off if he wouldn't have blurted out the fact that he didn't have a decent pair of boots, or a beanie, and Susan nodded knowingly, smiled broadly, and told him he was getting to the age where these things mattered.

He denied it, saying he never got anything new. And she said "mm-hmm" in that condescending way that really got his goat, but he was desperate enough to allow her to call a driver and go to the sporting goods store on Crazy Woman Creek.

The proprietor was a grizzled old man, who, by Titus's estimation, weighed at least three hundred, if not four hundred pounds. He was enormous, wearing a torn thermal knit T-shirt and baggy overalls, the white stubbles all over his face like bristles on a brush. Titus liked him, his booming voice and small brown eyes hidden under rolls of flesh, and the fact he dwarfed his own father, making him seem small and inadequate for once in his life.

Susan left the little ones at home with Isaac, saying they'd probably be back before Thayer woke up from his nap, but Titus could tell she was eager to get there and back as soon as possible. He was not going to take long, he never cared that much about anything he wore.

They were greeted by the tinkling bells above the door, the smell of leather and cardboard boxes, strong coffee and whatever Ted was cooking.

"Hey there!"

The voice was an assault on their senses, ricocheting off the log walls, knocking between aisles until the shoe and boot boxes rattled.

"Hello, Ted."

"If it ain't Isaac's wife. Susan, right? And his boy. Titus."

"You're right."

"So, how's everything up at the ranch?"

"Cold. Snowy."

"Yep, yep. So what can I do for you?" he boomed, leaning on the counter with hands like basketballs.

"Titus needs boots."

"We'll fix 'im right up."

Which couldn't have been farther from the truth. One pair was the wrong color, another didn't come up over the leg far enough, and so on.

Susan had never experienced buying anything for an adolescent, and certainly not one who had fallen so severely for one young lady named Trisha Mast. However, she knew nothing of the seriousness of the situation and became impatient, telling him he needed to just pick something, which only got her a glare from his dark eyes, so much like his father's. After a pair of boots were purchased, finally, there was the life and death decision of a beanie. Not too thick or thin, not navy blue or gray, and this one was too big, that one too tight.

She received many broad winks from Ted, but by that point she was feeling desperate to get back home to Thayer. She took a cleansing breath when they finally broke through the door into the brilliance of the snow-covered parking lot.

Titus sat in the back seat with his purchases, without saying a word the whole way home.

THAT EVENING, SHE watched the sunset, the color created in the swells and plains of the snow-covered land, colors no artist would ever imitate. The stark, unspoiled beauty of this great state was not for everyone, the isolation and loneliness of everyday life something you had to grow into. You had to accustom yourself to a slower pace, days when nothing mattered. If breakfast dishes weren't washed till nine o'clock, or sometimes not at all, it was no big deal. If laundry wasn't hung out by seven in the morning, there was no *fliesich* (busy) housewife next door left to wonder what was wrong.

All this Susan needed to learn. There was no hurry.

She had been raised to hurry. To accomplish everything in due time, to work hard, attend social gatherings and go to church, to regulate your days as much as possible.

And sometimes, probably more often than she cared to admit, she missed the energy of life back East, the tailspin of activities, the circle of friends and constant family drama.

She smiled to herself now, thinking of Rose and Liz, always a bit peevish about this or that. Peckish. They were like dear chickens, clucking around their allotted space, not always getting along. And Kate, so sweet and unassuming, always presenting a life of smooth sailing no matter what she endured. Yes, she was homesick, longed for family, but it passed and was replaced by her own family, her gorgeous homestead tucked against the backdrop of fir trees, the long driveway curving up to the buildings.

This was where she would spend her life, and here she was happy, with Isaac by her side. Well, sometimes he was by her side, she thought wryly. Mostly, he was in the woods.

But it was okay. Marriage, after a span of years, was okay. It wasn't always as she imagined it to be, but it was good and solid and comforting. It wasn't all starry-eyed romance, but there was beauty in the union of two different people, even in the disagreements, the selfishness, the mistakes made by two humans who were here on earth where the temptations and trials sometimes destroyed peaceful coexistence.

And now they were about to enter the life of parents to a teenaged son, definitely uncharted territory. Well, she'd face it with Isaac, put her hand in his. But she'd call on Darlene, too, that enterprising soul who had already worked her magic.

Praise God.

And so she watched the sun slide behind the tips of the fir trees and felt a sense of adventure. As the shadows crept across the land, changing the snow from blue to lavender to a deep indigo and gray, she closed her eyes and prayed for the Father's will to be done.

They would need God's wisdom to understand all the requirements to raise a young man who would overcome the sadness of his past and look to the future with courage and strength.

ABOUT THE AUTHOR

LINDA BYLER WAS RAISED IN AN AMISH FAMILY AND IS AN ACTIVE member of the Amish church today. Growing up, Linda loved to read and write. In fact, she still does. Linda is well known within the Amish community as a columnist for a weekly Amish newspaper. She writes all her novels by hand in notebooks.

Linda is the author of several series of novels, all set among the Amish communities of North America: Lizzie Searches for Love, Sadie's Montana, Lancaster Burning, Hester's Hunt for Home, the Dakota Series, The Long Road Home, New Directions, and the Buggy Spoke Series for younger readers. Linda has also written several Christmas romances set among the Amish: *Mary's Christmas Goodbye, The Christmas Visitor, The Little Amish Matchmaker, Becky Meets Her Match, A Dog for Christmas, A Horse for Elsie, The More the Merrier, A Christmas Engagement*, and *Love Conquers All*. Linda has coauthored *Lizzie's Amish Cookbook: Favorite Recipes from Three Generations of Amish Cooks!, Amish Christmas Cookbook*, and *Amish Soups & Casseroles*.

OTHER BOOKS BY
LINDA BYLER

LIZZIE SEARCHES FOR LOVE SERIES

BOOK ONE   BOOK TWO   BOOK THREE

TRILOGY   COOKBOOK

SADIE'S MONTANA SERIES

BOOK ONE

BOOK TWO

BOOK THREE

TRILOGY

Lancaster Burning Series

BOOK ONE

BOOK TWO

BOOK THREE

TRILOGY

HESTER'S HUNT FOR HOME SERIES

BOOK ONE

BOOK TWO

BOOK THREE

TRILOGY

THE DAKOTA SERIES

BOOK ONE

BOOK TWO

BOOK THREE

TRILOGY

Long Road Home Series

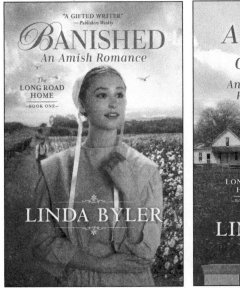

BOOK ONE

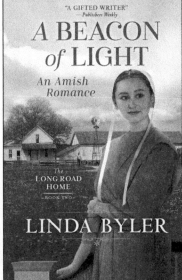

BOOK TWO

BOOK THREE

Buggy Spoke Series for Young Readers

BOOK ONE

BOOK TWO

BOOK THREE

CHRISTMAS NOVELLAS

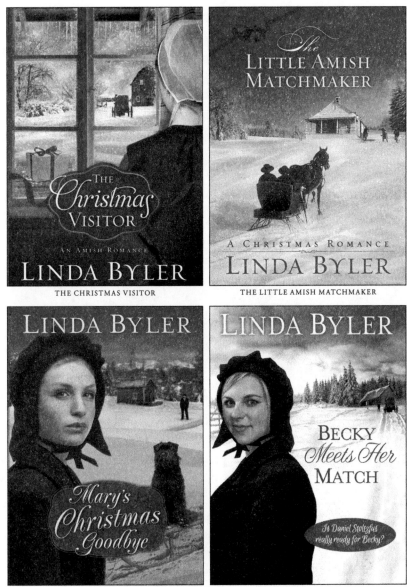

THE CHRISTMAS VISITOR

THE LITTLE AMISH MATCHMAKER

MARY'S CHRISTMAS GOODBYE

BECKY MEETS HER MATCH

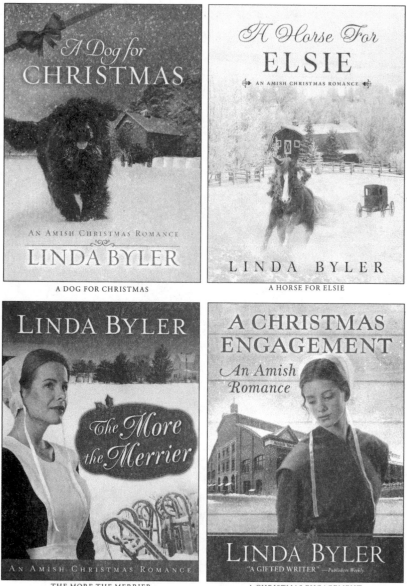

A DOG FOR CHRISTMAS

A HORSE FOR ELSIE

THE MORE THE MERRIER

A CHRISTMAS ENGAGEMENT

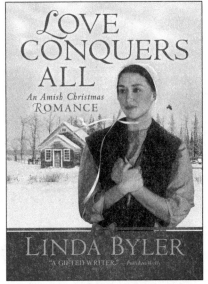

LOVE CONQUERS ALL

Christmas Collections

AMISH CHRISTMAS ROMANCE COLLECTION   AMISH ROMANCE AT CHRISTMASTIME

STANDALONE NOVELS

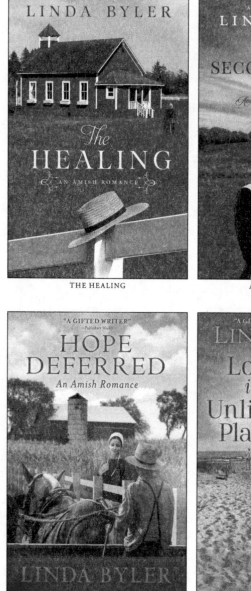

THE HEALING

A SECOND CHANCE

HOPE DEFERRED

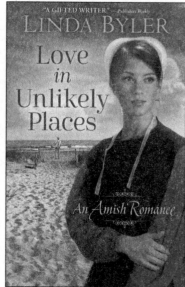

LOVE IN UNLIKELY PLACES